HARLEQUIN'S SUPPORT OF BIG SISTERS

Harlequin began sponsoring Big Brothers/
Big Sisters of America and Big Brothers and
Sisters of Canada in April 1988. Since then,
we have become the largest single sponsor of
Big Sisters Programs and related services in
North America.

This fitting association between the world's
largest publisher of romance fiction and a
volunteer organization that assists children and
youths in achieving their highest potential is a
wonderfully different kind of love story for
Harlequin. We are committed to assisting our
young people to grow to become responsible
men and women.

Brian Hickey
President and CEO

For more information, contact your local
Big Brothers/Big Sisters agency.

Dear Reader,

When I first considered writing one of the books for Harlequin's Big Brothers/Big Sisters of America series, I was rather apprehensive. Although many of my books have been populated with children, I'd never included the viewpoint of a child. But I was willing to give it a try, and lo and behold, less than a day later, Samantha Taylor, Vince Larusso and, last but not least, Frankie Lombardi were firmly entrenched in my mind.

I hope you enjoy reading *Nothing But Trouble* as much as I enjoyed writing it. While it's sad to realize there are so many children like Frankie who desperately need the friendship and guidance of a Big Sister, it's both uplifting and heartwarming to know there are people like Samantha willing to give a little time to make a big difference.

Nothing But Trouble is not just a story about a man and a woman on their way to making a lifelong commitment and happily-ever-after, it's also a story about a young girl and a woman who forge a relationship based on faith and trust. I think you'll discover, as I did, that *Nothing But Trouble* isn't so different, after all, from my other stories.

Because mostly. . . it's about love.

Best wishes,

Sandra James

NOTHING BUT TROUBLE

SANDRA JAMES

Harlequin Books

TORONTO • NEW YORK • LONDON
AMSTERDAM • PARIS • SYDNEY • HAMBURG
STOCKHOLM • ATHENS • TOKYO • MILAN
MADRID • WARSAW • BUDAPEST • AUCKLAND

Published September 1992

ISBN 0-373-70514-X

NOTHING BUT TROUBLE

"You're asking for a miracle,"

Vince said. "But I've seen this happen too many times to believe in miracles. Frankie's headed for trouble—big trouble."

For the longest time Samantha said nothing. Then she crossed the room and touched his forearm. "Then help me," she whispered. "Help me . . . to help Frankie."

The edge in his voice revealed his frustration. "I don't want you to end up hurt," he said. "I hope to God I'm wrong about Frankie, but what if I'm not? What if she stumbles and falls? You'll blame yourself, Samantha. I know you will."

She stared up at him, not caring that her heart was in her eyes. When she spoke, their lips almost touched. "If I do," she said softly, "will you be there to pick *me* up?"

CHAPTER ONE

FROM HER PLACE near the window, Samantha Taylor stared out at the dismal afternoon. The sky was a cold threatening gray. It was only the beginning of October, but the air already held the chill nip of winter. A short distance away, the buildings of downtown Chicago sat crowded and huddled together, as if braced against the wind the city was so famous for. In silent testimony, a particularly strong gust kicked up a swirl of dust on the street outside.

The strident peal of the bell proclaimed the beginning of the last period of the school day. It coincided with the opening of her office door.

"Here you are," said a voice that sounded disgustingly cheerful. "One Francesca Lombardi, signed, sealed and delivered."

Samantha turned. She eyed the file that had just been dropped on her desktop as if she'd just discovered a fly in her soup.

"I'm not so sure I should say thanks." She summoned a rueful smile. "Any chance you'd like to trade places with me for the next hour?"

Lou Rawlins pivoted in surprise. Tall and buxom, with steely gray hair, Lou was truly a godsend to the counselors and teachers at Lincoln Junior High. As usual, the sleeves of her blouse were rumpled, haphazardly rolled to her elbows. A pair of pink-rimmed glasses dangled from an eyeglass holder, resting on her ample bosom. In the two years since Samantha had joined the guidance counseling staff, she had yet to see the glasses perched where they belonged—on the bridge of her nose. Lou treated everyone with a warm motherly concern, but she was nobody's fool . . . and she was nothing if not outspoken.

At this particular moment, wiry eyebrows drew together over her nose. "What's the problem?" Lou asked in her usual forthright manner. "The last time Frankie Lombardi was in here, it was as quiet as a tomb. Some kids come into the office looking as if they hated the world and everyone in it—and they leave that way, too. I'm tempted to cover my ears, afraid I'll hear vases shattering and shouts that rattle the windows. But you—" Lou winked at her "—you've got the Midas touch. You're on the same wavelength with these kids."

That, Samantha reflected dryly, was a matter of opinion. Lou was right in observing that kids didn't always look forward to a visit with their guidance counselor. Some appeared frightened to death. Some just didn't give a damn. Others gave the impression they were armed and ready to do battle. Samantha saw her role as not just one, but many. She was mentor and advisor, partner as well as confidante, and occasionally even disciplinarian.

"I'm afraid I'm not on the same wave length with Frankie Lombardi," she said glumly. "Nothing seems to work with her." And wasn't that the truth, she amended silently. She'd tried kindness. Firmness. Gentleness and outright demand. Mr. Wells, the principal, thought the girl might relate better to a woman. He hoped Samantha might be able to achieve some kind of rapport with the girl and pinpoint her problem. But Samantha remained just as stymied by Frankie as he had been.

She had no explanation for Frankie's behavior. While Frankie's elementary school record was not exemplary, she hadn't been the problem child she'd been this year. Samantha was anxious to discover why, but Frankie had steadfastly refused to cooperate.

Lou tipped her head to the side. "What's she been up to this time? More back talk?" She sighed. "Mrs. Phillips said if it happens one more time, she wants her out of her class."

Samantha skimmed her fingers through honey-gold hair that waved sleek and shining to her shoulders. She had already pulled Frankie from one class and put her in another. She didn't want to have to do it again.

"Believe it or not," she admitted. "I haven't had any complaints from any of her teachers this week." She bit back an unexpected laugh when Lou pressed her palms together, closed her eyes and lifted her eyes heavenward in a gesture of thankfulness. "But," she added, "it seems Frankie has seen fit to expand her horizons."

Lou's brows arched in silent inquiry.

Samantha gave a telling sigh. "She stole some money from the cash register at a convenience store."

Lou whistled. "How'd she get out of it?"

Samantha shook her head. "She didn't. She's been convicted and assigned a juvenile probation officer. He wants their first meeting here at school with Frankie."

The situation wasn't at all unusual, but Lou snapped her fingers. "So that's why he phoned," she murmured. "Nick . . . no, Vincent Somebody-or-other . . ."

"Larusso," the younger woman supplied. As she spoke, Samantha grimaced. She usually wasn't prone to snap judgments, but she didn't think she liked Mr. Vincent Larusso. Their phone conversation yesterday had been short but definitely not sweet. He hadn't been rude, but he was just this side of brusque and right to the point. He was not, Samantha had decided, a man to mince words. When she hung up the phone, she had visions of a fire-breathing dragon.

Lou's voice drew her back from her musings. "Speak of the devil," she warned, "here she comes." With a jerk of her head, she indicated the hallway outside the office.

Samantha's eyes followed hers past the open door. Sure enough, there was Frankie Lombardi, her expression closed and belligerent. Her posture was unnaturally stiff as she marched toward them.

Lou grinned. "Looks like you'd better sharpen your battle-ax. This might be the one time you'll need it." She stepped back when Frankie entered, then quietly closed the door.

They were alone. Frankie halted just inside the threshold, her dark eyes flashing as they met Samantha's. Samantha squared her shoulders and met the girl's gaze unflinchingly. The silence was brief but all-encompassing. The two appeared to size each other up—weighing, measuring, storing.

It was Frankie who severed eye contact first. One well-worn sneaker toed the unevenly planked flooring. She didn't look at Samantha as she spoke. "The office sent a message you wanted to see me," she muttered.

"Yes, I did," Samantha confirmed pleasantly. She motioned Frankie to one of the two seats opposite her. Frankie waited until Samantha had assumed her seat behind the desk, then dropped into the chair nearest the window. Her notebook clattered noisily onto the floor beside her.

Samantha's lips tightened. Frankie had just confirmed what she already knew—that the girl would make this visit no easier than the others had been—and there had been four already this past month.

Samantha knew the score, however. Lincoln Junior High was situated in an area whose face was rapidly changing; like the many patchwork neighborhoods of Chicago, it was almost a city within a city. But now the corner bakery looked out upon a thriving fast-food restaurant. A dilapidated hotel shared the street with a newly restored brick-fronted town house. Some regarded the process as progress; others saw it as an invasion. There was friction between the long-time residents and the newer, trendier generation staking its claim. And that friction sometimes carried through to their children.

Complicating that was the fact that the school's students, seventh- and eighth-graders, were at an awkward stage in their life. They had evolved beyond the innocence of childhood, yet they were not yet adults. They were changing not only physically, but emotionally as well; some coped with those changes better than others.

Though it was also true that there were the proverbial bad eggs at Lincoln, it hadn't taken Samantha long to let them know that despite her soft voice and ready smile, she didn't hesitate to give as good as she got. Yet she was strangely reluctant to categorically dump Frankie Lombardi in with the rest of the "rowdies."

She released a long pent-up breath. No, she thought again. She didn't want to give up on Frankie...and she wouldn't let Frankie give up, either.

She flipped open the neat brown folder that Lou had delivered, wondering once more how she could get through to the girl. The name FRANCESCA LOMBARDI leaped out at her in bold black letters. *Francesca*. She struggled to hold back a smile. She couldn't imagine anyone calling the girl Francesca and getting away with it. Frankie was rather vocal on that particular issue and Samantha silently agreed with her. With her straight-as-a-board tomboy build, her tousled black hair and the surprising smattering of freckles dusted across her nose and cheeks, Frankie was an altogether fitting nickname for her.

Samantha sighed and folded her hands on the desktop. She decided to pave the way slowly and hopefully lighten the air.

"Frankie," she mused aloud, "you've been in here so often lately I'm beginning to think your name should be alongside mine on the plaque above the door."

Frankie didn't see the humor in her comment. Her jaw jutted forward. Par for the course, she said nothing.

Samantha curbed her growing frustration. *All right,* she thought silently. *If this is the way you want to play the game, we'll do it your way.*

"You know, don't you?"

The sound of Frankie's voice startled Samantha. Dark eyes stabbed into her, piercing and relentless. Her tone was just as accusing.

Samantha decided to ignore it. "About the theft charge? Yes, Frankie, I know. That's part of the reason I called you in here today."

Their eyes met and held. Samantha continued to study her as the silence stretched out. Frankie's manner was not openly hostile, but there was something cool—almost defensive—on the girl's face.

"I don't see what that has to do with you," the girl muttered finally. Her dark gaze dropped. She focused on a point just beyond Samantha's shoulder.

Samantha's finely arched, honey-gold brows shot up. "So you think I'm out of line—stepping in where I have no business? You may not realize it, Frankie, but what you do outside of school affects what happens in the classroom, and it's the same the other way around.''

The moment the words were out, Samantha could have bitten her tongue. Frankie wouldn't respond to fire-and-brimstone preaching. There was the chance it might even make her withdrawal even more pronounced.

And Samantha didn't want to build walls; she wanted to tear them down.

She rose and came around her desk, leaning back against the corner opposite Frankie. She considered and discarded a dozen different remarks before finally deciding to lay it on the line.

''I know you think I called you in here to give you a lecture—to tell you how disappointed I am that you would do such a thing,'' she stated evenly. ''Well, I can tell you what you expect to hear. I can slap your hands and make things tough for you here, but maybe we should wait until after you see your probation officer.'' There was a meaningful pause. ''He should be here any-time.''

For just an instant, Frankie appeared startled. ''He's coming here?''

Samantha crossed her arms over her sweater. ''Yes. He wanted a joint meeting among the three of us. I asked you to come by early to see if I could find out what's been troubling you lately.''

But as usual, trying to get the girl to open up was a lost cause. Frankie just slouched further in her chair. ''Nothing's bothering me,'' she said sullenly.

''No?'' There was an imperceptible tightening of Samantha's lips. With strained patience, she reached for Frankie's file and held it up before her. ''This tells me differently, Frankie. Your attendance this year is a downright disgrace."

Frankie straightened abruptly. "I had an excuse from home every time," she pointed out hotly.

Samantha couldn't quite restrain her skepticism. Frankie wouldn't be the first child to forge a note from home, and she probably wouldn't be the last. The attendance clerk had tried contacting Frankie's mother but had had no success since there was no phone.

"That may be," she said flatly, "but that's not the only strike against you. We had to reassign your gym class after you were accused of stealing—"

"Nobody ever proved I stole anything!"

No, Samantha thought sadly. But unfortunately she had her own suspicions.

"You've also had numerous detentions," she reminded the girl. "Your teachers complain that you don't pay attention. You're argumentative—"

"If you mean that fight with Melissa Stone—" anger kindled in Frankie's tone "—she had it coming! She thinks she's better than me, and I finally got tired of her rubbing my face in it!"

Melissa Stone, Samantha agreed silently, was an obnoxious little brat who perpetually had her nose in the air. But she hid a brief moment of triumph at Frankie's vehemence. By now she was ready to grasp at anything. Frankie's expression fairly shouted her indignant outrage, but Samantha didn't mind. She could deal with hostility. She could deal with antagonism. And this reaction was better than none at all.

"I know it's not easy to turn the other cheek," Samantha told her gently, "and I'm not saying you should have. But there's a better way than fighting." She paused.

"You're gaining a reputation as a troublemaker, Frankie. Is that what you want?"

There was no reply. Samantha fought a restless impatience while Frankie continued to stare at her. She was well aware of what she represented to the girl—a tall confident woman who had the upper hand and knew it. But Samantha didn't want to be an imposing authority figure who demanded and accused. She wanted Frankie's respect, but she didn't want the girl to fear her.

"You know," she remarked casually. "These little discussions of ours are going to have to stop. I'm the one who ends up doing all the talking. It would certainly be nice to hear a voice other than my own."

Frankie didn't rise to the bait. Whatever reaction she'd hoped for—good, bad, indifferent—was conspicuously absent. Dark, fathomless eyes stared back at her. The child didn't even blink.

Her triumph proved extremely short-lived. Samantha leashed her impatience and resumed her seat behind the desk. She posed her next question in a tone that held more curiosity than anything else. "Do you dislike me, Frankie?"

For long uninterrupted seconds it appeared the girl intended to be as tight-lipped as usual, but then she shrugged.

"Do I scare you?"

Frankie's pointed little chin lifted skyward. She defended herself staunchly. "I'm not scared of anybody."

And that, Samantha thought with unwilling humor, was that. Tough talk from a tough little cookie. Her lips twitched but thankfully she didn't smile.

"Tell me something, Frankie. You live with your mother?"

Her nod was terse. Samantha had suspected that, since her school records made no mention of her father. She was playing for time, and hoping against hope that Frankie would let down her guard just a little.

But Frankie's back had gone ramrod stiff. Samantha experienced a curious tug on her heartstrings. On one plane of thought, she couldn't help but notice the way Frankie's jeans were patched on both knees—and they were far too short as well. Her dark blue sweatshirt was faded and worn threadbare in several places. On another level, she realized that Frankie resented her questions, so she probed as gently as she could.

"No brothers and sisters?"

Outside, a fierce gust of wind rattled the windowpanes. Inside the small office, the pall was deathly quiet.

But Samantha wasn't yet ready to throw in the towel. She leaned forward slightly. "I'm curious," she said again. "Any brothers and sisters?"

Frankie shook her head. "It's just the two of us, me and my mom." She relinquished the information grudgingly.

Samantha's gaze had yet to leave her face. Since the Lombardis had no phone, she had sent out a letter to Frankie's mother over a week ago. She had yet to hear from her, though, which made her think perhaps Frankie's mother didn't give a damn about her daughter.

But there was something in the girl's expression, something that made her wonder... "What does your mother think of your being picked up for stealing?"

Frankie looked stunned for an instant, then her gaze dropped abruptly to her lap. But for just an instant, Samantha could have sworn a fleeting shame flitted across her features.

She tugged at a fold in her jeans, over and over and over again. At last she raised her head. Samantha had no trouble interpreting the rigid set of her thin shoulders. Distrust was plainly etched on her young face.

"Frankie," she said softly. "I'm concerned about you. I want to help you, and to do that I need to find out the reason you've tumbled so far downhill this year. You're an intelligent girl. Too smart to be doing the things you've been doing."

She hesitated, feeling her way carefully. "I know kids sometimes get themselves in hot water for any number of reasons. They're mixed up, or maybe it's to spite their parents. Or maybe they're just out for a lark because they think there's nothing better to do." There was a brief pause. "I can't help with a solution until I know the problem."

She held her breath, waiting expectantly. Frankie was looking at her rather oddly; Samantha was almost afraid to hope that she might finally have reached her.

And she hadn't.

All of a sudden Frankie's face froze over. She jumped up and whipped around her chair. Thin fingers grasped the wooden back so fiercely her knuckles showed white.

"You think I'm no good, Miss Taylor. Do you think I don't know that?" Her anger was laced with a furious resentment. "You say you want to help me. Well, I know better. And I know why. Because it's your job, Miss Taylor, and that's all it is! The minute I walk out this door you won't give me another thought till the next time you have to *bother* with me."

Samantha met her anger with a steady calm. Inwardly she wondered how she managed it. She had always prided herself on her tact, but Frankie was sorely testing her limits.

"If I thought you were no good, Frankie, I wouldn't be here talking myself blue in the face. Believe me, I've got better things to do with my time." As low as her voice was, the words were delivered with stinging impact.

She took a deep breath and counted to twenty, because ten just wasn't enough. "You couldn't be more wrong, but apparently that's something you'll have to discover for yourself." She pointed toward the chair. "Now please, sit down!"

Frankie sat.

The girl was too stunned to disobey. For a fraction of a second, startled surprise was mirrored on her features. Samantha had no intention of gloating, however. She suspected it was going to take all the wit and skill she possessed to get through to Frankie.

There was a dull ache in her temples. She rubbed it absently before turning her attention back to the girl.

"I'm sorry that had to happen," she told her quietly. "I want to help you, but you're not making it very easy for either of us."

Frankie stared down at her knees. Her feet were tucked under the chair, as if she were preparing to flee. Her profile was shadowed, so Samantha had no clue what she was thinking. But Samantha had the strangest notion that if Frankie turned away now, she would stumble and fall until she hit rock-bottom.

It was a long way down...but the climb up was even longer.

Samantha moved without conscious thought. She stopped beside her and laid a hand on her shoulder. Frankie tensed at the contact, but Samantha paid no heed.

She spoke softly, almost imploringly. "I'm willing to give you the benefit of the doubt, Frankie. I want to believe in you. Can't you do the same for me?"

The air was suddenly very still. After the longest time, Frankie met her gaze hesitantly. Samantha's throat tightened oddly. A dozen different emotions flashed across the girl's face in that moment. She saw pride, a world of it—and a hint of hurt and confusion as well. But the bleak acceptance that followed cut into her like a knife.

The girl's eyes lowered. "I . . ." She cleared her throat and Samantha sensed how difficult this was for her. Her voice was scarcely audible as she finished, "I'll try."

Samantha gave her shoulder a light squeeze. "That's all I'm asking."

Indeed, it was more than she had hoped for. Samantha realized she had won this round, but victory was far from close.

The intercom on her phone buzzed. Samantha turned and reached for the receiver.

It was Lou. "Mr. Larusso's here."

Samantha didn't bat an eye. Mr. Larusso, she decided grimly, could just cool his heels for a few minutes. She wasn't through with Frankie just yet.

Her eyes never wavered from Frankie's face as she spoke to Lou. "Please tell him I'll be with him in a few minutes."

But it seemed the time she so dearly wanted was for naught. She decided to backtrack and do some more digging about the girl's home life. But once again, Frankie's jaw thrust out. The girl's responses—when she chose to say anything at all—were monosyllabic and grudging. Clearly she felt Samantha was intruding. A few more questions and Samantha knew she was getting no-where fast.

With a sigh of exasperation she buzzed Lou and asked her to show Mr. Larusso in. Perhaps he, she conceded dourly, could succeed where she had failed.

It seemed she had barely hung up the phone when the door opened. Samantha turned and got her first view of Frankie's probation officer.

"Samantha Taylor? I'm Vince Larusso." He was all business as he stepped forward and shook her hand.

The handshake was brief; their fingers barely brushed, yet Samantha found the contact oddly unsettling.

Her first impression was one of size and strength. Her little office seemed smaller yet. And she was tall for a woman, nearly five-eight. Even in her heels she had to tilt her head slightly to meet his eyes. And if he seemed big to her, what would Frankie think?

Poor Frankie, who was one of the smallest eighth-graders in the school... It didn't take a second inspection to ascertain that the shoulders filling his black turtleneck hadn't been achieved by padding.

Nor did he resemble the fire-breathing dragon she'd expected. His hair was dark, darker even than Frankie's. She placed his age at somewhere in his mid-thirties. His eyes were a startling light shade of brown, almost gold. His features were ruggedly configured; high cheekbones rose above a square jawline. The contours of his mouth were too thin and stern-looking to appeal to her, yet she couldn't deny that he was passably good-looking in a rough sort of way.

He didn't take the chair she offered him. He dropped his blazer over the arm and angled one narrow hip against the worktable shoved beneath the window.

Those incredible golden eyes fixed on Frankie. "Well, well. So you're the little girl with sticky fingers. Tell me, Francesca. How many times did you pull your little stunt before you got caught?"

His tone was so silky-smooth and pleasant, it took a moment for the words to sink in. How she stopped her jaw from dropping, Samantha didn't know.

She stopped where she was, a step away from her chair. Vince Larusso had folded his arms across his chest and calmly awaited Frankie's response, one dark eyebrow hiked imperiously.

She was half-afraid to look at Frankie, but the girl drew her gaze like metal to a magnet.

Dimly she heard Frankie bound to her feet. She faced her nemesis with a bravado that was almost laughable considering the difference in their size.

Samantha couldn't believe it when Frankie stalked over to him and wagged two fingers beneath his nose. "Two things. First of all, I am not a little girl. Second, my name is Frankie—*not* Francesca. Got it, Larusso?"

Samantha stood as if she were shell-shocked. Her eyes darted between the two. Frankie's glare was blistering. And Vince Larusso had gone absolutely still.

Samantha had only one thought. She had been glad that round one was over...

But round two was just beginning.

CHAPTER TWO

THE SILENCE WAS STIFLING. No one moved; no one said a word. It was as if the entire world were holding its breath.

Vince Larusso began to applaud. The sound seemed overly loud in the small room. Stunned, Samantha fixed wide questioning eyes on him. He was smiling, she noted incredulously, a smile of genuine amusement that took years off his age and softened the craggy planes of his face.

"So it's Frankie, is it? Well, Frankie, I hope that little speech made you feel better because if I were you, I wouldn't count on it happening again."

A dull flush began to creep into Frankie's thin cheeks. Samantha sensed that while her color was rising, so was her temper.

Vince Larusso didn't appear to notice—or else he didn't care. His actions were completely nonchalant as he removed a pair of wire-rimmed half lenses from the inside pocket of his jacket and slipped them on. He peered at Frankie over the rim.

"Would you mind taking a seat? I'm sure you're anxious to get this finished." As polite as his tone was, there was something less than pleasant in the way he spoke; just the slightest hint of sarcasm.

Frankie flung herself into the chair where he'd dropped his blazer. "Ain't that the truth," she muttered.

His lips still smiled, but not his eyes. Frankie made no attempt to veil her hostility as she glared at him. Samantha didn't know whether to laugh or cry. If she'd thought there were sparks before Vince Larusso arrived, then the room was now engulfed in a conflagration the likes of which Samantha had never seen. She held her breath, certain another explosion was imminent.

But he merely leaned back slightly and laced his fingers across his abdomen, disregarding Frankie and focusing on Samantha. "Does she have any problem areas here at school?"

Samantha snapped back to attention when she saw he addressed her. "We were just discussing that when you arrived."

"And?"

She resisted the impulse to add her glower to Frankie's. Instead, her fingers smoothed the pleat in her skirt and adjusted a fold in her sweater. She was rather amazed to realize she was stalling.

"Mrs. Taylor?"

"Yes, yes." This time she couldn't disguise her impatience. "And by the way, it's *Miss* Taylor, not *Mrs.*" She didn't notice until it was too late that her reproof was almost identical to Frankie's.

One winged black eyebrow quirked. "Miss Taylor—" he emphasized "—would you care to clue me in on Frankie's recent performance in school?"

Her gaze flew to his. It didn't occur to her until that moment that he would misconstrue her adamancy in clarifying her marital state. She experienced a squirming discomfort. Good God! Did he think she was making some kind of play for him? His expression of amused tolerance didn't help—she sensed he was laughing at her.

His reaction was unexpected. His no-nonsense attitude toward Frankie had somehow convinced her that he was tough and hard to the bone. But while she welcomed the realization that perhaps there was a hint of softness in him after all, she didn't appreciate being laughed at.

Her chin tilted. "There are some areas that could use some improvement." *And boy, was that an understatement.* Though her tone was even, she was aware she was still hedging.

The tilt of his head and his unwavering gaze conveyed an unspoken message—he expected her to continue.

Samantha hesitated. His scrutiny was disturbing. And why she felt compelled to defend Frankie, she couldn't say. She glanced at the girl, but Frankie's concentration was wholly on Vince Larusso.

She cleared her throat. "I've been rather concerned about her attendance."

"I see. Playing hooky, is she?"

Samantha's back stiffened. It was no wonder Frankie's dander was up. No one's temper was more placid than her own, but she was beginning to feel it bristle.

"No." She met his gaze coolly. "But she's missed numerous school days this year."

"How about grades? Is she passing?"

There was a weighty pause. "No," she admitted finally. She emitted a heavy sigh. "There's no doubt that she's extremely capable. But she doesn't appear to be applying herself . . . and there have been a number of altercations . . ." Her voice very low, she went on to cite several instances.

When she'd finished, Samantha distantly noted that Frankie was now staring out the window. A pang went through her. Damn! she thought. What had she done?

She shouldn't feel like a traitor yet that was exactly how she felt.

And Vince Larusso had turned toward Frankie. His tone, like his expression, betrayed nothing of his thoughts. "Is there anything you'd like to add, young lady?"

For a moment it seemed Frankie wouldn't answer. She refused to look at him; she appeared to be deliberately ignoring him. Finally she gave an insolent shrug.

There was a slight tightening of Vince's lips. "I assume that means no." He flipped open a notebook on the corner of the desk and began to write. "In that case, we'll set the terms of your probation now. First of all, you'd better stay on the right side of the law—and that means no more stunts like the one you pulled several weeks ago. Secondly, I'll be closely monitoring your school attendance. Miss Taylor here will be reporting any absences to me. You can rest assured someone will be checking up on you to see if they're legit."

He didn't bother to look at her as he spoke. "Third, about your grades. Anything less than a C in each class is unacceptable. Fourth, I'm giving you a curfew of nine o'clock. You'll also need to report in to me—" he lifted his head and frowned over at Samantha "—do you have any objection to having the meeting take place here at school?"

Samantha's head was whirling. "That's fine," she murmured.

"First Monday of every month? Right after school?"

She nodded.

Once again the pen scratched madly. "All right, then. We'll meet here in Miss Taylor's office the first Monday of every month. Finally, Frankie, under no circumstances are you to associate with Joey Bennett—"

"Joey!" The name burst from Frankie's lips. She twisted around in her chair to stare at him.

"Joey Bennett," he stated matter-of-factly. "The boy you were with when you—"

"I know who he is! Why can't I see him?"

At this, Vince raised his head and grimaced. "The reason," he stated evenly, "is patently obvious. Joey Bennett is the worst influence someone like you can have—and you were with him when you committed the theft, Frankie. So if Joey Bennett is a buddy of yours, you'd better take a little more care in choosing your friends from now on. And by the way," he added, his tone almost conversational, "I'll be sending a list of these terms to your home so your parents know what's going on."

For the longest time Frankie said nothing. Samantha sat very still, aware of the tension in the room, even if Vince Larusso was not. He began to lower his gaze once more but all at once Frankie bounded to her feet.

"Who do you think you are?" she flared. "You—you can't do this. You're not my father!"

Something flickered in his eyes. "Lucky for you," he offered with a faint smile. "I'd probably have given you a well-deserved spanking long ago."

She confronted him boldly, almost brazenly. "I've never been spanked in my life."

"It shows, too."

The force of Frankie's anger had propelled her forward, fists jammed at her sides. "You—you don't like me and I don't like you!" she cried. "I want another probation officer."

"Sorry," he said mildly. "No can do."

Samantha's shoulders sagged. One step forward, two steps back. She despaired silently. Vince Larusso had just managed to undo what little headway she'd managed to gain with the girl.

His voice was suddenly hard; it dropped into the air with the weight of an anchor. "You just don't get it, do you? You broke the law, Frankie. That changes the rules. That puts the ball in *my* court and what it boils down to is this—we play the game my way, Frankie. My way or not at all."

"Your way or not at all! What's that supposed to mean?"

He didn't bother to sugarcoat his explanation. "It means that if you don't behave yourself—if you break any of the terms of your probation—you can say bye-bye to your home and family and hello to Juvenile Hall." His smile held no mirth. "Do us both a favor, Frankie. Be a good girl and don't get yourself in more trouble."

Frankie blanched. Her lips barely moved as she whispered, "Juvenile Hall? You mean I...I'd have to *live* there?"

His thumb up, he pointed his forefinger at her. "You got it, kid."

Samantha felt as if a giant hand had closed around her heart. Frankie looked like a lost little girl who had just forsaken her last hope of ever finding her way home.

He snapped the notebook shut. The sound was like a gun going off. "Now," he said briskly, "any other questions?"

Frankie shook her head.

"You can go then."

The girl snatched up her books and rushed out the door. But just before she bolted, Samantha caught a glimpse of her face. Her breath caught sharply as she saw the one thing in the world she'd never expected.

Tears.

FRANKIE SHOVED the heavy wooden door shut with the bottom of her foot. A perverse satisfaction shot through her when it closed with a noisy thump. She could almost hear the echoing thud bouncing off the walls inside. She wasted no time sprinting down the wide stone steps.

But when she reached the sidewalk below, her step faltered. She turned and gazed back over her shoulder. She thought she'd swallowed the lump in her throat, but suddenly it was back, bigger and harder than ever.

She didn't want to, but all at once she remembered how much in awe she had been the very first time she had ever seen Lincoln Junior High. It was huge and sprawling, built of soaring limestone walls. Though the building was only two stories high, to Frankie it had seemed like a hundred. And with its squarely angled corners and craggy towers, she'd been certain it was a medieval stone castle from some faraway place.

She had often fancied she was the princess who lived in it; that she was pampered and adored, surrounded by knights in shining armor. That her father was a handsome, generous king and her mother a beautiful queen who hadn't a care in the world...

Scowling fiercely, Frankie spun around. It was a stupid dream anyway, she told herself harshly. There was no such thing as knights in shining armor—and a princess was the one thing she would *never* be. If she was going to do something as silly as dream, why couldn't she at least be like the other kids—the girls whose fondest wish was to become a pop star like Janet Jackson? Or the boys who played at being a daring adventurer like Indiana Jones, or a fearsome soldier like Rambo.

Her head down, she marched forward, thoroughly disgusted with herself. She never even saw the figure rounding the next corner until it was too late.

"Watch where you're going!" snarled a young male voice. "Or else I'll...oh, it's you." There was an abrupt change in his tone.

Frankie had already recognized the scarred leather jacket that Joey always wore. She hesitated, then began to step around him.

"Hey! Where you going so fast?"

She stopped, then risked a glance at him. Joey was fifteen and towered over her by nearly a head. It was only in the past few months that he'd finally begun to really fill the shoulders of his coat. She wasn't afraid of him, though. Sure, he was no saint. But Frankie had known Joey for a long time. He wasn't mean or uppity to her like some of the kids at school were. He always played straight with her; he never pretended to be something he wasn't. And he was the one who had introduced her to Phil, the man who owned the pawnshop on Market Street. And without Phil...

She deliberately cut the thought short. Her "sticky fingers," as Larusso called it, was something she didn't want to think about right now.

Still, she couldn't quite meet Joey's gaze. "I'm not supposed to talk to you," she muttered, as if that explained everything.

But Joey had no trouble guessing her meaning. "Hey, you must have seen your probation officer."

He sounded so amused Frankie sent him a fulminating glance before she stalked forward again.

Joey fell into step beside her. "Hey," he chided. "This isn't like you. What did he say that's got you scared sh—"

"Joey!" She whirled on him furiously.

Joey merely laughed and tweaked her cheek. "You're funny, ya know? You don't think a thing of walking into a store and coming out with your pockets stuffed full, but I keep forgetting certain words are a no-no with you."

That, Frankie found herself admitting, was likely because she'd never heard such words pass her mother's lips. An unwilling smile edged her lips as she reconsidered. Or perhaps she had and she just didn't know it. Her mother's lapses into her native Italian were rare, but they did happen occasionally. And Frankie's command of Italian was rather limited. As Mama liked to say, "If you live in America, you speak American."

Joey's voice interrupted her musings. It appeared he wasn't to be denied. "So tell me. What else did he say?"

"That I wasn't supposed to hang around you, for one thing!"

"Who's gonna tell? Me? Or you?" He spread his hands wide and sneered. "I suppose he told you if you're a bad girl he's gonna lock you up and throw away the key."

Frankie's expression was answer enough. Joey threw back his head and laughed uproariously. "Talk, Frankie. That's all it is—cheap talk. And you're a first-timer. They got bigger fish to fry than you."

Why was he boasting? She couldn't resist a little dig. "Like you?" she asked archly. After all, she was the one who'd been caught. The police had let Joey go when the store owner fingered her, but his name must have turned up somewhere in the police report. Otherwise, how would Larusso have known she'd been with him?

But Joey merely grinned and winked at her. "Yeah. Like me."

They walked across the railroad crossing, leaving Lincoln Junior High behind. Frankie cast a last look over her shoulder at the school grounds. For the first time the school seemed gray and faceless and forbidding. She couldn't prevent the slow burn that simmered along her veins.

First there was Miss Taylor. She wasn't snooty like Mr. Wells, Frankie admitted grudgingly. But that was the only concession Frankie was willing to grant right now. Even Miss Taylor had to tell her what a problem she was! And then she had tried to make up for it by coming out with that sappy little speech!

I want to help you, Frankie, and to do that I need to find out why you've tumbled so far downhill this year.

It was just as Joey said, she told herself indignantly. Talk. Cheap talk. No doubt Miss Taylor had just one thing in mind. She'd be like some of the kids at school— drawing her in, including her and pretending to be nice— and all the while laughing at how gullible she was. But Frankie knew better now. No one would ever get the chance to dump on her again.

Then there was Larusso. What was it he'd said about her grades? *Anything less than a C in each class is unacceptable.*

Unacceptable, she mimicked in her mind. *He* was the one who was unacceptable. And she would never forgive him in a million years! He had made her feel foolish and hurt; she wasn't proud of what she'd done but did he have to rub her nose in it?

There was a word for men like him, she thought blackly. She fumbled around in her limited vocabulary and managed to find it . . . arrogant, that's what he was.

Her smile was smug. "Larusso," she murmured aloud, savoring the thought, "you're an arrogant bas . . ." She caught herself in the nick of time. The description wasn't a flattering one and if Mama had heard her, she'd have washed her mouth out with soap.

And once was quite enough, thank you. Her lips and tongue burned in remembrance of that not-so-long-ago day. She had come up with a rather fitting—and immensely satisfying—label for her absentee father. Unfortunately Mama had taken immediate exception to it.

It was worth spending the next hour at the bathroom sink, gargling and spitting.

Joey glanced over and caught her unholy grin. "Now that's more like it." He clapped a hand on her shoulder and ran an eye over her worn jean jacket. "You could use some new threads, Frankie. Wanna give it a go?"

The cash she'd stolen—or tried to steal—rushed into her mind. At the memory, a faint bitterness crept through her. She had intended to give the money to Mama so she could buy another uniform. Mr. Mullins, the owner of the bakery where Mama worked, insisted that all his employees wear the same starched white dress. It irked Frankie, especially since Mama didn't even work at the front counter. But Mama had only one, so she had to wash and dry it six nights a week.

Joey prodded her again. "You coming, Frankie?"

In spite of Joey's assurances, she couldn't forget Larusso's warnings as easily as she'd have liked. She shook her head. "I think I'll pass this time," she muttered.

But Joey didn't seem to have heard. He stared out beyond the railroad tracks. A broad smile creased his face. "Hey, there's Pete."

Frankie followed his gaze. Sure enough, there was Pete Renfrow, lounging against the hood of a shiny black car. As usual, he was surrounded by a group of boys and several girls.

"Did I tell you about his new car?" Joey sounded as boastful as if it were his own. "It's a Camaro, and it's got

all the bells and whistles. You know what Pete always
says—he wants nothin' but the best.''

Frankie fell silent, but she knew what Pete said, all
right. Lately Joey quoted Pete the way Mama quoted
their last parish priest, Father Anthony—*Padre Antonio*
as Mama always called him.

Frankie wasn't sure she liked Pete. Joey had introduced them a few weeks ago. Pete was nineteen, but most
of his friends were younger, around Joey's age. As far as
she knew, Pete didn't have a job. But she knew from Joey
that Pete always had plenty of money—she couldn't help
but wonder how he came by it—but she wasn't sure she
wanted to know, either.

Joey nudged her. "Hey, why don't you come and take
a look? Pete won't mind if you hang around for a while."
He gave a sly grin. "Maybe we can both go steal our-
selves some new threads."

Frankie lagged back a step and shook her head.
"Maybe some other time," she muttered.

She sensed his disapproval, though surprisingly, he said
nothing. He shrugged and deserted her at the next corner in favor of Pete.

One thought kept playing through her mind as she
watched him saunter down the street. There was one very
big difference between herself and Joey, she realized for
the first time. Joey stole because he liked the risk and he
liked the thrill.

She did it because she had no other choice.

Frankie couldn't stop the tired feeling that seeped
through her. Her shoulders sagged as she trudged along.
They didn't understand, any of them. Not Miss Taylor.
Not Larusso. Not even Mama. But what grated was her
certainty that they would *never* understand, even if she
tried to explain.

Damn him anyway! she thought suddenly, fiercely. Damn Larusso and his interference in her life. She jammed her fist against her palm in sheer frustration. Thanks to him, she would have to lay low for a while.

But the next instant a secret smile crept across her lips. She might have to pay the price later, but right now she didn't care. Larusso was so arrogant he'd never dream that a kid like her would even *think* of trying to get even....

JUST AS VINCE LARUSSO was on Frankie's mind, the girl was also on Vince's mind. It was difficult to concentrate on Frankie Lombardi, though. Samantha Taylor might have proved a rather pleasant distraction, if only she'd allow him to enjoy it. Instead she was making him feel guilty as sin.

And he didn't even know why.

Frankie had no sooner made her grand getaway than Samantha's phone rang. He gleaned from the one-sided conversation with the secretary that an irate parent was on the line and wasn't to be dissuaded. She took the call but not before she'd pointedly asked him to wait until she was finished.

He took her up on her suggestion and located the coffeepot in the teacher's lounge. He was gone for about ten minutes and it was another ten minutes before she defused the problem with the parent.

He found it disconcerting as hell to hear how pleasantly she spoke to the caller while she glared daggers at him. He finally moved to the window and sipped his coffee in order to escape her drilling stare. He had the feeling it had something—everything—to do with one Francesca Lombardi.

He was still at the window when the receiver dropped back into its cradle. He turned in time to see her lean back in her chair and close her eyes in an expression of acute relief. But the instant she opened her eyes and glimpsed his smiling regard, her mouth turned down at the corners. That silently accusing gaze damned him once more.

"You shouldn't frown so much, Miss Taylor." He admonished her gently. "Frowning causes lines, and a pretty lady like you wouldn't want that, would she?"

Her eyes narrowed. "You're trying to soft-soap the wrong person," she informed him bluntly. "You should have tried it with Frankie instead."

Vince sighed, a sound of genuine regret. He lifted his hands and tapped his fingertips together lightly. "Frankie," he repeated with a rueful smile. He pulled off his glasses and dropped them on her desktop. "That's really what this is all about, isn't it?"

Her smile was tight. "Very perceptive, Mr. Larusso. It's too bad you're not a little more tactful as well."

Her meaning was unmistakable. A pity, he thought to himself. He had no objections to prolonging his encounter with the very pretty Miss Samantha Taylor...if only the subject were not Frankie Lombardi.

His smile faded as he resigned himself to the business at hand. "Believe it or not," he told her softly, "I'm the last person to argue with the merits of tact."

"You could have fooled me!"

Her unladylike snort nearly made him laugh, but he knew he didn't dare. "You think I came down too hard on her?"

"Too hard?" she repeated sweetly. Her palms slapped against the desktop. She shot to her feet with the force of a rocket. "You're damn right I do! She's just a kid, only thirteen years old. You treated her like a—a criminal!"

Vince blinked. For a woman with such gentle features, she had one heck of a temper. She looked as if she'd like to tear him apart and feed him to the vultures. But the fact remained, he had done what he thought was right. More importantly, he'd done what was necessary... for Frankie's sake.

"Does the label really matter?" His voice was very quiet. "We can call her a juvenile delinquent, or we can call her a criminal. We can call her Rebecca of Sunnybrook Farm for that matter. But that won't change what she did. Frankie Lombardi broke the law and now she has to stand up and face the music."

Samantha couldn't remember when she'd been so furious. How could he be so cold?

"And that's all there is to it, I suppose." Her tone was as scathing as her expression. "Open and shut, just like that? Well, let me tell you something, Mr. Larusso. Frankie may act like she's the toughest kid on the block, but inside there's a little girl that bleeds like all the rest of us."

There! Now she'd told him. So why didn't he look convinced? Instead he regarded her with open skepticism.

"You," he pronounced flatly, "feel sorry for her."

Samantha's temper sparked. "So what if I do? Did you look at her—I mean, really look at her? The condition of her clothes? How thin she is? It's obvious she doesn't have much. And she comes from a one-parent family. Maybe no one at home gives a damn. Maybe there's no one there who cares where she is or what she does! I guess I do feel sorry for her," she concluded feelingly. "But a little honest emotion is better than feeling nothing at all!"

A dangerous glint had appeared in Vince's eyes. He rose slowly to his feet; they faced each other across the width of her desk. "Like me, I suppose?"

His tone was dangerously low, but Samantha didn't back down an inch. "Like I said before, Mr. Larusso, you're a perceptive man."

They confronted each other in resolute silence, but there was no denying the battle lines had been drawn. Vince felt his jaw harden. Score one for you, Samantha Taylor, he conceded darkly. She had struck a blow—and a low one, at that.

The muscles in his cheek tensed. "I'm afraid my job doesn't put me smack dab in the middle of a popularity contest. But believe me, it's better that these kids know I mean business right from the start. The only way to get through to them is to talk their language. If I have to stoop to their level to get the job done, then by God, that's what I'll do."

"You scared that poor girl half to death!"

His laugh was gritty. "Not a chance. Kids like Frankie don't respect authority and they don't fear it. Besides, what is it this age is known as? Oh, yes, the *formative* years. Well, in a way that's right. Because she's only thirteen years old and already she's gotten her feet wet. The next few years will tell if she's going to take the plunge into deeper waters. Let's just hope she got my message loud and clear."

"Oh, I think she did." Samantha glowered at him. "In fact, you did more than that. You even made her cry!"

Vince lifted his eyes heavenward. A stab of dark humor hit him; he felt a reluctant grin tug at his lips. "My dear Miss Taylor," he drawled. "She really has pulled the wool over your eyes, hasn't she? Didn't it ever occur to you that Frankie probably knows all the moves by now?

How to turn people like you up and around and inside out?''

"No, it hadn't," she snapped. "But apparently it's occurred to you!"

No, Vince thought with a pang. He had a much better source. A much better source indeed . . .

"They don't stay innocent long in these streets." His voice was very low and deliberate.

But Samantha didn't look convinced. She looked as staunchly opposed to him as ever. Vince experienced a spurt of pure frustration. How could either one of them do Frankie Lombardi any good if they were at cross-purposes?

He sighed, struggling for a patience that had never come easy. Samantha Taylor was as stubborn as Frankie was conniving!

"Let me ask you something. Do you think she knows right from wrong?"

For a second she looked startled; then she bit her lip, clearly uncomfortable. That, Vince decided, was a good sign. She gave a reluctant nod.

"So do I. But it didn't stop her from stealing a considerable amount of cash from that convenience store." He studied her for several seconds. "Did she tell you how she did it?"

Samantha shook her head.

"Then maybe this will convince you 'that poor girl' isn't as guileless as you think. She went up to the counter to buy a pack of gum. When the clerk opened the register, she asked about an item on the shelf below the opposite side of the counter. As soon as the clerk turned her back, she grabbed a wad of bills from the till." He grimaced. "It's the oldest trick in the book. The trouble is, it works a lot more often than you'd think."

Samantha grew cold inside. The oldest trick in the book? It sounded rather daring to her. She winced as she acknowledged that Frankie was bold and brash enough to carry it through.

But it wasn't what she saw on the outside—it was what she *didn't* see in Frankie that touched a chord of compassion deep inside her.

She bit her lip and glanced across at Vince. Her voice was very small. "I didn't say she was guileless."

Vince merely smiled crookedly. "Still think I came down too hard on her? Is it unreasonable to require that she stay out of trouble? Or keep her grades up—" He stopped when he saw her suddenly frown. "What?"

She perched a hip on the desk and folded her arms in front of her. "That boy you mentioned," she said slowly. "The one you said she couldn't associate with."

"Joey Bennett."

"She was with him when she stole the money?"

Vince nodded. "That's what the police report said. My office has been working with him since he was ten years old. It's all penny-ante stuff so far, but one of these days..." His grim expression told the tale only too well.

Samantha's indignant anger had long since fled. "I'll admit I may have reacted rather hastily." She relented graciously but she wasn't ready to concede victory just yet.

Vince found himself on the receiving end of a mildly reproving look. "But it's a good thing you're not a doctor," he heard her say. "Because your bedside manner could stand a whole lot of improvement."

Vince gave an uneasy laugh. The lack of heat in her voice took away the sting, but he regretted the harsh words they'd exchanged. He had no objection to being on the same side as Samantha—and he was most definitely looking forward to seeing her again.

He gave a low chuckle and reached for his jacket. He slipped it on and began adjusting the collar. "I promise a definite improvement the next time I see you. In the meantime, if there's any other problem with Frankie, just give me a call at this number."

His fingers dipped into the inside breast pocket of his blazer. His expression grew puzzled, then faintly alarmed. Rather baffled herself, Samantha frowned as he thrust his hand into the other two pockets on the front of his jacket, and then his slacks as well.

"What is it?" she said quickly. But already she had half an inkling. His gaze veered straight to the chair where his jacket had been lying the past hour...the chair Frankie had last occupied.

Her heart sank. She sincerely wished she hadn't asked....

His features were dark and as fierce as a thunderhead. "Why, that little... My wallet's gone," he muttered hotly, incredulously. "Dammit, she stole my wallet!"

CHAPTER THREE

FRANKIE TRUDGED past a stone-fronted town house with ornate but rusted wrought-iron railings. At the corner, church spires towered over row after row of apartments. She climbed the steps of her building and nodded a hello to the ruddy-cheeked woman sitting at the top of the porch. As usual, Mrs. Talarico gave a beaming, gap-toothed smile.

"Francesca!" The woman gave the girl a hug that threatened to squeeze the breath from her. "I hardly see your mama anymore," she said in thickly accented English. "She is not sick again, no?"

Frankie paused, one hand on the rough concrete railing. "She started working another job in the evening a few days ago." Her eyes darkened as she admitted, "Even I don't see her much anymore."

"Another job!" Mrs. Talarico shifted her considerable bulk to peer up at her. "Where?"

"Doing cleanup work at an office building."

"She is still at the bakery?"

Frankie nodded. Mama had started there about two weeks ago. She knew that while Mama was glad to be working again, the pay was less than she'd made at the restaurant.

"She is so thin! Too much work is not good for her, I think. If she is not careful, she will—how you say—catch her death." The woman clucked disapprovingly. "You send her down when she has the time. I will fatten her up, eh?''

Frankie nodded and summoned a wan smile. Inside the building, she plodded up the stairs, the lines in her forehead betraying an unnatural worry for one so young. Was Mrs. Talarico right? Was two jobs too much for Mama?

Frankie couldn't remember a time when Mama had been really strong and stout. Her mind, yes—but not her body. Her asthma always bothered her more during the winter—colds and flu never seemed to pass her by. And then Mama had been so sick... It was silly, but sometimes she was almost afraid to hug her—she had the craziest sensation that Mama would shatter into a million pieces.

Her shoulders slumped as she opened the door to their tiny one-bedroom apartment. "Mama?"

"Here, Francesca!"

The voice came from the kitchen. Despite the fact that Mama insisted on speaking English at home, her voice still bore an accent that was only slightly less heavy than Mrs. Talarico's.

Frankie dropped her books on the nearest chair. Half a dozen steps carried her across the floor. She found her mother at the stove, stirring a simmering pot of marinara with a wooden spoon.

Anna Lombardi sent her daughter a beaming smile. Frankie returned the smile in full measure, but Mrs. Talarico's words lingered. Was it her imagination—or did Mama look tired?

"You are home early," her mother observed.

Frankie's smile vanished. She'd been so upset over Miss Taylor and Larusso that she'd almost forgotten ... "Joey's mother didn't need me today," she muttered.

God, how she hated the way the lie sprang so easily to her lips. Yet what choice did she have? She had to come up with a source for the money she got from stealing, and that was the only one she could think of. Was it her fault no one would give her a job? She'd gotten laughed at, shooed out the door and told to come back when she was sixteen or had an employment certificate from the State Department of Labor. She'd soon discovered she had to be fourteen for that—and had to have a birth certificate to prove it.

She recalled how smug she'd been, so sure she could get around it. Joey knew someone—who knew someone else—who could dummy up her birth certificate. But then Mama had told her she didn't have a copy. And the price the man wanted was ridiculous—way beyond what she could pay. Lying about her age was impossible—she hardly looked twelve, yet alone sixteen!

Still, her conscience spurred her toward the truth. "I...uh, I had to see my probation officer today, too."

Anna's eyes widened. She replaced the lid on the pan and set aside the spoon. "I should have been with you, no?" She gave a heavy sigh. "But I just got home only a few minutes ago and—"

"It's all right, Mama. Besides, Mr. Mullins probably wouldn't have let you off early anyway." Frankie was heartily glad Mama hadn't been with her. She'd have been all the more embarrassed.

Mama held out her hand. "Come. You must tell me what happened. And about this pro—" Her brow furrowed as she stumbled over the word.

"Probation officer." Frankie rolled her eyes. She would have liked nothing more than to drop the subject but she obediently followed her mother into the living room. Mama patted the spot next to her and she reluctantly sat down.

"So, *cara*, you like him? It was not as bad as you thought, no?"

Mama's expression was anxious. Frankie couldn't stand the thought of disappointing her again. Mama had been so horrified when she learned about the theft charge, Frankie still cringed in shame whenever she thought about it. Yet not once had Mama scolded or lectured her. And Frankie knew why...

It cut like a knife knowing Mama didn't blame her; she had blamed herself.

So she shook her head and even managed a faint smile. "It was all right," she murmured. She couldn't bring herself to say she liked Larusso, though; she couldn't even say his name. With a name like Larusso, if Mama even suspected he had a *thimbleful* of Italian blood, she'd have loved it. Instead she told her the rules he'd laid down, with the exception of one.

She didn't tell her she wasn't supposed to see Joey.

When she'd finished, Mama patted her cheek. "You are a good girl, Francesca. This I know, just as I know you will never do such a thing again." She started to say something else, but then her thin shoulders slumped.

Frankie frowned. "What is it?"

Mama pressed her lips together. "This money that you have made baby-sitting for Joey's mama. You should keep it, *cara*, and buy something for yourself—"

But Frankie shook her head firmly. "I don't think of it as my money, Mama. It's *ours* and I want to help when I can. Besides, it hasn't been that much anyway." She hesitated. "I just wish I could get a real job so I could do more."

This time it was Mama who cut her off. "You have given so much already, *cara*. When I think of all the school you have missed because you stayed home to take care of me... I don't mind washing dishes and windows and scrubbing floors, but I don't want that for you, Frankie. I want you to have the chance to *be* somebody."

Frankie wanted to squirm in shame. *Be* somebody. She was a thief, she realized miserably. Yet was it so wrong? She had hurt no one...and she had done it to help Mama.

She couldn't look her mother in the eyes. "I wish you didn't have to work this night job," she muttered.

Mama waved aside her protest. "It is just for a while. Just until I can repay the back rent that we owe to the landlord. And those bills to the doctor."

Frankie clamped her jaw tight to keep from spitting out a word she knew Mama wouldn't like. Their landlord hadn't kicked them out when Mama lost her job at the restaurant. But the minute Mama was back on her feet and found the job at the bakery, he'd turned around and increased their rent. That was part of the reason she had taken the janitorial job in the evenings.

But Frankie felt she'd explode inside if she didn't say something. "It's not your fault you got sick and that bozo at the restaurant fired you," she said hotly.

Her eyes darkened as she recalled the past few months. Mama had caught a horrible cold in August and just couldn't seem to shake it. She'd spent three weeks in September flat on her back in bed, scarcely able to lift her head.

Mama reached out and touched her hand. "I am only doing what I have to," she said quietly.

Frankie stared at the hand lying on hers. Mama's skin looked tissue-paper thin, stretched over bones so fragile they looked as if they'd snap if she squeezed too hard.

She couldn't prevent the seething resentment building inside her, growing stronger with every breath. It wasn't fair! a voice inside raged. Her father had walked out on them years ago and never looked back—not even once. It wasn't fair that he'd left Mama alone to take care of the two of them. Frankie couldn't remember a time when money hadn't been short, but things had never been as bad as they were right now.

Mama touched her cheek gently. "You are thinking about your papa," she said quietly.

"I have no papa," Frankie denied fiercely.

"Oh, but you do, *cara*. You are strong and brave and full of pride here—" her hand lifted to touch the silky black strands on Frankie's forehead "—like me." Her voice was as gentle as a summer breeze.

"But you are like your papa here." She touched Frankie's breast with her fingertips. "His head was filled with dreams of seeing the world. And he made me happy, *cara*, he did." Her sigh was as soft as a summer breeze. "Oh, yes, *cara*, you are much like your papa, I think. Like him, you have a restless heart."

A distant faraway look had settled in her mother's eyes, giving Frankie a glimpse of something that both angered and frustrated her. She pressed her lips together to stop the bitter words from pouring out but the effort was useless.

"But he left us," she burst out. "He left us and he never came back! You should hate him for leaving us alone. But you don't, do you? Sometimes I think you still love him!"

A sad, wistful smile curved Mama's lips, a smile that tore her heart in two. "Oh, Francesca," she whispered. "How can I *not* love him? He gave me *you*—he gave me all that is precious in this world."

It was a poignant, bittersweet moment for both of them. Frankie didn't know when she'd loved her mother more. When Mama reached out and gathered her close, Frankie clung to her mother as if she feared Mama would disappear any moment. But even as she felt her mother's trembling fingers slide through her hair, over and over, she fought back helpless tears of angry despair.

Her breath caught raggedly. It shouldn't have hurt knowing that Mama would forgive her for the awful things she had done, but it did—God, how it hurt! Mama seldom spoke an angry word to her. She had never—ever—screamed at her the way Joey's mother did. Mama was never jealous; never wanted more than what they needed, the way Frankie sometimes did. And she remembered only the good things that happened—and never the bad. Was it a gift? Or a curse?

But her eyes were so dry they seemed to hurt when Mama left a few minutes later. Frankie begged her to stay, but Mama gently refused. When she opened the door, a sharp draft from the hall rushed into the room, proclaiming the inevitable advent of winter.

It was an unwanted, sorely unwelcome reminder—Mama had never liked the frigid Chicago winters. She was cold, always cold... She would wish for spring, and joke that someday soon, they would go where the sun always shines....

Once again, Mrs. Talarico's words echoed in her mind. *If she is not careful, she will catch her death...catch her death...*

This time it was Frankie who shivered.

VINCE WASTED NO TIME charging out of Samantha's office. She grabbed her coat and hurried after him. He stopped in the hall when he realized she was right at his heels. She didn't give him time to ask her intention. "I'm going with you," she stated firmly.

Hands on his hips, Vince surveyed her incredulously. "What! You don't trust me, do you!"

If she didn't, she certainly had good reason. He'd looked like a man possessed as he stormed out of her office, his face like a thundercloud, every hard line of his body taut and determined.

She arched a honeyed eyebrow. "Can you blame me? Watching you and Frankie together was like watching a pair of contenders in a boxing match."

He snorted. "And poor little Frankie doesn't stand a chance against a heavyweight like me, I suppose. Put your mind at ease. Much as I'd like to, I promise I won't wring her scrawny little neck."

"Right." A smile tugged at her lips. "At least not until after you have your wallet back." Indignant outrage sparked in his eyes but she didn't give him a chance to voice it. "I'll come along to referee—" she couldn't resist teasing a little "—but knowing Frankie, you may end up needing a bodyguard instead."

She nearly laughed when he muttered, "You're probably right."

Ten minutes later they drove slowly down a potholed street, past a dignified stone church. Restless and impatient, Vince stared over the steering wheel of his car with narrowed eyes. Turning the next corner, he was the one who finally spotted the address.

"Wait! I think it might be that brick building on the corner." He glanced down at the scrap of paper Samantha had brought. "That's it, all right."

He had barely pulled over to the curb than he was out the door and rounding the front fender. When he swung the door open for her, Samantha decided his goodwill stemmed more from his desire for her to hurry than anything else.

Almost from the time they'd left the school, Samantha had been struggling to hold back a full-fledged smile of genuine amusement. Vince Larusso possessed the air of strength and confidence of a man who was sure of himself and his place in the world. The idea of such a man being bested by a young girl—a girl of only thirteen, no less—struck her as humorous.

She ventured a glance at him as they hurried along. She was relieved that the fiery blaze in his eyes had dissipated; she mentally crossed her fingers and hoped that Frankie didn't decide to see how much it would take to rekindle it.

Closer to the apartment building, she noticed that the exterior brick was weathered and faded, cracked and crumbling in numerous places. Several children playing in a gravel lot turned to regard them curiously as they mounted the wide stone steps. Samantha smiled at them then preceded Vince inside the entrance.

"What if Frankie isn't here?" she murmured once they were inside.

"She has to come home sooner or later."

Samantha bit her lip, suddenly glad she had come after all. His grim tone didn't bode well for Frankie.

Samantha had to make one last stand. "What if you're wrong? What if Frankie didn't steal your wallet?"

A sudden twinkle lit his eyes. "In that case, I'll gladly eat humble pie."

Her brows shot up. "Anything she cares to dish out?"

"Anything," he vowed gravely.

That, Samantha decided, was something she'd like to see.

Vince glanced at the address. "Apartment 404," he murmured, then pointed toward the far corner. "Let's take the elevator."

But the elevator wasn't working and they had to take the stairs.

Samantha was puffing when they reached the fourth floor. Vince glanced over and caught her in the midst of drawing a deep grateful breath of air.

"Why, Miss Taylor, did climbing all those stairs wear you out? Maybe you're spending too much time cooped up in that office of yours." He grinned unexpectedly.

The flutter of her heart had nothing at all to do with the overexertion—and everything to do with his wickedly attractive smile. She hastily revamped her earlier opinion. Vince Larusso wasn't just passably good-looking.

He was nothing short of spectacular.

She pretended to eye him disgustedly. "And I suppose you're in tip-top shape?"

"I certainly hope so."

She slipped her hands into the pockets of her coat. Tongue-in-cheek, she murmured, "Is that from chasing down all the juveniles you manage to scare away?"

His laugh was low and husky and oddly pleasing to her ears. "Only when the need arises," he promptly assured her.

She wasn't sure if he was kidding or not.

The shadowed hallway seemed alive with ghosts as they walked along. Samantha shivered a little, feeling suddenly somber in such stark surroundings, Vince, too, grew silent, and she sensed he felt it, too. They stopped before the last door at the end of the hall. Chipped brass letters posted on the wall beside the door revealed it to be Apartment 404.

Vince nodded toward the door. "Would you care to do the honors or should I?"

"I will," she said quickly. There was no doorbell, so Samantha stepped forward and knocked firmly three times. Vince remained where he was.

Behind the closed door, there was a dull thud and the sound of running footsteps. The door was thrown open and Frankie stood there, her expression so bright and eager Samantha almost didn't recognize her. "I knew you'd change your mind—" she began.

The sentence dropped off. Surprised pleasure abruptly transformed into wary caution in the blink of an eye. "Miss Taylor." Frankie's tone was faint, her expression one of obvious discomfiture. "What are you doing here?"

Vince stepped into view. "Hello, Frankie," he said calmly.

Frankie's reaction was lightning quick. She started to shove the door shut but Vince's hand shot out. Samantha felt herself shoved forward just as his palm slapped against the door, thwarting Frankie's attempt to close them out.

The bottom dropped out of Samantha's stomach. She scarcely noticed Frankie; it seemed her entire being was focused on the man behind her. He was so close she could feel the wool of his slacks sliding against her nyloned calves; the woodsy scent of after-shave teased her nostrils. For a fraction of a second, she stood paralyzed, rooted to the floor like an ancient tree.

His breath danced by her ear. She felt the rush of air and knew he spoke but she scarcely heard the words he directed at Frankie.

"We have some unfinished business, young lady. We can take care of it now—" there was a long drawn-out pause "—or I can call the police and let them handle it."

Samantha took a hasty half step to the opposite side of the doorway, wondering what madness had come over her. It was silly to be so—so aware of Vince Larusso as a man. Especially when she didn't think she even liked him!

But she heaved a wordless sigh of despair as her gaze bounced between Vince and Frankie. Vince looked about as yielding as a brick wall. His profile was stark, the contours of his mouth rather grim. Frankie prickled visibly at his air of cool detachment.

She stretched out a hand to the girl, her eyes softly imploring. "Please, Frankie. Can we come in for just a minute?"

Frankie scowled but she pulled the door back and stepped aside so they could pass by.

Vince wasted no time stating their intentions. "You don't need to bother showing us to a chair," he said mildly, "We'll only be staying long enough to collect my wallet." He crossed his arms and confronted her with a cool stare, deliberately waiting.

Samantha wasn't sure if she should laugh or cry when Frankie began to smirk. She knew then that Frankie was guilty.

Frankie offered a mocking smile. "Lost your wallet, huh, Larusso? Gee, that's too bad."

Vince was the picture of control. "Isn't it, though. Of course if I don't get it back soon, and without anything missing—" one dark eyebrow arched warningly "—there'll be hell to pay."

Frankie's dark eyes smoldered dangerously. Her lips tightened, and for a moment, Samantha feared she intended to deny it. "Just a minute," she muttered finally. She didn't waste the opportunity to fling a speaking look at her audience before she walked over to a small closet beside the front door.

Vince said nothing; Samantha took a quick look around the small apartment. A matchbox-size kitchen was visible through an arched doorway. One other door led off the living room, probably a bedroom. The living room was sparsely but adequately furnished, everything neat and tidy. The furniture, though, was definitely on the shabby side, but very clean . . . much like so many of Frankie's clothes.

Samantha frowned. There was something vaguely disturbing about the observation, but she couldn't quite put her finger on it.

Frankie appeared once more. Her posture was anything but cowed and defeated as she walked straight across to Vince and dropped his wallet into his palm.

Vince overlooked the rampant challenge in her expression; instead he opened his wallet. "You'll have to forgive me for not wanting to wait, but I think I'd better take a little inventory."

And he proceeded to do just that, inspecting the contents of his wallet with an attention to detail that had Frankie bristling.

Finally he snapped it shut. "Nothing's missing," he said briefly. Samantha felt some of the tension seep from her limbs. But she couldn't help wondering if that would have been the case if they hadn't shown up so soon, and the thought was like a pebble in her shoe.

She stepped forward. "Your mother isn't here, is she?"

Frankie's gaze swung to her, clearly suspicious. She shook her head then asked bluntly, "Why do you want to know?"

Samantha purposely adopted a light tone. "I just thought it might be a good time to meet her as long as we were here." She managed to hide her displeasure. It seemed she was right after all—Frankie was simply left too much on her own.

Vince was already waiting at the door. Samantha glanced over and caught his eye. "Would you mind if I spoke to Frankie for just a minute?"

Neither Frankie nor Vince looked thrilled at the prospect. Vince finally gave a reluctant nod. "I'll wait outside."

Frankie shot him a withering glare as he left. When they were alone she exploded. "He acts like he's afraid you shouldn't be alone with me! Well, he ought to be afraid," she muttered, "'cause now I know where he lives!"

She was just spouting off steam, Samantha realized. She smiled slightly, but her mind was off and running. So Frankie *had* looked in Vince's wallet. But she hadn't taken anything. Why? she wondered. She'd had the chance before they came . . . and she hadn't taken it.

Samantha wished she knew. And she wished that Frankie hadn't been alone . . . *where* was the girl's mother?

Now wasn't the time to ask, though. Because Samantha was well aware that what she was about to say would undoubtedly strike sparks off Frankie's temper.

She sighed and quietly studied the girl. In spite of her secret amusement over Frankie's boldness, what she had done was wrong. And it really was no laughing matter.

"Frankie," she said quietly, "why did you steal his wallet?"

"Because of the way he acted . . . laying down the law the way he did! He made me feel like a fool." Her lower lip thrust out. "He deserved it, Miss Taylor. You know he did!"

So she had done it to get back at him; to bring him down a peg, exactly as Samantha had thought. Unfortunately Frankie wasn't the type to roll over and play dead. Like a child who was hurt—and determined not to show it—she struck out blindly, without stopping to think of the consequences.

And it only added more fuel to Samantha's suspicions—that beneath Frankie's tough exterior was a heart that could hurt and bleed like any other.

She wasn't so different from any other kid after all.

She reached out and laid a hand on Frankie's shoulder. She was pleasantly surprised when the girl didn't draw back. "Frankie, you're going to have to try to get along with him."

Frankie's eyes shot sparks of fire. "Why should I?"

"Because the harder you make it on him, the harder he'll be on you." She raised her brows to emphasize her point, then went on quietly, "You may not like it, and I may not like it, but that's the way the cookie crumbles." She smiled and pinched her cheek. "Do you know what I'm trying to say?"

For an instant Frankie looked ready to argue; then her eyes lowered abruptly. She rubbed the toe of her tennis shoe across the worn carpet. "I guess," she muttered.

Samantha gave her shoulder an approving squeeze and turned to leave. Her fingers were curled around the door handle when she heard Frankie's voice.

"Miss Taylor?"

She turned. "Yes?"

"I really didn't intend to steal anything *in* his wallet. And I was gonna give it back." She hesitated. "Do you believe me?"

Frankie's tone was grudging, yet there was something very vulnerable in the way she stood very still, awaiting Samantha's reaction.

Even as she wondered if the girl was even aware of it, the naked entreaty in Frankie's eyes reached all the way into Samantha's heart. And suddenly it really didn't matter *what* she believed . . . as long as she believed in Frankie.

"I do," she said softly. And maybe she was being a sucker—an easy mark—but it was worth it when Frankie duplicated her smile.

When Samantha stepped back into the hall, Vince surprised her by poking his head inside once more. "Frankie!"

The girl's head appeared from behind the door. "Now what?" She looked as annoyed as she sounded.

"Next time," he said very quietly, "please make sure you know who's at the door before you open it."

This time there was no retort, not even the merest hint of defiance from the girl. Frankie merely nodded and closed the door. Samantha couldn't decide if it was the deadly serious look on Vince's face or his use of the word "please." He waited until he heard the sound of a bolt being slid before he turned back to Samantha.

She couldn't help but smile as they descended the stairs. "You know," she said smugly, "I think you're as bad as she is."

He frowned.

Samantha waved a hand in the air. "She wants us to think she's as tough as nails. That she's hard-nosed and bold and brash—"

"She is," he injected dryly from the step behind her.

Samantha went on as if she hadn't heard. "And you," she continued, "want her to think that you're as tough as she is . . . tougher, in fact. But I'd say that inside there's a guy with a—''

"A marshmallow heart?" Vince had no trouble with her interpretation. His mocking smile was directed solely at himself. He had the feeling if he told Samantha Taylor a few of the tales of his disreputable youth, it might have curled that very pretty hair of hers.

They had reached the main floor by now. Vince shouldered the door open and followed her through. "I'm not so sure I'd go that far," he said once they were out on the sidewalk. "But where Frankie is concerned, I'm not foolish enough to see what isn't there."

Samantha stopped short. There was something in his tone . . . "And I am?"

Touché. Vince congratulated himself grimly. Just when he'd decided he'd like very much to see this lady again, he had to stick his foot in his mouth.

He hadn't meant to put it quite so bluntly, but Samantha didn't know that. In a way, he realized, it was easier for him to get his point across at gut level with kids like Frankie than it was with someone like Samantha. There was an air of freshness about her, a youthful naïveté that was sweet and pure . . . and just a little intimidating.

Maybe because he'd had precious little experience with it.

He knew instinctively what kind of life she'd led. More than likely, she'd had a picture-perfect childhood—raised in the suburbs by parents who loved each other; living in a house with a swingset in the backyard; coping with nothing more worrisome than passing the next geometry test.

It was the kind of life he'd never had—the kind of life Frankie had never had.

He gestured vaguely. "Look," he told her, his voice very low, "I just don't think it's wise to get your hopes up where Frankie is concerned. Because if you do, you may end up disillusioned."

The wind whipped her hair over her cheeks. She raked it back impatiently and fixed him with a glare.

"What makes you such an authority?" she demanded.

"I've worked with this age group for fourteen years," he said quietly. "How about you?"

God, how she hated his knowing look! "Two," she snapped. "And I suppose you think a paltry little thing like showing a little humanity is no substitute for experience!"

"Ah, my bedside manner again," he murmured. He rubbed his chin and adopted what he hoped was a suitably wounded expression. "And I thought I did so well this time! Did I shout at poor Frankie without realizing it?"

Samantha stared. Why, he was teasing! It suddenly struck her that while she stood here fuming at him, the only thing she'd proved was that her fuse was considerably shorter than his.

She bit her lip, but before she knew it she was laughing aloud, and Vince was joining her.

"I owe you an apology," she said ruefully as they started down the sidewalk once more. "But when I look at Frankie, I don't see the worst in her. I . . . I'm trying to see *behind* that. I guess I'd like to think that her halo's just a little tarnished." There was a brief pause. "But you still think I'm too softhearted, don't you?"

"Only if you still think I'm too hard-boiled," he responded quickly.

"Then let's just say the jury's still out on both counts." She tipped her head to the side and regarded him with a crooked smile.

It was a smile that seemed to reach out and grab hold of his heart. And all of a sudden he couldn't help but wonder...

If he'd had someone like Samantha Taylor in his life all those years ago, would things have turned out differently? Maybe he wouldn't have been as wild...as careless. And maybe Tony might still be alive...

His thoughts slid abruptly to Frankie Lombardi. *Had* he come down on her too hard? For just an instant, he felt a pinprick of doubt. And if he had, was it because she reminded him of someone long gone...but never forgotten?

He almost wished he could have been indifferent toward Frankie Lombardi. Because he couldn't deny that back at Samantha's office, for a frozen moment in time, Frankie had made him think of Tony.

His gut tightened in painful remembrance. Even her militant stance had been familiar—her head thrown back, legs splayed wide in careless defiance... And those dark mutinous eyes that seemed to burn into his soul... Frankie even possessed the same volatile, fiery nature as Tony...

Frustration ate at him like acid. How, he wondered for the thousandth time, did one teach these kids that nothing was more dangerous than the recklessness of youth?

It was one of life's many lessons, he mused bitterly. They had to learn it for themselves. Only by then, it might be too late...

The way it had been too late for Tony.

No, Vince thought again. He hadn't been too hard on Frankie. His way was the best way—the only way.

Samantha was as quiet as he was during the short drive back to the school. She watched as he shoved the gear-shift into park and switched off the engine. But she made no move to get out so Vince turned to look at her.

He smiled slightly when he spied the triumphant light in her eyes. "You look like the lady who just found the formula for world peace."

"Not quite." She laughed. "But I may have hit upon one for our friend Frankie."

His brows rose questioningly.

She tapped her fingers against the leather of her purse. "I think part of Frankie's problem may be that she has too much time on her hands. But I also think she needs a friend, someone to give her a push in the right direction when she strays from the path."

With Frankie, that might prove to be rather often. But Vince kept his opinion to himself. Instead he hitched his elbow on the seat, trying hard not to look either too amused or skeptical. "I thought that was my role," he said with a faint smile.

Samantha's eyes sparkled with an unholy light. "I don't mean to sound sexist," she said with a grin, "but this calls for a woman's touch."

Vince frowned. "What do you mean?"

Samantha took a deep breath. She could hardly contain her mounting excitement. The idea had been whirling around in her head ever since Frankie had left her office.

"You know the Big Brother/Big Sister program?"

He nodded, his expression thoughtful. "That's probably a good idea. There's only one problem, though—or rather two."

"What?" Samantha couldn't stand the thought of any stumbling blocks; this could be the best thing anyone could do for Frankie.

He offered a pained smile, only half joking. "Number one, Frankie may not like the idea. Number two, I hate to be the one to point this out to you, but Miss Sweetness and Light doesn't always have the sunniest disposition. It would probably take a saint to put up with our tarnished little angel."

"In that case," she informed him primly, "you may call me St. Samantha."

His expression was precious. She nearly laughed as his eyes widening in slow-growing comprehension. "What are you saying? That you want to be her Big Sister?"

"As someone so recently said—" she grinned her satisfaction "—you got it, Larusso."

CHAPTER FOUR

ONCE HER MIND was made up, Samantha was not a woman to waste time. As soon as she entered her office the next morning, she sat down and began flipping through her Rolodex, searching for Lynette Marshall's number.

Lynette was a caseworker with the Big Brothers/Big Sisters of America Chicago Metropolitan Office. The two women had met shortly after Samantha started working at Lincoln Junior High. Since that time, she had made numerous referrals to Lynette; there were a number of children here at school that she felt could benefit from the program. Last year, Samantha had gone one step further and become a volunteer Big Sister herself for a girl named Lila Walker.

Like Frankie, eight-year-old Lila was a child left too much on her own. She had been extremely quiet and introverted when Samantha was first paired with her. It had been a challenge to try to draw Lila out of her shell, but somehow she'd managed to do exactly that. Unfortunately Lila and her mother had moved to Indianapolis. Their final day together had been several weeks ago.

Lynette hadn't yet called to advise her of a potential match with another girl; Samantha hoped she wasn't too late....

Lynette chuckled when Samantha asked how the matchup was going. "Well, you're the eager beaver, aren't you? I wish we could find more volunteers like you. But it looks like you're one step ahead of me. I've been at a workshop all week so I'm afraid I haven't had a chance to go through my list of referrals yet."

Samantha gave a silent prayer of thanks. "Then maybe I am one step ahead of you after all." She plunged ahead hurriedly. "There's a girl here at school that I'm working with. I'd like to get her involved with the program as soon as possible." She went on to tell her about Frankie's recent bout with the law, and the situation at home.

"Sounds like this is just what she needs," Lynette commented.

"My thoughts exactly." Samantha gave a tentative laugh. "But there's one more thing—I realize this may be a little unorthodox, but if I can get Frankie into the program, *I'd* like to be her Big Sister." She held her breath and waited.

Silence followed her announcement. Samantha had the feeling she'd caught Lynette by surprise. She hoped it was no more than that.

Thank heaven Lynette didn't keep her waiting long. "It is a little unorthodox," Lynette said cheerfully, "but we've had a few cases like this from time to time so it shouldn't be a problem, as long as Frankie's accepted into the program and she and her mother approve the match. Have you spoken to either of them yet?"

"Not yet," Samantha stated quickly. "First I wanted to make certain there wasn't a problem if I asked to be her Big Sister."

"I have no objection to you broaching the subject," Lynette said. "If Frankie and her mother decide they'd like to get her involved, have Mrs. Lombardi contact me and we'll get things rolling."

That was all Samantha needed to hear.

THE SHARP RAP on the door sent a jolt through Anna. Try as she might, she couldn't help it. A loud, unexpected sound—the shrill of a siren, the slamming of a door—often made her heart hammer wildly, her palms grow cold with dread. Her mind would scurry back, to the days when she had been so afraid that her baby would be taken from her; that she would be sent back to Italy and never see her Francesca again...

"Mama?" Her daughter looked up from where she sat cross-legged on their bed. "Did I hear someone knock?"

The rap came again. Anna flashed Francesca a smile and hurried to the door. She told herself her fears were stupid and foolish; that it was concern for their safety that made her slide the bolt, but not the chain.

But she knew better.

Easing the door open a crack, she peered through the opening. "Yes?"

"Mrs. Lombardi?" The voice was low and clear. It belonged to a tall well-dressed woman with honey-colored hair that bobbed gently to her shoulders.

"Mrs. Lombardi, my name is Samantha Taylor. I'm one of the guidance counselors at Lincoln Junior High." Despite the barrier between them, the woman looked her straight in the eye. "If you have a minute, I'd like to talk to you about Frankie."

The chain slid free. Anna motioned her inside. "Come in," she invited. She spoke in thickly accented English.

Samantha breathed a sigh of relief as the door closed behind her. She'd told herself on the short drive here that chances were good she wouldn't find Frankie's mother home. Indeed, she hadn't really expected to find her here.

Nor was Anna Lombardi what she expected.

Somehow she'd convinced herself that Anna Lombardi would be a great hulk of a woman—not this soft-spoken, diminutive being who looked as if she'd blow away with the next breeze. Why, she barely came to Samantha's shoulder!

She cut short her perusal when she saw that Anna was regarding her with a blend of surprised curiosity mingled with no small amount of worry. The woman started to say something, only to turn aside with a dry, shallow cough. Only a few seconds passed before she was able to speak again. "So," she murmured. "You know my Francesca?"

Francesca. Samantha would have smiled, if Frankie hadn't chosen that moment to step from the bedroom.

Anna turned slightly and saw her daughter. Samantha could almost see the silent question running through her head. "I'd like it if Frankie could join us," she said quickly, "since she's the reason I'm here." She offered Frankie a quick smile.

Frankie didn't smile back. Smoldering eyes met hers, wordlessly accusing. The girl gazed at her as if she had come bearing tales. In that moment, a vague assumption sneaked into Samantha's mind—and one which accounted for her mother's surprise. No doubt the letter she'd sent had never reached Anna—but she was suddenly very sure Frankie had read it. No doubt her mother would never see the list of probationary terms Vince had promised to send, either. Yet how could she earn Frankie's trust if she betrayed her now?

Anna touched her arm gently and pointed to the sofa. "You will sit, no? And you, too, *cara*." She gestured to her daughter, who stiffly took the chair on the opposite wall.

Samantha sat down on the sofa along Frankie's mother. "Mrs. Lombardi, I'm not sure if you're aware of it, but I saw Frankie in my office yesterday, along with her probation officer, Vince Larusso."

Just the mention of Vince's name was enough to make Frankie visibly bristle. Her expression grew as dark as a thunderhead. Samantha, however, experienced an entirely different reaction when she said Vince's name. The tiniest of shivers edged up her spine. It was a feeling that wasn't at all unpleasant...until she wondered what Vince Larusso would say if he were aware she were here right now.

Anna darted a quick glance at her daughter. She spoke before Samantha had a chance to continue. "The money she stole—I swear it will not happen again...she is not a bad girl, this I know with all my heart...and maybe it is my fault—"

"It's not your fault, Mama, you know that! I did it, not you!" In a flash Frankie was off her chair and kneeling before her mother.

Stunned by Frankie's vehemence, Samantha could only watch as Anna laid her hand on Frankie's cheek. There was something very telling about that gesture, something that made Samantha glance away from this very private moment.

"You are too much alone, *cara*. If only I had been here—"

Frankie's shoulders seemed to sag. "You would be if you could," she said, her tone both bitter and resigned. "But I know you can't, Mama."

Samantha swallowed; she couldn't think when she'd been so ashamed. Lifting her eyes, she glimpsed a startling maturity in Frankie's young features. She also realized how mistaken she had been to harbor the notion that Anna might not care about her daughter.

It was even more apparent that Frankie loved her mother very much. For Samantha this was a rather humbling acknowledgment.

She studied the other woman quietly, mentally calculating. How old was Anna? Late thirties? Early forties? Surely no more, and yet... Her hair was as black as a crow's wing, swept back into a small knot at her nape. Was it the severe hairstyle that made her seem older? Her skin must have been pretty once, but now there were lines around her eyes and mouth. Her heart-shaped face was thin, almost gaunt.

She reached out and touched Anna's shoulder, feeling as if she were intruding but aware the timing couldn't be better for what she had to say.

"I take it you work long hours, Mrs. Lombardi." She probed very gently. "So you're not at home with Frankie as much as you'd like?"

Anna's gaze dropped to her hands; she nodded. Frankie jerked around so that she sat cross-legged on the floor. She spoke up, sounding half defiant, half angry—and extremely defensive. "It's not her fault! She works at Mullins Bakery from six until three, Monday through Saturday. And then she goes out at five again and cleans an office building."

Samantha's mind reeled. Anna was working six days a week, and two jobs yet! No wonder she looked so tired and haggard.

She took a deep breath, choosing her words very carefully. The last thing she wanted was for either of the Lombardis to think she was criticizing.

"Mrs. Lombardi, Frankie has had some problems in school this year, but she and I have discussed them and I'm hopeful things will improve there." She winced at Frankie's expression. The girl looked as if she'd stabbed her in the back. She tried to soften the words with an apologetic smile and turned to her mother.

"It's also true that sometimes children get into trouble when they're left on their own too much. And sometimes there's not much a school counselor can do. But in Frankie's case, I think she could use the support—and friendship—of an adult. Someone she could talk to and go places with. Someone," she said softly, "like a big sister. That's why I'd like to suggest getting her into the Big Brother/Big Sister program..." She went on to explain in more detail.

"Finally," she finished, unable to keep the excitement from her voice. "If you think this is something you'd like to do, I'd like to see how you feel about me being Frankie's Big Sister."

Frankie had twisted around so that she was positioned between Samantha and her mother. That was something she clearly hadn't expected. "What kinds of things would we do?"

Samantha felt like doing cartwheels. She'd been so afraid Frankie would veto the idea hands down. Thank heaven her tone was cautious, not skeptical. Nor did she appear to be unwilling.

"Depending on what you like to do," she responded lightly, "lots of things. Play games, watch TV or a movie. If you like sports, we could go see a high-school basketball game sometime. Or we could do something else, whatever you want." Samantha paused. "I want to be your friend, Frankie," she said softly. "That's what really matters."

Frankie's lashes slid down to shutter her expression. Samantha had the strangest sensation the girl was embarrassed.

"I guess it wouldn't be so bad," she relented at last. She glanced up at her mother. "What do you think, Mama?"

Samantha had been so caught up in worrying about Frankie's reaction that she'd nearly forgotten about Anna. She was a little stunned to find that Anna looked uncomfortable.

Anna gestured vaguely. "How would we do this? There are papers to fill out? People to see?"

Samantha was suddenly very glad she'd brought along a copy of the forms. She bent and retrieved one of the forms from her satchel, then showed it to her. "There's a questionnaire for you and Frankie to fill out," she explained. "As you can see, it's concerned with Frankie. Activities she's interested in, her personality and behavior and health. What she likes to do, that kind of thing."

She leaned back in her seat. "There's an interview with a caseworker, too, since they'll also want to make certain that you understand what to expect, and that you approve of Frankie and I being matched up."

Anna wet her lips. "Who would do this—this interview?"

"A woman named Lynette Marshall. I've known her for several years. In fact, I already spoke to her about the possibility of me becoming Frankie's Big Sister." Her eyes were encouraging. "Lynette is really very sweet and easy to talk to. Certainly no one to be afraid of."

No one to be afraid of. Now why had she said that? Why did she think it was exactly what Anna needed to hear? And why was Anna so nervous? Her hands twined together in her lap, over and over again. She wondered dimly if Anna were even aware of it. And she looked like a woman torn in two.

Indeed Anna was torn. She could never regret what she had done—never. Only she had been so alone, except for Francesca. Afraid to trust in anyone, for fear of being discovered. And so she had kept her daughter close...too close?

A wrenching pain gripped her heart. Francesca was so strong. So brave. And she really *was* a good girl despite her quick temper.

She didn't want more trouble for Frankie. She didn't want her to grow up as cowardly and fearful as she. Yet Anna couldn't quite banish the threat that she might be discovered...

She reminded herself how careful she had always been; how she never drew attention to herself. She had taken jobs no one else would take to put food in their mouths. She made trouble for no one.

There was no reason to believe that anyone knew. In all this time, no one even suspected. Only Padre Antonio had known, though he would never have revealed her. But Padre was gone....

Now they had no one.

Anna silently prayed for the guidance and faith that had yet to fail her.

"Mrs. Lombardi, I realize I've caught you by surprise with this. And I hope you know I'm certainly not trying to replace you. I'd just like to be there sometimes for Frankie...when you can't be. I want to help Frankie. Most of all, I want to be her friend." Samantha reached out and squeezed Frankie's shoulder. Frankie dropped her eyes, but Samantha's smile didn't waver as she glanced between mother and daughter.

Anna focused on the other woman with all of her being. Her voice was so quiet, so reassuring. Her eyes so calm and blue.

She trusted this woman—Samantha. She didn't know how or why, she just did. Nor did Anna question herself any further. When she believed, she believed with all of her heart.

Samantha rose to her feet. Her gaze encompassed both Anna and Frankie. "Please think about it, will you? If you decide it's what the two of you want, Lynette asked me to have you contact her." She stepped forward and handed Anna a business card with Lynette's address and phone number.

Anna had risen as well, but she was already shaking her head. "We do not have to think about it. I will call this woman—" she drew back and waved the card "—tomorrow from the bakery."

She surprised Samantha by seizing her shoulders and kissing her on both cheeks. "You will be good for my Francesca, this I know." She drew back and beamed down at Frankie.

Samantha sought Frankie's gaze as well. "Frankie," she said quietly. "I want you to know I won't be offended if you decide you'd rather have someone else for your Big Sister."

The girl appeared startled. She shook her head quickly. "I'd rather have you than someone I don't know," she said earnestly.

Samantha smiled; her eyes conveyed her thanks. It wasn't until she was back in her car that a sobering thought entered her mind. She exhaled slowly, sending the fringe of bangs on her forehead aflutter. On one hand, she was glad that Frankie's home wasn't the battleground she had feared. It was also a relief to know there was plenty of love and caring in the Lombardi household.

But she hoped that Frankie hadn't agreed to be a Little Sister simply to please her mother.

THE THOUGHT bothered Samantha over the next week. She saw Frankie only once. The girl was in the cafeteria, sitting at a table with her hands crossed over her books, her chin resting on her hands as she stared out the window. She'd been tempted to go over and talk for a few minutes. But just as she stepped toward her, another girl came up and sat down next to Frankie. And thankfully none of Frankie's teachers found it necessary to send her to the office.

She didn't know if Anna Lombardi had contacted Lynette Marshall yet. Just over a week had passed since her visit to Frankie's home. Samantha thought of asking Frankie, but she didn't want either the girl or her mother to feel she was railroading them into something they didn't want. She decided to bide her time a few days longer, and then call Lynette to see if she'd heard from Anna Lombardi.

She was pondering that very possibility on Thursday afternoon when her phone rang. Pivoting away from the filing cabinet in the corner, she grabbed for the phone on the opposite corner of her desk. "Counseling, Samantha Taylor speaking," she answered crisply.

"Samantha? This is Lynette Marshall."

"This is certainly timely. I was just thinking I should give you a call." Samantha switched the receiver to her other ear and settled her hips against the corner of her desk.

"About Frankie Lombardi, I'll bet." Before she had a chance to respond, Lynette went on lightly, "Congratulations, Samantha. Looks like you've got yourself another Little Sister."

"So Anna Lombardi did reach you after all!"

"Last week," Lynette confirmed. "I interviewed her and Frankie yesterday afternoon at their apartment. By the way, Anna seemed very impressed with you."

A glow of satisfaction warmed her veins. "What did you think of them—Anna *and* Frankie?"

"Anna struck me as a woman who has far too much on her shoulders," Lynette said promptly.

"My thoughts exactly." Samantha's tone was almost grim.

"Frankie's more of a puzzle." Lynette paused thoughtfully. "She was rather quiet, but I have the feeling she isn't always that way." There was a low chuckle. "You should have seen her face when I explained our Big Sisters aren't to be viewed as baby-sitters. She looked like she was ready to explode!"

"Frankie can be rather volatile," Samantha admitted. "But I hope that's not going to be a problem."

"Anna also let me know she wouldn't always have money to give to Frankie for movies and things like that. She seemed relieved when I explained that was fine—it's the time and companionship you can give Frankie that's worth far more."

By the time Samantha hung up the phone, she was feeling rather pleased with herself. Yet a twinge of unease sneaked up her spine as she thought of Vince Larusso. He had agreed that a Big Sister might be just what Frankie needed. But he'd been less than enthusiastic when she'd mentioned she wanted the role for herself.

And somehow that made victory just a little less sweet.

CHAPTER FIVE

THE SKY OVERHEAD was a seething mass of rain clouds. In the late afternoon gloom, Lincoln Junior High School appeared gray and faceless, its looming stone towers stark and forbidding.

Vince rubbed the back of his neck wearily and stared up at the craggy outline, wondering what on earth he was doing here. He had a pile of files on his desk awaiting dictation. Half a dozen phone calls to make.

Business, he reminded himself. This was strictly business.

The huge wooden door creaked eerily behind him. His footsteps echoed quietly through the deserted halls. Seconds later he stopped and spoke briefly to the secretary who had announced him last week. She shook her head and pointed him toward the only office with its light still burning. Scant seconds later, he knocked once and stepped inside.

Suddenly he knew exactly why he was here. And it didn't have a damn thing to do with business.

Her hair swirled around her shoulders as she turned her head, silky strands the color of sunlight pouring through honey. Her eyes widened slightly, as incredibly blue and clear as he remembered—and he remembered all too vividly.

He couldn't help the puddle of heat that settled smack dab in the middle of his stomach.

She couldn't help the way her voice came out husky and breathless. Nor was she certain she should be glad to see him. But she was. She was, indeed ...

"Why, Mr. Larusso. What brings you here?"

You, he wanted to say, but didn't.

Instead he slipped his fingers into the pocket of his slacks. "I thought I'd stop by and see how Frankie's been doing."

"Aha." Her tone was light. "So this is an official visit then."

The merest hint of a smile quirked his lips. "Not exactly," he murmured. "But I wouldn't put it past Frankie to orchestrate a palace revolt in record time."

There was something rather disturbing about that statement. It sounded as if he had tried and convicted Frankie and written her off as hopeless before the girl even had a chance to prove herself.

Samantha didn't want to believe that of Vince. Damn, but she didn't.

She wrinkled her nose at him. "Frankie," she announced, "has been a perfect little angel since the last time you saw her."

"I believe the word was tarnished, not perfect," Vince amended dryly. Dark heavy eyebrows rose a fraction. "With a saint to watch over her, what else could she be?"

If she hadn't seen the faint light dancing in his eyes, she might have been offended. As it was, Samantha could only laugh.

Hearing it, Vince experienced a feeling that was part pleasure, part pain. The sound was so open, so honest and ... carefree. He couldn't remember the last time he had laughed like that....

Maybe he never had.

"Am I keeping you from something?" Some*one* was what he really wanted to say.

She shook her head. "Not really. I mean, I have a dozen things I could be doing, and probably *should* be doing. But to tell you the truth I was just thinking about calling it a day."

He admitted to a sliver of disappointment. "I'll walk you to your car then."

"Oh, I didn't bring my car today. I walked."

"Where do you live?"

She gave him her address.

"That's a long way from here."

"Not really." She took a perverse satisfaction in disagreeing. He'd folded his arms across his chest, a thoroughly male posture that sent out a warning even before he spoke.

"You have to go through a rather bad area to get there."

Samantha bit back a spurt of irritation. Being the youngest of four daughters had had its disadvantages, one of which was being coddled and babied till she was sure she was smothering. But she'd been on her own for years now and she had discovered she liked depending on no one but herself.

Her chin came up. "I walk more than I drive or use the CTA, Mr. Larusso. And I do it because I happen to like it."

There was no denying the challenge in both her voice and her expression. Vince felt like throwing his hands in the air. On one plane of thought, it struck him that Samantha Taylor was the independent type. He didn't mind. He'd certainly never cared for clinging vines. But on another plane of thought entirely, he wished she would stop calling him Mr. Larusso. He wanted her to say his name. Vince. He wanted to know what it would sound like coming from her lips.

His gaze deliberately veered to the dismal gloom beyond the window. "You like walking two miles in the rain?"

Her nose tilted even higher. "I have an umbrella."

"And I," he said pointedly, "have my car." He straightened abruptly.

This time it was Samantha who wanted to throw her hands in the air. He was the protective sort, no doubt about it. She should have expected it, she realized, remembering how he'd warned Frankie against opening the door to strangers. Well, that was fine where Frankie was concerned, not so fine with her... Her jaw dropped.

He'd moved to the coat tree in the corner and was holding out her coat for her to slip into. Her umbrella was already tucked neatly under his arm.

Her jaw closed with a snap. Without a word she crossed to where he stood and thrust her arms into her coat.

Vince overlooked her closed expression as she pivoted before him. A whiff of perfume teased his nostrils. The rustle of her skirt against her legs reminded him rather keenly that it had been a long time since he'd been this close to a woman. Oh, there had been relationships over the years. But nothing lasting. No one who had been really... special.

He watched as she flipped her hair out from beneath her collar, conscious of an odd tightening of his body. Right now he liked what he saw very much... too much, perhaps?

Neither one said a word as they exited the building together. The light misty rain falling turned the world the color of pewter. Vince suspected he didn't dare comment about the fact that she'd given in so easily.

At the corner parking lot she abruptly pivoted and headed in the opposite direction. Vince was too stunned to react for a moment. "Hey," he called out finally. "My car's over here."

He was still standing where she'd left him, his expression rather bewildered. Samantha flipped open her umbrella, turned and smiled brightly. "Who said I was riding home with you?" She was still smiling as she began striding forward once more.

It didn't take long before she realized she wasn't alone. When she did, her smile withered. She stopped short and glared at him. "What," she demanded, "do you think you're doing?"

"You won't ride with me," he pointed out smoothly. "Therefore, I'll walk with you instead." He reached out and tapped the end of her pert little nose. "Please don't waste your breath arguing."

He was maddening. Exasperating. Yet all at once Samantha felt a bubble of laughter threatening to erupt. "Why not?"

"Because," he said softly. "I don't like to lose—and I rarely do." There was something vaguely disturbing about that statement . . . her mind groped fuzzily. It sounded like something Brad might have said . . . And yet the teasing in Vince Larusso's eyes robbed his claim of arrogance.

His gaze lifted toward the leaden-gray sky. "Since you won't share your umbrella with me, you sure you won't humor me and let me give you a ride home—especially considering you're a saint and all? I could use a few points with someone upstairs."

Unbidden, a smile escaped. "You," she accused without heat, "are a persistent man."

"Stubborn, too, I'm told."

"Anything else I should know about?" Tongue-in-cheek, she raised her brows.

Innocuous as the question was, a curious pang ran through him. *If you only knew,* he thought. *If you only knew.*

With an effort he kept his smile in place. "I wouldn't want to scare you off just yet." He nodded back in the direction of the parking lot. "Shall we?"

Samantha paused. She hadn't forgotten her shock at his bluntness that day in her office with Frankie; she had sensed a harshness in him, a harshness that bordered on ruthlessness . . .

Brad had been hard sometimes, she remembered suddenly. Methodical and fastidious and inflexible. But ruthless? The comparison gave her pause. Still, she had also glimpsed a hint of Prince Charming in Vince Larusso, and she couldn't shake the feeling he wasn't as hard as he sometimes appeared.

In answer she held her umbrella out so he could duck under it. They reached his car just as the heavens opened up.

The pelting downpour hadn't eased any by the time they reached Samantha's house. A wind-driven sheet of rain blasted against the windshield as she pointed out her driveway.

Her mind was racing. Should she ask him in? Would he expect her to ask? A nagging little voice reminded her he'd given her no reason to even think he might *want* to . . . Something seemed to plunge heavily inside her. Disappointment? Surely not. Why, she wasn't even sure she liked him!

But she couldn't deny that merely looking at him made her stomach tighten in a most peculiar way. It was strange, because she'd never thought she could be in the least attracted to a man as rough and earthy looking as Vince Larusso. And certainly not one who could be so—so abrasive sometimes.

He was peering through the murky gloom toward her house, affording her the chance to study his profile. His hair still glistened with dampness, making it appear blacker than black. She stared with mute fascination at the strong column of his neck. The contrast between the bronze of his skin and the whiteness of his shirt was striking.

"This looks like a nice place."

Samantha gave herself a mental shake and followed his gaze. As always, the sight of the narrow two-story clapboard kindled a swell of pride inside her. Initially she'd been drawn to the neighborhood, which was old and well established. She'd fallen in love with the towering oak tree in the front yard, but the house had needed a lot of tender loving care when she'd bought it. With a little remodeling on the inside, some elbow grease and numerous coats of paint on the outside, the result had made a world of difference.

"Thanks," she said softly. "My dad always said there's nothing like owning your own home. And it's all mine—or at least it will be when the mortgage is paid off a good many years from now."

The satisfaction in her voice had the strangest effect on Vince. He thought of the north-side apartment he'd graduated to over the years. It wasn't a luxurious high rise, but it was altogether nice and comfortable. He'd never really thought of it as anything more than the place where he ate and slept . . . until now.

His eyes had shifted to her. "You'll be soaked by the time you reach the door," he noted with a frown. "Maybe you should wait until the rain lets up before you go in."

He had echoed the very thought that was running through Samantha's mind. But coming from him, the suggestion made her smile. She couldn't resist teasing him. "You know you're doing it again," she chided gently.

His eyes flickered toward her as he reached out to switch off the ignition. "Doing what?"

"Letting that marshmallow heart show through."

His smile was rather derisive—but directed solely at himself. That she might think he was soft was almost laughable. She wouldn't say it—much less think it—if she knew the things he'd done. . . .

"Well, well," he murmured. "And here I thought I was being a gentleman." He hitched his elbow on the back of the seat and turned to regard her. "Is it too much to hope that you've changed your mind about my terrible bedside manner?"

She chuckled. "That doesn't seem to be a problem unless Frankie's around, which reminds me . . ." She decided this was as good a time as any to tell him. "Remember I mentioned that I'd like to try to get her into the Big Sister/Little Sister program? I just got a call today that she's been accepted. And guess who's going to be her Big Sister?"

His eyes flickered. His tone echoed his disbelief. "Not you."

Samantha winced. She'd thought that might happen, but somehow she managed to maintain her cheerfulness. "Oh, yes. Me!"

The smile on his face was wiped clean.

She could feel his eyes drilling into her, silently accusing. The atmosphere in the car grew stifling. For the longest time, the only sound was the furious drumbeat of rain on the rooftop.

Finally he let out a long, pent-up breath. "Good Lord," he muttered. "I can't believe you actually went through with it!"

Her pretense at good humor faded. He'd managed to spark her usually placid temper—again.

"You said yourself it was a good idea." Her tone was as stiff as her spine.

"I don't doubt that it is. But you're not out in never-never land where every story has a happy ending. Kids like Frankie aren't scared off easily. Most of the time they go from bad to worse—"

"But I could make a difference," she argued. "If I didn't believe that I wouldn't even think of trying to help her. You, on the other hand, are the most cynical man I've ever met!"

He gave a short laugh. "Cynical? I'd prefer to call myself a realist. And you really are a saint, aren't you? You're certainly determined to be a do-gooder."

Samantha's jaw closed with a snap. "You make it sound like a dirty word, and it isn't! Besides, what about you? You seem to have given up on her. You're supposed to be helping kids like Frankie. Or is it just a job to you? Do you really care what happens to her—to other kids like her?"

Vince felt he'd been slapped in the face. The tension spun out as their eyes locked in silent combat. A part of him wanted to lash out at her, but there was suddenly a tight constriction in his chest. It wasn't just a job to him. It could never be that—not after Tony.

He didn't want to argue with her. Damn, but he didn't.

His eyes searched her face. She continued to confront him in resolute silence.

He stretched out a hand. "You're angry," he said, his tone very low. "I said something you didn't want to hear, didn't I?"

Samantha shoved open the car door. "On the contrary," she stated curtly. "You said exactly what I expected you to say." She was frustrated and angry. Most of all, she was disappointed. "Thanks for the ride, Larusso."

The door slammed shut. Her back was ramrod straight as she stalked toward the house.

Vince watched until she disappeared in the gloomy gray mist. So, he thought wearily. They were back to that again. Larusso. *Mr.* Larusso.

He couldn't prevent the dismal bleakness that seeped like blood onto his soul. He hadn't meant to argue with her—he really hadn't! But it was too late now to change what had happened.

And Vince had come to the conclusion a long, long time ago that he couldn't change what he was...any more than he could change what he'd once been.

HALF AN HOUR LATER Vince entered his apartment. Swift purposeful steps carried him straight to the phone in the living room. But once there, he made no move to pick it up.

"Damn!" Before he even knew what he was about, he'd slammed the newspaper on the coffee table. Both the word and the gesture exemplified his pent-up frustration.

It did little to relieve the tension coiled within him.

Outside the wind howled an eerie melody. The rain continued its monotonous rhythm against the windowpanes. Both were a fitting accompaniment to the storm churning away inside him.

He dropped into the worn leather chair at his right, not bothering to switch on the light. God, but he wished he could empty his mind of that damned scene with Samantha! It was none of his business what she did or didn't do with Frankie. So why had he bothered to warn her? Why did he even care? And why was he angry that she had flung his warning right back in his face? Let her find out for herself that life wasn't always right or fair. Yet he couldn't rid himself of the feeling that somehow he'd hurt her.

Vince didn't understand it, any more than he understood the strange restlessness that had plagued him these past few weeks. He had learned the hard way not to look too far ahead—dreams were for the foolish and the young. But he'd been feeling strangely out of tempo; for the first time in longer than he cared to remember, he was just a little unsure of himself and his next move.

He leaned his head back wearily. Where Samantha Taylor was concerned it certainly appeared he could do or say nothing right. As he had since the day they'd met, he felt driven by a need to see her again that was almost compulsive.

And this he didn't understand, either. Vince had never lied to himself. He wasn't a terribly social man. He was even somewhat of a loner. He'd grown accustomed to being alone. He had accepted it as an inherent part of his life.

But he felt suddenly hollow, so devastatingly empty he felt he would crumble to dust with the slightest touch. And he wondered what—if anything—could possibly fill that bottomless chasm inside him.

There was a tiny linked chain around his neck. His fingers closed absently around the small silver crucifix that rested against his chest; it was several moments before the feel of cool metal registered against his fingertips. After all these years, it was as much a part of him as his arms and legs. He hadn't removed it since the day they'd laid Tony in the ground.

Yet to touch it, to stroke it as he did now, brought no comfort—no surcease from the bitter wave of remembrance that battered him. Tony's image was imprinted forever in his mind—always laughing, always the daredevil. So damned *alive* ...

He closed his eyes and let the crippling pain wash over him. He told himself it hurt no more than it had all those years ago... it hurt no less, either.

The movement of his fingers stilled. "Oh, Tony," he said aloud. "We didn't live life. We played with it—toyed with it the way no one should ever *ever* do..." And then a quirk of fate, a fleeting moment in time...and that life was no more.

There would be no second chance for Tony. Only fate had taken a perverse satisfaction in reminding Vince that although it was too late for Tony, it wasn't too late for him.

On that note, he straightened. Fingers that weren't entirely steady plowed through the tumbled darkness of his hair. Finally switching on the light, his gaze slid unerringly toward the telephone.

Five minutes later, Samantha's phone began to ring. She picked it up on the second ring. "Hello?"

"Samantha?"

Shock held her rooted to the floor, one hand poised on the handle of her refrigerator; she'd know that voice anywhere. Why had he called? And what did he want? Was he about to chew her out—again?

"Larusso." Her voice sounded nothing at all like her own. "I didn't know you had my num—"

"You're in the phone book." It was less an explanation than an accusation.

The corners of her lips twitched; her smile appeared from nowhere. She edged her way onto the chair. "Let me guess," she said dryly. "You don't approve."

"You got a call from an irate parent that first day in your office," he reminded her. "What if he or she decided to start harassing you at home?"

She sighed. "That hasn't happened yet, Mr. Larusso, and I seriously doubt it will."

There was a long silence. "You're probably right," he muttered. "But that's not what I called to tell you."

Samantha blinked, surprised that he let the subject drop so easily. Still, she couldn't quite prevent the note of caution in her voice. "Oh? Then why did you call?"

There was another lengthy pause. "To tell you I was sorry—and I am . . . sorry, that is."

He sounded—tired somehow. Against her will, against all her better judgment, her heart went out to him. She could almost see him, sprawled in a chair, long legs stretched out before him.

"So am I," she said softly. "I lost my temper."

There was a small silence. "Happens a lot, does it?"

His tone carried a faint but unexpected trace of underlying amusement. Samantha had the strangest feeling she'd just lifted a tremendous weight from his shoulders.

"To tell you the truth, no. Except with you," she admitted ruefully.

"Well," she heard him murmur. "As someone once told me, a little honest emotion is better than nothing at all."

Samantha frowned. There was something rather familiar about that statement ... "Oh, my. I did say that, didn't I?" She was glad he wasn't there to witness her incriminating blush.

The laugh they shared seemed to dissipate some of the tension, but Vince's tone turned serious again a moment later.

"I shouldn't have been so abrupt. It's just that I hate to see you get hurt."

The last thing Samantha wanted was another argument. "I'm a big girl," she said lightly. "I can take care of myself."

There was a fractional hesitation on the other end of the line. "Can you?" he asked slowly. "Please don't take this the wrong way, but I can't help but wonder if your background is anything at all like Frankie's."

Past experience warned her to be on guard, but Samantha was more puzzled than anything else. "I'm not sure what you mean?"

"Did you grow up here in the city?"

"Oak Lawn."

"What about your parents? Divorced and at each other's throats? Or married and living together?"

"My parents have been married nearly forty-five years!" Why, it was laughable to think of her parents at each other's throats. Sure there was an occasional spat— her father joked that he had to keep her mother on her toes. But Samantha didn't doubt that they were every bit as much in love as the day they'd married.

"So you never had to fend for yourself much? You had a stable home life?"

"Very," she affirmed calmly. "I was brought up to respect the same values and principles as my parents."

"What about friends? Did you ever hang around with anyone your parents disapproved of? Someone who liked to test the limits of the law maybe?"

Her smile was long gone. She had an inkling where this conversation was leading; she hoped she was wrong. "No," she told him evenly. "And I wasn't inclined to sample the forbidden fruit, either." If her tone was just a little short, that was too bad.

It was just as he'd thought, Vince concluded. She'd had a picture-perfect childhood. He wasn't sure if he was relieved or disappointed.

"I'm well aware of how fortunate I was to grow up the way I did," she added quietly. "But that doesn't make me blind to someone else's problems—or totally unaware of what people are capable of."

She sounded very staunch and unwavering—and yes, even stubborn. Vince decided it was time to throw in the towel, at least for now. "Aha. I know when I've been beaten, so maybe this would be a good time to say goodnight."

Samantha hadn't expected him to give up so easily. Had she said something to put him off? She hoped not. She liked him, she realized. When they weren't arguing over Frankie, she liked him quite a lot. In a way, he was a lot like Frankie. She'd already decided neither one of them was as uncaring and insensitive as they sometimes appeared.

"Hey, Larusso?"

"Yes?"

"Thanks for calling." Her voice was as wispy-soft as cotton.

His was just as low. "No problem."

There was a seemingly endless silence while both seemed to hold their breath, as if they were waiting...waiting.

He wanted to ask if he could see her. Now. Tomorrow. It didn't matter when. He prayed for some sign she felt the same. But she gave nothing away...

Neither did he.

"Good night," he said finally.

"'Night, Larusso." Was that a trace of regret he heard in her voice? Or the wistful imaginings of a lonely man?

He hung up the phone slowly, unable to control the bitter texture of his thoughts. It wasn't like him to feel sloppy or sentimental; it wasn't like him to feel sorry for himself. Only he couldn't deny that during those few minutes on the line with Samantha, he hadn't felt so—so stark and empty.

You've been alone most of your adult life, an insistent little voice reminded him. *Tonight's no different than any other night.* But it was, and he couldn't lie to himself any longer.

That vague restless stirring inside was back—and this time with a vengeance.

CHAPTER SIX

"NOBODY SAID you had to do this. Besides, you probably have a million other things to do."

The day was destined to be a disaster. Samantha was suddenly very sure of it. Frankie had just climbed into her car and sat huddled as close as possible to the passenger door.

Samantha battled a sense of helpless frustration. It was difficult to overlook the girl's hostile mutter and closed expression, but she knew she had to try.

"Look at me, Frankie." Beneath her quiet tone was an implicit demand the girl couldn't ignore—and she didn't.

Frankie's gaze slid back to her. There was a pointed little thrust to her small chin, but Samantha paid no heed. "Maybe this is as good a time as any to let you know I don't scare easily," she said evenly. "I grew up with three older sisters and I didn't get through it by rolling over and playing dead. Most of the time they tried to coddle me and smother me to death, but once in a while they thought they could walk all over me just because I was the youngest." There was a significant pause.

If anything, the girl's chin angled higher yet. "What's that got to do with me?" she demanded.

Samantha smiled slightly. "Maybe nothing. But I'm just trying to let you know I learned very early not to give up easily."

Frankie's gaze was smoldering. "You're just here because you feel sorry for me!"

For an instant Samantha was taken aback. Vince had accused her of being a do-gooder. Was that what Frankie thought, too?

She sighed. "Frankie, I thought we settled this. I'm not trying to pass judgment on you or your mother. I thought you wanted the two of us to do things together. You told Lynette you did. Or have you changed your mind?"

The resounding "yes!" she expected never materialized. Frankie said nothing, but her lashes dropped. If anything, the girl's withdrawal became even more pronounced.

Samantha began to pray for a patience that all at once seemed in short supply. "You told me once you didn't dislike me," she reminded the girl.

Frankie didn't deny it; nor did she confirm it. She merely swallowed and turned her head aside to stare out the window. "Why," Samantha asked softly, "do I have the feeling you're trying very hard *not* to like me?"

Because she was! The answer tore through Frankie's brain, making her want to squirm in shame. The worst of it was that she didn't even know why! She'd gone along with this for one reason and one reason only—she thought it was what Mama wanted. It really hadn't mattered that it seemed important to Miss Taylor.

But now, the thought caused a twinge of guilt. She wasn't sure she believed Miss Taylor when she said she wanted to be her friend. Mama was the only one who'd ever really cared about her. Still, Miss Taylor didn't snap at her or tell her she was lazy and no-good. Frankie knew that's what some of the teachers thought—one had even told her so, and it really burned her. They thought they knew everything, but they didn't know anything at all about her!

She grudgingly admitted Miss Taylor didn't seem like that type. But she *had* been nice to Mama, so maybe she deserved at least a chance.

Samantha had already decided to take a rather risky gamble. "I'm not going to force you into something you don't want," she stated quietly. "You can go back inside right now if that's what you want."

Frankie's knee was wagging back and forth. She crossed her arms over her chest, then jammed her hands into the pockets of her faded denim jacket, only to cross her arms again. At last she shook her head.

"I...uh...I don't have anything better to do anyway," she muttered.

Samantha wasn't sure whether to laugh or cry. Instead she reminded herself that wars weren't won in a single battle. The analogy was a disturbing one. She wasn't at war with Frankie; just the opposite, in fact.

She wasn't sure Frankie knew it, though.

Hoping her smile didn't appear forced, she regarded the girl once more. "Have you thought any more about what you'd like to do today?"

Frankie shrugged. "I dunno," she muttered. "Whatever you want."

Her answer was no more than Samantha expected. She tapped her fingers lightly against the steering wheel and regarded the clear blue skies outside. The weather had turned unseasonably warm for October. After the rain of the past few days, it was especially welcome.

"It's a shame to waste all this sunshine," she mused aloud. "There's a park just a few blocks from my house. Maybe we could go for a bike ride." She glanced over to gauge Frankie's reaction. For just an instant, there was an unexpected leap in Frankie's dark eyes. But it disappeared so suddenly she might have imagined it.

"I don't have a bike," she said grudgingly.

"My neighbor has one she hardly ever uses. I know she'd let us borrow it because I've done it before when my niece is visiting."

Frankie's thin shoulders slumped. She stared at the floor, her voice barely audible. "I've never had a bike, Miss Taylor. I—I don't even know how to ride one."

Samantha almost didn't catch the tiny break in her voice. When she did, it was her undoing. A tight band of emotion seemed to encircle her chest. To her, having a bike was as much a part of childhood as nursery rhymes and cartoons.

She laid a hand on Frankie's shoulder. "If we could do anything you want, Frankie, what would it be?"

For the longest time Frankie said nothing. Then she sighed, a tiny whisper of sound. "I wish we could have a picnic," the girl murmured. "You know, just like what you see on TV, with hot dogs and a blanket spread out under a tree..." She caught Samantha's eye. "It's kinda cold right now, though. I remember we had snow the end of October last year."

Samantha hadn't missed the wistfulness on her face. Seeing it, she swallowed a pang. What else had the girl missed out on? "One never knows this time of year," she admitted. "And I'm afraid the ground's a little too soggy today for a picnic." Even as she spoke, she made a mental note of Frankie's wish. "Is there anything else you'd like to do?"

She held her breath and waited. Frankie seemed lost in thought.

The silence spun out. Just when she'd begun to give up hope, Frankie darted her a cautious look. "We can do whatever I want?"

Samantha nodded. "Within reason, of course," she added with a grin.

Frankie took a deep breath. "I wish—I wish we could make chocolate chip cookies."

Samantha blinked. She wasn't sure what she'd expected the girl to say, but that certainly wasn't it. "You want to make cookies?"

Frankie nodded. "When I was little, Mama and I used to do things like that," she admitted haltingly. "But Mama just doesn't have the time anymore..." She bit her lip.

Samantha shoved the keys into the ignition. "Then this is your lucky day," she said airily. "Because I just happen to have the best recipe for chocolate chip cookies this side of the Mississippi...."

That was how they spent the afternoon.

Frankie was rather quiet, but Samantha didn't expect her to shed her wariness so soon. Trust would not come so easily or quickly to a girl like Frankie—she knew better than to expect it.

It was while they were on their way back to Frankie's that the girl popped an unexpected question. "Do you really have three sisters?"

"I certainly do," she chuckled. "Beth, Kay, and Pat. My parents were certain that after three girls, they'd have a boy when I came along. The only name they had picked out was Sam. When they realized they had another girl, they decided to call me Samantha instead. Only at home everyone still calls me Sam."

She risked a quick glance at the girl. Frankie's mouth had long since lost its sullen droop, but she wasn't smiling...didn't she *ever* smile? It seemed such a little thing, but it made Samantha's heart catch painfully to realize she'd never seen Frankie smile—really smile.

"That reminds me," she said softly. "When we're not at school, Frankie, I'd like you to call me Samantha—please, not Sam!"

She didn't get the rise out of the girl she'd hoped for. Frankie nodded, but said nothing.

They stopped in front of Frankie's building a few minutes later. Samantha decided not to press her luck by asking if Frankie had had a good time. Frankie seized on the tin of cookies she offered her as if they were gold; that was reward enough for Samantha.

On the drive home she wondered what Vince would say when he learned they'd spent the afternoon baking cookies. Just the thought of him sent a strange little shiver dancing up her spine. The next instant a reluctant smile curved her lips. Vince seemed to think there would be more pain than gain in helping Frankie walk the straight and narrow. She only hoped Frankie wasn't tempted to stray too far from the path—or too often.

Her mind still on Frankie, she strode through the back door into the kitchen. She stopped short, sorely tempted to walk back out. Frankie had offered to help wash the dishes before going home, but Samantha had firmly refused. She had wanted to treat Frankie like a guest on their first day together.

She groaned when she saw the disaster they'd created. Dozens of cookies lay cooling on the tabletop. There was flour scattered the length of the countertop. Two large cookie sheets jutted from the sink. Beside them was a stack of sticky bowls.

All at once she didn't care if there were pots and pans stacked to the ceiling. Her gaze slid to the table and the neat rows of cookies; a purely impish spark appeared. She'd resisted the temptation all the while Frankie was here. Now there was no one to see and she felt like a kid in a candy store.

The first one tasted marvelous, the second even better. The third...

The peal of the doorbell made her jump. Her head jerked around guiltily before she was galvanized into action. She hurried toward the living room, scrubbing her hand across her mouth and swallowing hastily. Reaching for the doorknob, she idly wondered who—

"You really should ask who's at the door before you open it," stated a familiar voice.

Her eyes collided with those of Vince Larusso. Two things skittered through her mind in that instant. The first was that she was glad to see him, and the reason why didn't really matter. The second was that he'd voiced that same warning to Frankie—and it was then that she'd experienced the first stirrings of warmth toward him.

She was feeling that same warmth now, but for an entirely different reason. Dressed casually in jeans and a plaid cotton shirt, a scarred leather jacket thrown over one arm, he exuded a sheer male presence that nearly took her breath away.

She leaned against the doorframe. A slow smile crept across her lips. "You know, Larusso, I'm beginning to think you have something against the standard greeting."

A teasing light appeared in his eyes, making them look almost pure gold. "You're looking at a guy who grew up on the streets," he claimed lightly, "I must have missed my lesson in charm school."

What he lacked in charm, he made up for in wholly masculine appeal. The thought swooped out of nowhere, making her feel rather flustered. It didn't help when he smiled straight into her eyes. For a heart-stopping moment, she was sure he had no trouble reading her mind.

He held up her umbrella. "You left this in my car. I'd have returned it yesterday, but it rolled under the seat and I didn't notice it until today."

Her gaze slipped past him toward the cloudless blue sky. "I hadn't missed it yet." Her laugh was rather breathless. "But thanks for bringing it by." She reached for the umbrella. Their fingers barely brushed. To Samantha, the contact was electric.

"Would you like to come in?" The question was out before she could stop it, and then she didn't want to.

Their eyes touched—and something else, too, something deep inside. "I don't mind if I do," he murmured easily.

He was scarcely through the door before her heart set up a furious clamor. She resisted the impulse to run for the nearest mirror. With her luck there were probably crumbs on her lips, flour on her nose or the seat of her jeans where she'd absently dusted her hands before she took Frankie home.

"Would you like a cup of coffee? Or maybe tea?"

"Coffee wouldn't taste bad. But only if it's not too much trouble." Vince could scarcely tear his gaze away from her.

Her state of mind didn't improve when he followed her into the kitchen. She wondered desperately what it was about Vince Larusso that made her feel so off balance. She'd never felt like this with Brad, or any other man for that matter. She couldn't shake her awareness of his presence. Like a shadow in the sun, she couldn't reach out and touch it, but it was there.

He leaned back against the counter and hitched his fingers in the back pockets of his slacks. Samantha filled the coffee carafe with water, trying not to notice how the movement stretched the fabric of his shirt across his chest. Without a suit jacket, he didn't appear quite as big. It hit her right in the pit of her stomach how nicely put together he was. Despite his height, his body was lean and trim, not at all heavy.

Once the coffeemaker was ready, she began to clear the table so they could sit down. "You'll have to excuse the mess," she said absently, layering cookies in the clear glass jar. She turned and started to offer him one only to find he'd already reached out and stolen one for himself.

His expression turned sheepish. "And you'll have to excuse me," he said by way of explanation. "I can't remember the last time I had homemade chocolate chip cookies."

One hand jammed on her hip, she awaited his verdict. "Well," she prompted. "How are they?"

His grin made her heart stop. "Manna from heaven." He reached for another.

An unholy light danced in her eyes. "I'll make sure I pass on the compliment to the cook the next time I see her."

He frowned blankly. "You didn't make these?"

She stifled a smile. "No," she said mildly. "Frankie did."

He nearly choked on the mouthful he'd just taken. His gaze slid to the half-eaten cookie in his hand. "Hell," he muttered. "There's probably arsenic in this!"

His expression was precious. She stuffed the last of the cookies into the jar and patted his shoulder. "Not to worry," she chuckled. "I supervised."

He smiled weakly. "That's supposed to make me feel better? You don't like me any more than she does."

That's where you're wrong, she thought silently. She knew he was kidding, of course. But it didn't stop her from acknowledging that she liked him, despite what promised to be an ongoing feud over Frankie. Indeed, she suspected she could like him far more. . . .

She wiped off the table, filled two cups with coffee and offered one to him. He sat down across from her. "So," he said finally. "Frankie was here today."

Samantha nodded and reached for the sugar. She half expected a crack about her do-gooder image, but he remained silent. She glanced at him, surprised to discover his eyes on her face, his expression rather tentative. He looked as if he very much wanted to say something but couldn't decide if he should.

That was exactly how Vince felt.

"Spit it out, Larusso," she invited, laughing. "Whatever it is you want to say, it can't be that bad."

Vince smiled slightly. His thoughts were suddenly tinged with bitterness. It was a long time since he'd met anyone utterly without guile; maybe he never had. But Samantha wore her feelings openly. Like a well-plotted map, her features were a direct route to her every thought, her every nuance of emotion.

It was inevitable that he should be reminded . . . they were nothing alike, not at all. He held tight to his emotions as closely as he guarded the secrets in his soul. He didn't dare take them out and examine them too closely—he knew he wouldn't like what he found. And so he ignored them, and buried them deep inside where no one would ever see.

"I have the feeling," he murmured, "that you'd rather not know."

"Sure I do," she protested. "Say whatever's on your mind. I can take it on the chin, I promise."

Could she? Vince stared into his cup. There was a time he'd have thought nothing of crushing someone like her under his heel. But Samantha was different, and he wasn't sure yet if it were a blessing or a curse.

"Now I'm really curious, Larusso. Do I have to beat it out of you?"

That made him smile, but it was a smile that didn't quite reach his eyes. "Sometimes honesty commands a high price," he murmured.

"What price?"

"You'll probably boot me out on my ear," he said dryly.

"I'm not the violent type."

"Lady—" this time there was just the hint of a smile in his voice "—you just threatened to beat me."

She raised both hands in a conciliatory gesture. "Never," she vowed. "Besides—" she quirked a brow "—you're bigger than me."

Vince shook his head and sighed. "All right, then. I found it—" he seemed to be searching for the right word "—disturbing to think that you had Frankie here."

She frowned slightly. "Here?"

"At your home," he clarified. "At least until you get to know her better."

Her smile was wiped clean. Vince swore silently. Damn! He should have known this would happen. Hell, he *had* known! It was why he hadn't wanted to say anything.

Her stare was blistering. "Maybe you'd like to explain that, Mr. Larusso. Or does this have something to do with—how was it you put it—Frankie's sticky little fingers?"

Mr. Larusso. He felt like grating his teeth. Vince! he wanted to shout. My name is Vince!

Instead he laced his fingers around his mug and met her gaze evenly. "Are you aware that many residential burglaries are committed by juveniles?" He posed the question very quietly. "They tag along to a friend's house—or the friend of a friend. They check the place out—ask to use the bathroom maybe—to see if there's anything of value around. They look to see where things are kept, where the exits are—"

She shot to her feet like an arrow. "I don't think I like what you're saying. I could understand it if Frankie were from a family of thieves or something. But I met her mother and I'd stake my life that the woman doesn't have a deceitful bone in her body."

He shook his head. "Half the time the parents don't even know what's going on."

"But Frankie's never done anything like that..."

That we know of, he amended silently.

"...and I refuse to believe she'd break into my house just to steal something!"

His smile held no mirth. "They don't always have to."

The sound she made was one of pure disgust. Two steps carried her to the sink where she dumped out the remains of her coffee. She whirled around again, her posture unnaturally stiff.

"What do you have against Frankie?" she demanded. "Or are you always so—suspicious?"

Vince was stung. He couldn't ignore the stab of guilt that twisted inside him. He'd been thinking a lot about Tony lately. Was it because of Frankie Lombardi? His mind rejected the thought as ridiculous.

His heart said otherwise.

But he refused to believe he had singled her out, the way Samantha had just accused him. If anything—because of Tony—he was that much more determined not to see her dragged down any further.

He shoved his fingers through his hair, suddenly feeling as old as the heavens. He understood what Samantha was feeling right now. He'd been in her place a hundred times—wanting so badly for a child to succeed, only to see that child completely turn his back. A hundred times he'd tried to steel himself against the hurt he felt . . . and a hundred times he'd failed.

"Look," he said finally. "I know I seem overly cautious to you—hell, maybe even paranoid!"

Samantha's eyes sparked. He certainly had that right!

"Sometimes too much trust is as bad as too little." He looked up at her suddenly. "Just don't fool yourself into seeing something that isn't there—or forget what *is* there."

Watching him, listening to him, Samantha felt her anger slipping away. It was as if she could see the faint lines in his forehead deepen. And he sounded as frustrated as he looked. Yet whenever they talked about Frankie, it was as if some invisible barrier sprang up between them. She sensed an underlying hardness in his manner that both puzzled and dismayed her. Yet right now, he looked so tired, so defeated, that she felt a curious tug on her heart.

All at once she felt compelled to rationalize her behavior as well as her anger. "Frankie and her mother are struggling just to get by," she said quietly. "I don't think Frankie has had it easy. And believe it or not, she's very protective of her mother." She shook her head help-lessly. "Maybe she's had to grow up too fast, because sometimes I get the feeling it's as if there's a forty-year-old trapped inside her body. Why, she's never even had a bike!

"It's like she's on the edge of a cliff," she went on feelingly, "and I want to pull her back. And I want her to have the chance to do things she hasn't had the chance to do." Her troubled gaze sought his. "Is that so hard to understand?"

No, he thought. God, no. He wanted to explain, he really did. But it didn't matter that he'd exchanged his colors for a suit coat. There was a part of him he couldn't escape—a part of him he couldn't hide, no matter how hard he tried. Deep inside, he was the same kid who was tough and hard because if you weren't, you were shoved aside and trampled upon.

If only he could tell her about Tony. If only... but he was afraid she'd cringe in horror, and he didn't want that to happen. Not yet. Maybe when she knew him better she would understand, and not judge him. But right now he wasn't sure he could find the right words, at least for her.

And maybe there was a better way.

He rose to stand before her. "Are you busy for the rest of the afternoon?"

His voice was rushed and hurried, even a little ur-gent. She shook her head.

"Good. Because there's something I'd like you to see that might help you understand where I'm coming from." He grabbed her coat from the chair where she'd draped it earlier and dropped it on her shoulders. He hustled her outside and into his car so quickly her head was spinning.

It wasn't long before she saw he was headed for the south side of town. "You know," she said lightly, "there's a law against kidnapping."

He chuckled. "That's not my style."

Samantha silently agreed. Vince was too direct and forthright to resort to subterfuge. That was clear right from the start.

The neighborhood they entered into was old and run-down. Dozens of old frame buildings seemed to lean upon one another. Finally they stopped in front of a ramshackle old building next to a dilapidated tenement. Two stories above, threadbare curtains flapped through an open window.

Vince wasted no time getting out. Samantha opened the passenger door. Why had he brought her here? she wondered. He hadn't liked the idea of her walking home through what he called a "bad" neighborhood. This one was downright dangerous. She shivered and slipped on her jacket. All at once the waning afternoon sunlight seemed cold and bleak.

He joined her on the sidewalk. She glanced uneasily past his shoulder, where half a dozen unruly, restive-looking youths had taken possession of the sidewalk in front of the building.

"You sure you're on the right block, Larusso?" She was only half joking.

"Around here they all look the same." He most definitely was not joking.

His stride took him toward the entrance. Her heart sank as she saw they had to pass directly by the group of youths. Samantha kept apace with him and tried not to stare, but they were so young—some no older than

Frankie. They were just kids, she thought numbly, kids who had no doubt witnessed enough harshness to last a lifetime; kids who had lost their innocence far too soon.

A little shock ran through her when her eyes picked up the glint of steel. One of them was carelessly brandishing a switchblade. He intercepted her glance, flicked the blade up in the air and caught it, smiled nastily and shoved it in his boot.

Fear prodded her blindly forward but she stumbled on a crack in the sidewalk. Behind her, strong fingers closed around her arm. She was grateful when Vince's hand remained there; she instinctively edged closer as he guided her past the group, walking by them bold-as-you-please. When he opened the door, she rushed inside. Her heart was beating so fast she could scarcely breathe. It didn't matter how young they were, these kids frightened her.

"Aren't you afraid your car will be gone when we go back out?" Why she was whispering, she had no idea. But her ominous surroundings seemed to demand it.

"It'll still be there." He ushered her up the stairs.

"But those kids outside. They're—why, they're hoods! They'll probably have it stripped in—"

They're hoods . . . the words echoed off the chambers of his mind, dull and empty. Her reaction was no more than what he'd expected, far less than what he'd hoped for. Yet he couldn't blame her, because she was right....

That was the hell of it.

He cut her off more abruptly than he intended. "They won't. They know me."

Samantha gasped. How? How did they know him? Her head jerked around to confront him, but the question died in her throat. His expression was cool and remote, revealing nothing of his thoughts. Her imagination ran wild until she realized how obtuse she'd been. He was a probation officer; he saw kids like these day after day.

"Here we are," he murmured. He pushed open one of two cracked and peeling double doors. His hand at the small of her back, he gently pushed her through.

She found herself standing in a huge room filled with an assortment of workout equipment. The noise was the first thing she noticed. Amidst the clanking and heaving, the grunts and groans, she spied several boys around sixteen or seventeen, and a couple of older men. All reflected that same hard-to-the-bone defiant spirit as the kids outside. In the corner, a huge muscle-bound man lifted a hand in greeting. Vince gave a brief salute in return, then lowered his head to her ear.

"That's Al," he said, his voice very low. "He runs this place with a grant from the city."

She gave a shaky laugh. "So the purpose of this visit is inspiration? You brought me here so that I'd want to look like him—and then you wouldn't think twice about me walking home again from school again." As scared as she'd been, she was relieved to find her sense of humor hadn't deserted her.

Vince seemed to relax as well. "Now there's a thought," he murmured. The next instant he stepped behind her. His hands on her shoulders, he guided her around a quarter-turn. "See that kid there? The one with the red bandanna around his head? His name is Danny Rodriguez. A year ago he robbed a convenience store and knifed the clerk who was about to raise a silent alarm."

Samantha gave a shocked little gasp. "Why is he here? Why isn't he—"

"Locked up somewhere?"

She nodded, unable to take her eyes from the boy, who couldn't have been more than fifteen.

Vince's tone was grim. "He was for a while. But he's a juvenile, remember. The system has only so much room. Besides, rehabilitation is the key word. Change their behavior—change their way of thinking." His voice took on a cutting edge. "It's easy for the guys at the top to dictate to the rest of us. They think we can pull a kid out of his home, give a few pretty little speeches and everything will be fine and dandy. They don't realize that sticking a kid right back into a neighborhood like this just starts the whole damned cycle all over again. And that's where the real battle is."

That he felt very strongly about it was obvious. Samantha wasn't about to argue. She had encountered much the same problem in her own job.

She said nothing when he proceeded to point out another boy who was on probation for assault charges. He then ushered her across the hall into a gymnasium where a group of kids were shooting baskets.

"See the redhead sitting on the bleachers? He's had repeated burglary and theft offenses starting from the time he was seven."

"Seven! That's hardly more than a baby!"

His laugh was short and harsh. "Kids grow up quick around here if they grow up at all." With nary a pause he pointed to the teenager who'd just lobbed the basketball through the air. "Rob there helped carry out a nifty little armed robbery. No knives this time—" his matter-of-fact tone was chilling "—just a very convenient Saturday night special."

Samantha swallowed, fighting a churning swell in her stomach. She knew things like this went on, yet seeing these boys and knowing what they had done made it much more real. Much more deadly and horrifying.

And all the more heartbreaking.

It was a moment before she realized several boys had disengaged themselves from the others. They swaggered toward them.

"Who's the babe, Larusso?"

"Hey, Larusso! Get your—" the word was shockingly graphic "—over here and shoot some hoops with us!"

Vince was unperturbed. He glanced at Samantha, relieved to note that her face had gone from pale to blooming with color. "Later," he called out.

Someone hooted. "Aw, come on, man!"

"Hey, leave the man alone! Can't you see he got better things to do?"

There was a round of guffaws. A lewdly yelled suggestion made her shift uncomfortably. Another made her avert her eyes and stare at the dingy brown wall. She had no intention of objecting when a long arm appeared in her line of vision and pushed open the door.

"Your true colors are showing," he murmured once they were out in the pitted hallway. "You're blushing."

His smiling regard spurred her defensiveness. "It was stuffy in there."

They started down the steps. "You mean you're not embarrassed?"

"Of course not!" She reconsidered when he raised his brows and gave her a long, sideways glance. "Well, maybe a little."

He laughed. "Maybe a lot."

The betraying rush of color deepened. She felt compelled to explain. "They thought I was your—"

"I know." They were at the outside exit. He reached around her shoulder and placed his palm flat against the door but made no move to open it. "Were you offended?"

His tone was very low. All trace of amusement vanished in that instant. Samantha turned slightly, a movement that succeeded in bringing them just a breath apart. They touched nowhere, yet she could feel their closeness through a nerve-shattering awareness. All she could think was how his shoulders stretched to fill the worn leather of his jacket.

Her eyes strayed helplessly to his face. There was a guarded tension in his features. Though she didn't understand why, she sensed her answer was important to him.

She shook her head. "I wasn't offended." The words were no more than a breath of sound. They were all she could manage at the moment.

Raucous male voices and the echo of footsteps on the stairs reached her ears. Vince stepped back; the spell was broken.

She shivered and instinctively edged closer to Vince as they stepped through the doorway. Miraculously his car was still parked at the curb, untouched.

She didn't speak again until she was settled in the seat. "Those kids inside. They seem to know you rather well."

Now he was the one who looked embarrassed. "I coach basketball here a couple of times a week."

"For the kids that were here today?"

"Mostly."

"Are you their probation officer? Any of them?"

He hesitated. "Just one who wasn't there today. One of the guys I work with is assigned to several of the kids there."

She twisted around in her seat so she could see him better. It was, she decided, rather refreshing to have him under the gun for a change.

"Why," she mused aloud, "do I have the feeling you're not there just to coach basketball? That you're there to straighten their heads out instead?"

"Sometimes I feel like bashing their heads together."

His low grumble made her smile. "You don't make pretty little speeches, I'll bet." She remembered what he'd said inside.

The merest hint of a smile curled his mouth. "No," he agreed. "Not pretty. This is neutral territory, I guess. They know who I am and what I do, but they don't hassle me. I do what I can, when I can, and try to let them know I'm available if they need someone to talk to. It gets them off the streets for a while, and if we're real lucky, it could be a change in direction for some of them."

"I see," she said lightly. "Do I dare accuse you of being a do-gooder?"

"Don't you dare," he said gravely. "You'll ruin my reputation if you do."

Amusement flickered between them, but Samantha couldn't rid the image of those hard-bitten angry young faces that kept flitting into her mind. Her smile faded.

"Larusso." His name was unusually somber. "What do you think will happen to those kids? Say, in three or four years."

His answer was a long time in coming. "Their record will be expunged when they turn eighteen. With a whole lot of luck, they'll stay clean. But all too often they end up in prison."

"What about Danny Rodriguez?"

"I'd like to believe that won't happen."

"But chances are against him keeping clean and staying out of prison." It was more a statement than a question.

"Yeah," he said heavily. "I guess they are. Because all too often these kids go from bad to worse."

"And you feel that's where Frankie's headed."

His voice was carefully neutral. "Your words, not mine."

"But it's true, isn't it?" She was quietly insistent. "That's why you brought me here, isn't it? To prove that you're right about her and I'm wrong—"

"No." His denial was swift and emphatic. "This has nothing to do with either of us being right or wrong, believe me." He grimaced and darted her a quick hurried glance. "I just wanted you to see what you're up against. Because if you don't go into this with your eyes wide open, you could be letting yourself in for a big fall. It's easy to get caught up in these kids' problems, not so easy to let go." His sigh held a note of weary frustration. "It'll be a miracle if any of them turn out straight."

Samantha's gaze fell to her lap. His message was implicit—he was warning her not to get her hopes up too high. On one level, she appreciated his concern. But she wondered what he would say if he realized he'd only made her that much more determined to drag Frankie back from the hole she'd begun sliding into.

She raised her head. "If that's how you feel—" her voice rang out as clear as a bell "—then why bother? Why even *try* to help them out? Is it worth all the pain and anger and frustration?"

They had stopped for a red light. For the longest time she thought he hadn't heard—or had chosen to ignore her. Then all at once she had the strangest sensation he was a million miles away. Even as she watched, a curious bleakness seeped into the strong, proud lines of his profile.

There was an odd tightening in her chest. He looked so—so empty and alone. It spun through her mind that there had to be a reason . . . and then even that thought was lost when he finally spoke.

"Is there a price tag on life?" His voice was very quiet, almost whimsical. "I don't know. I'm not sure I want to know. But if even one of those kids goes straight, I'll rest a little easier at night."

He glanced over, caught her wide-eyed gaze and gave a sheepish little smile. Samantha knew then that he had forgotten her presence completely.

Neither spoke throughout the remainder of the drive; there didn't seem to be the need. For some strange, indefinable reason, Samantha felt very close to Vince just then. She even dared to hope that perhaps they weren't so far apart where Frankie was concerned after all.

Darkness was complete by the time Vince angled his car into her driveway. Somehow she wasn't surprised when Vince said he'd walk her to the door.

On the back porch she opened the screen, fitted her key into the lock and turned it. She made no move to open the door. Instead she turned and smiled up at him.

"Would you like to stay for a while? I can't promise much in the way of dinner but I'm sure I can scrape together something."

Her heart was racing, she realized. They stood only a breath apart. It was impossible not to be conscious of him as a man, a very attractive man. This was the first time she'd felt anything at all like this since she'd broken off her engagement to Brad, yet that awareness both fascinated and confused her. Vince wasn't the kind of man she was usually attracted to; certainly he was nothing at all like Brad. Brad had been cool and so utterly in control she'd sometimes wanted to scream.

Vince Larusso, on the other hand, was hot-tempered and volatile. There was a tough uncompromising masculinity about him that was unlike anything she'd ever encountered in a man before—a masculinity that both fascinated and confused her.

It also scared her just a little. Vince was…rougher, for lack of a better word. Bolder and more abrupt. And she couldn't quite banish the notion that despite the "marshmallow" heart she teased him about, he possessed a ruthlessness she didn't think she liked.

So why had she asked him to stay? And why was she standing here praying that he wouldn't refuse?

But if Samantha was in chaos, so was Vince. There was something going on inside him, something that was going to take getting used to. It was as if everything inside were being rearranged. He wasn't sure what it was, or why it was happening—only that it was. It frightened him a little, because he was used to being in control.

Yet he wanted to stay. He wanted it very badly. Conversely it was for that very reason that he knew he wouldn't.

Finally he shook his head. "I can't," he said, shifting uncomfortably. "I'd really like to. It's just that—" He broke off, wondering if she would understand.

Something must have shown in his expression. "You're going back there, aren't you?" Her eyes never wavered from his. "To the gym?"

He nodded. "I told them later," he said, his tone very low. "I know I didn't promise, but I hate to let them down."

Samantha had just decided she'd just made another fascinating discovery. Vince Larusso was a man with principles and standards—tough ones, she suspected. Well, she liked that in a man. She especially liked it in him.

"You don't have to explain." She felt she was smiling clear to her heart. "Maybe you'd better get back before they decide you've deserted them after all."

Her smile made his breath catch. The urge to linger was overpowering. He felt like a lap dog at the feet of its mistress. Not until she had opened the door and stepped inside did he jam his hands into his pockets and force himself to move away.

"Vince?"

She called after him softly, a voice that sent tingling currents feathering up and down his spine. He'd wondered what his name would sound like on her lips....

Now he knew.

But it only made him hunger to hear her say it again and again, a hundred different ways. Playfully. Passionately. All husky and soft and breathy, like just now.

Slowly he turned and faced her. Through the darkness, their eyes connected.

"Please be careful," she whispered.

His lips smiled; his eyes didn't. In all his life, he couldn't think when anyone had asked that of him. Because no one had ever cared, except perhaps Tony... The empty spot on his soul seemed emptier still.

He raised a hand. "I'll be in touch."

CHAPTER SEVEN

A TEPID LATE-MORNING SUN glittered down on the small figure huddled on the stone steps.

A voice hailed her. "Frankie! Hey, Frankie!"

Frankie turned her head in the direction of the voice. Joey was striding leisurely down the sidewalk toward her, his jacket tucked under his arm despite the nippy north wind.

"Hi, Joey." She edged over slightly to make room for him.

He sat down next to her. "Where ya been lately?"

Frankie's lips tightened. "You're the one who hasn't been around all week," she said stiffly.

He shrugged. "Yeah, well, you know how it is. I've been pretty busy."

"I looked for you down at Phil's yesterday but you weren't there." If she was mad, Frankie couldn't help it. Joey was her best friend, only she hadn't seen him even once this past week. She wasn't dumb enough to fool herself. She knew why. He'd been with Pete.

Her accusing tone didn't bother Joey in the least. He grinned and propped his elbows on the steps behind him. "We spent all day yesterday just cruisin' in his car. It's a neat car, Frankie. Man, you oughta see it."

"Yesterday? You skipped school?"

Joey glanced over and caught her frown. "So what? Who needs school anyway? That's what Pete always says."

Frankie stared out into the street.

"Hey, what's the problem? Pete's an all-right guy." This time Joey sounded a little miffed.

Frankie slipped her hands into the pockets of her coat, shivering a little from the biting wind. She sighed, feeling Joey's stare. "You really like him, don't you?" she asked quietly.

Joey's eyes gleamed. "Who wouldn't? Pete's one smooth operator, Frankie. When he talks, everybody listens. And he's got everything he wants—that car. And man, is he a slick dresser!"

"You told me once that he doesn't have a job."

Joey snorted. "Why should he work when he doesn't have to?"

"So where's he get money for all this stuff?"

Joey tapped his temple. "He's got it where it counts. He's a lot like Phil, only smarter. Plus he's got the perfect setup." A slow grin spread across his features. "He gets what he wants and he barely lifts a finger. 'Maximum reward for minimum effort' is how Pete puts it."

Frankie tugged at a loose thread in her jeans. So Pete was involved in peddling stolen goods, just like Phil. She couldn't say she was surprised. And apparently he found someone else to do his dirty work for him, like Joey and the other kids who were always hanging around him. No doubt stealing wasn't the only thing he was involved in.

Joey nudged her. "Hey, why don't you come with me today? Pete won't mind, 'cause I already talked to him about you. He said he can always use an extra pair of hands." He winked and laughed.

Frankie wasn't laughing. "I can't," she muttered.

Joey's smile faded. "How come?"

Frankie hesitated. She was tempted to go with him, but Miss Taylor was supposed to pick her up any time now. It irritated her that the thought of standing her up made her feel almost guilty. Joey was her best friend. Miss Taylor wasn't.

"'Cause I'm waiting to meet somebody." She looked away as she spoke.

"Who?"

Frankie sighed. "Her name's Miss Taylor. She's a counselor from school." Her voice very low, she explained about the Big Sister/Little Sister pair-up.

"Why's she bothering with you?" he demanded when she'd finished.

The edge in his tone made Frankie stiffen. "'Cause she wants to, that's why."

"Cripes. She sounds like Mary Poppins." Joey rolled his eyes. "Wake up, kid. She's probably only doing it to make herself look good. That's the only reason anybody does *anything* for somebody else."

Frankie's chin jutted out. She didn't know why she was so steamed. Joey had just stated what she'd been telling herself all along.

Joey stood. "Well, Frankie? You comin' with me or not?"

"Nope." She ignored his snapping gaze. If Joey was a little upset, so what? Maybe he'd know how she'd felt all this week when she'd wanted to talk to him and he hadn't been around.

"Well, then," he said snidely, "have a blast with Mary Poppins."

He flung his jacket over his shoulder and spun around. Frankie was still glaring after him when she heard the sound of a car door. She turned her head to see

Miss Taylor heading toward her. It gave her a start to see her dressed in jeans and a sweater, just the way it had last week.

"Hi, Frankie. Are you all set?" Her smile was syrupy sweet, the girl noted disgustedly. Joey was right. She was a regular Mary Poppins.

"I'm ready." Frankie picked herself up from the steps.

Inside her car, Samantha slid the key into the ignition. Her tone was deliberately casual as she glanced over at her passenger. "Who was that boy you were talking to?"

Frankie froze. She was sorely tempted to snap "None of your business!" but she stopped herself. Instead she looked deliberately out the window. "A friend," she said shortly.

But Samantha had already noticed the mottled flush creeping into the girl's cheeks. "Joey Bennett?" she asked quietly.

Frankie's head whipped around. Her expression fairly shouted defiance. "What if it was?"

Samantha fought a spurt of helpless frustration. The question was as good as an admission of guilt. Some sixth sense had warned her the boy was Joey Bennett the instant she saw Frankie talking to him. She hadn't meant to start off their day together like this. Yet she had to know for certain if the boy was Joey.

She made no move to start the car's engine. Instead she shook her head and regarded Frankie. "You're not supposed to be seeing him, Frankie. You know that."

"I didn't go looking for him." *This time,* a little voice reminded her. "He was the one who came up and started talking." At least she wasn't lying, though for the life of her, Frankie couldn't understand why it mattered. Sure, it hurt to lie to Mama. But it had never mattered with anyone else. So why did she feel like ducking her head and hiding her head in shame?

Yet some devil inside her made her do just the opposite. "You're gonna tell Larusso, aren't you?"

Samantha didn't back down from Frankie's furious glare. The girl was leery of her; she didn't trust her. A pang swept through her. Was it just her? Or was it because she was an adult?

She took a deep breath and prayed she wasn't making a very big mistake. "I could," she said calmly. "But I'll let it slide this time because I think you deserve the benefit of the doubt." Frankie looked relieved. "But don't think you can wheedle your way around me just because we see each other outside of school. Is that understood?"

When Frankie gave a tiny, nearly imperceptible nod, Samantha's heart twisted. *Oh, Frankie,* she thought, *I'm not the enemy. Can't you see that?*

"All right now." She deliberately lightened her tone. "What are we going to do today?"

Frankie shrugged.

This time Samantha was prepared, however. "I thought you might say that. You haven't had lunch yet, have you?"

"No."

She smiled her satisfaction. "Good. Then you're in for a surprise."

Slowly, almost reluctantly, the girl's eyes were drawn to her face. "What kind of surprise?" she asked after a moment.

Samantha chuckled and started the car. "You'll see," she said airily.

In reality, she was far less sure of herself than she sounded. At her house, they stepped into the kitchen.

Samantha immediately called a halt. "Close your eyes," she commanded.

Frankie squinted up at her as if she'd lost her mind.

Samantha sighed. "It won't be a surprise unless you close your eyes."

"*What* won't?"

"It won't be a surprise if I tell you, either," she said dryly. "Come on, now. Chin up. Hands out. Eyes closed, and don't you dare open them until I tell you!" She found herself on the receiving end of another long, suspicious stare before the girl finally complied. Samantha took her hand and led her toward the living room, where she positioned her just inside the doorway. "Stay right there," she instructed.

She rushed across the floor. "Okay, Frankie. Open your eyes."

Wide dark eyes flew open. Samantha was half-afraid to see her reaction. Instead she moved to stand at the edge of the gaily colored plaid blanket spread out on the floor in the center of the room.

"Voilà," she announced dramatically. "One picnic coming right up. One picnic basket filled with all kinds of goodies. One portable grill to fix our hot dogs and roast marshmallows. We even—" with a flourish she pointed to the potted palm strategically placed at the edge of the blanket "—have a shade tree!"

For long, drawn-out seconds, Frankie stared. Samantha held her breath until she thought her lungs would burst. "Well?" she asked with a lightness that far belied her anxiety. "What do you think? Is this or is it not just what you ordered?"

Frankie edged forward as if she were in a trance. Slowly she knelt down on the blanket. Her hand came out to touch the wicker basket with a touch that was almost reverent.

Her gaze veered suddenly to Samantha. "Just like on TV," she said with a grin.

Samantha was suddenly sure her heart would burst instead. Her plan was a success. She'd surprised Frankie. More, she was almost certain she'd delighted her. But best of all, she'd made her smile—an honest-to-goodness, real-life smile.

She used the portable grill outside on the back porch to grill their hot dogs. But they ate them in the living room, sitting cross-legged on the blanket.

She reached for another handful of potato chips and dropped them on her plate. "When I was a kid," she mused, "my dad used to barbecue almost every Sunday. I used to sit in the grass and make little necklaces and bracelets from dandelion stems."

Frankie looked startled. "Dandelions! But they're weeds!"

Samantha grinned. "Yeah. I know. My mother never failed to inform me at least twenty times the next morning when she found wilted dandelion stems in my jewelry box."

Frankie stared down into her cupful of lemonade. "I never did that," she said in a small voice.

Samantha's heart twisted. Frankie didn't have a bike—she didn't know how to ride one. Coaxing gently, she learned there were other things Frankie had never done. Playing baseball in the park. Touch football in the fall. Swinging on a swingset or going down a slide.

All were things she'd done a hundred times as a child and never thought twice about. She suddenly felt rather selfish for having taken them for granted all this time. But she was more determined than ever to see that

Frankie had the chance to experience all that she had missed.

Frankie put her cupful of lemonade up to her lips. "This is . . . nice," she murmured. An unexpected spark flared in her eyes. "The only thing that's missing is bees."

"Count your blessings." She laughed and tipped her head to the side. "We'll have to do this again in the summer. Outside. In a *real* park. And maybe your mother could come along, too. We could see if she likes dandelion necklaces any more than *my* mother."

Frankie's eyes lit up. "That'd be neat," she started to say. All at once, however, her smile faded. Her features grew almost brooding. "Except Mama might not be able to come if she's still working two jobs," she muttered.

Samantha frowned. "Has she been doing that long?"

Frankie mulled for a moment. "About a month, I guess. She had a job for a long time as a waitress, but then she was sick most of September so she got fired."

So Anna *had* been sick in September, when Frankie had been absent from school so often. At least she knew for certain Frankie's excuses were legitimate. She listened intently as Frankie went on.

"We were already behind on the rent when the landlord raised it." She scowled. "Mama found a job at the bakery but she said she needed another one to help pay the bills for when she went in to see the doctor."

"I noticed her cough when I was there," Samantha observed quietly. "Did she have bronchitis?"

"I think that's what it was. But she always coughs a lot in the winter. She says it's because of her asthma. Mama doesn't like it when it's cold. She likes it when the sun shines and it's warm," she added, almost as an afterthought. "She says she always catches more colds in the winter."

Which no doubt aggravated her asthma, Samantha deduced grimly. Her sister Pat had had asthma as a child, but she'd outgrown it. But she remembered her mother fretting and hunting out the vaporizer because Pat had nearly always wheezed whenever she caught a cold.

"So her health has never been good."

It was more a statement than a question. Frankie looked vaguely uncomfortable. "Mama doesn't really like doctors and hospitals, either. That's why when she went to the doctor in September I knew how sick she really was."

Samantha set her paper plate aside, both curious and concerned. "Why doesn't she like doctors?"

Frankie wrapped thin arms around her knees and drew them up to her chest. "I think it might have something to do with Father Anthony—he used to be the parish priest. He got real sick and had to go to the hospital." There was a small pause. "He never got out."

Samantha's breath caught. "He died?"

Frankie nodded and stared out across the room. "Mama cried a lot when he died," she said quietly.

And Anna, because of the inexplicable workings of the human mind, perhaps associated doctors and hospitals with death and dying.

"Frankie." She decided to risk pressing her luck. "Is that what happened to your father, too? Is he dead?"

Frankie's expression underwent a lightning transformation. One minute she looked pensive, even sad. The next she looked angry and as hard as obsidian. "He ran out on Mama and me when I was just a baby. He never came back, so I don't know where he is—" there was no mistaking the bitterness that fed the words "—and I don't *want* to know."

Samantha was aghast. "But what about his family? Didn't they know where he went?"

Frankie explained curtly. "Mama met him when he was in the Army stationed in Italy. Then he came to Chicago to work at some fort here. After a while he ran off. That's all Mama ever told me so I don't think she knew much about his family."

"And she doesn't have any other family here in this country?"

Frankie shook her head. "Mama's parents and brothers died in a fire when she was just a kid. She went to live in an orphanage outside Rome after that."

So all these years it was just the two of them ... The scenario was suddenly stark and vivid in her mind. Time and circumstances had transformed Frankie into a child well versed in the harshness of life. Her mother was frail and sickly; they'd had to struggle for what little was theirs. If Frankie was hard-nosed and worldly, it was no wonder. No doubt she had had to watch out for both of them, herself and her mother.

Yet one thing was very clear. No matter how tough and careless Frankie appeared, she cared about her mother very much.

More than anything, Samantha wanted to reach out and wrap the girl in her arms ... if only she dared! But she was well aware Frankie didn't trust her, and perhaps the reason had its roots in her father running out on them. She also knew that Frankie had to discover for herself that she cared—really cared—before the girl would ever begin to trust her. And that would take a great deal of time and patience.

She had plenty of both.

The pall that had descended was almost stifling. Everything had gone so well today, Samantha hated to ruin it by dwelling any further on Frankie's mother or father. A change of subject was definitely in order.

"Hey, you know what? No picnic is complete without roasting marshmallows." She didn't need to feign the tiny smile flirting at her mouth. The mere mention of marshmallows made her think of Vince, something she'd been doing quite a lot of this past week.

She chuckled at Frankie's skepticism. "What if I don't like them?"

"You'll have fun roasting them anyway," she said airily. Rising to her feet, she crooked her finger.

Unfortunately the coals in the grill outside were stonecold. Samantha decided to be creative and try toasting them over the electric burner of her stove. She was delighted to find that Frankie loved roasted marshmallows as much as she did. Unfortunately her fourth one plopped onto the burner. A thin plume of smoke preceded an acrid aroma. Samantha had no sooner switched off the burner than the smoke alarm emitted a screeching whine.

Frankie grabbed the dishrag and carefully tried to remove the marshmallow from the burner. Samantha grabbed a chair and yanked the cover off the smoke alarm, her fingers clumsy as she hurriedly tried to disconnect the battery.

Neither one heard the pounding footsteps tearing up the back porch.

Samantha finally succeeded in jerking the battery from its berth. The sudden silence was almost as earsplitting as the smoke alarm. She opened her mouth to laughingly tell Frankie that this was certainly one picnic she would never forget—

"What," demanded a low male voice, "is going on here?"

Both females whirled around. Samantha wasn't sure who was more startled, her or Frankie. The sweep of her gaze took in the tall formidable figure filling the doorway, hands braced high against the doorframe.

"Samantha? I nearly broke my neck getting in here when I heard all the noise. And your door wasn't locked, either!"

There was no escape from that burning golden gaze. Vince looked both confounded and furious as he confronted her. She might have laughed if she hadn't been so embarrassed.

"We were roasting marshmallows," she said weakly. "And then the smoke alarm went off."

He looked from one to the other and back again. "Marshmallows," he repeated. She heard a long sigh and saw his arms drop back to his sides. "A symbolic gesture, I take it," he muttered.

She hopped off the chair and gestured over her shoulder. "We were having a picnic," she said, as if that explained everything.

"In here?" His gaze veered beyond her to the crazy scene in her living room—furniture pushed aside, the remains of their lunch littering the blanket.

"It was fun," she informed him tartly.

Across the room, their eyes met and held. "Then it looks like I came just a little too late, doesn't it?" One dark heavy brow hiked roguishly upward. Not until then did she realize he was silently laughing at them.

His smile completely disarmed her. Samantha was unable to do anything but smile in return, an odd little flutter in her heart.

Unfortunately Frankie wasn't so inclined. Entranced as she was, several seconds passed before a movement to the side of her reminded her of the girl's presence. Frankie was staring at Vince, her expression sour enough to curdle milk.

A flurry of panic struck when Vince transferred his attention as well. "Hello, Frankie," he greeted lazily. "I was hoping you'd be here."

The girl shifted her weight from one outspread leg to the other. She muttered something under her breath that sounded like "I'll just bet."

Vince, however, was looking rather amused. Based on past experience, Samantha wasn't sure if that was good or bad. "Don't you want to know why?" she heard him ask.

Frankie's gaze veered directly to Samantha. Samantha was startled at the wordless accusation burning in her eyes. Clearly she expected her to tell him about Joey.

There was a long, drawn-out silence before Frankie glanced back at Vince. "I guess," she muttered shortly, "seeing as you're just dying to tell me."

"Good. Because I have something for you." His mild tone gave nothing away, but Samantha had seen the way his lips compressed tightly for just an instant. He was obviously trying hard not to let Frankie rattle him.

Did she dare hope it was because of her?

Vince beckoned to her, started to turn and then thought better of it. "You'd better get a jacket." His gaze took in both of them. "This might take a while."

It was Samantha who retrieved their jackets from the front closet, her curiosity thoroughly aroused. Frankie, however, followed Vince outside with all the enthusiasm of a man approaching a firing squad. She stood on the bottom step of the porch, her hands jammed into the back pockets of her jeans. Vince moved around to the back of his car and lifted the trunk. Samantha paused on the step behind Frankie, watching as he bent to lift something from inside.

A dull red frame and two tires flashed into view. He wheeled it around the fender and halted expectantly.

Frankie frowned. "So what? It's just a bike."

"Smart girl," he said dryly. "If you noticed that, you also noticed it's not new, and it's not a fancy ten-speed." His tone was casually offhand, his expression anything but as he awaited Frankie's reaction.

For once Frankie's features betrayed none of her characteristic belligerence. She peered at Vince uncertainly. "I don't get it," she said slowly. "Are you lending it to me or something?"

His lips quirked. He shook his head. He had yet to take his eyes from her face. "It's yours," he said softly.

Frankie stared at the bike. "Mine?" she echoed faintly. Her gaze trickled slowly to his face. She swallowed, her voice low. "Why?" was all she asked.

Vince shrugged. Samantha sensed he was feeling every bit as awkward as Frankie. "Weather permitting, you won't always have to walk to school—" there was a meaningful pause "—which will give you more time to study."

Watching the exchange, Samantha's throat grew achingly tight, but there was a warm glow spreading inside her. When she'd told Vince that Frankie didn't have a bike, she'd never dreamed he'd do something like this.

Samantha's hands came up to rest on the girl's thin shoulders. "Why don't you give it a spin?" she urged.

Frankie didn't make a move. Her head drooped like a rag doll's. She stared at the toes of her sneakers. "I don't know how," she muttered.

Vince arched a brow. "Come again," he said calmly. "I didn't catch that." He'd heard her perfectly well. He knew from the way Samantha's eyes widened that she was well aware he'd heard.

Frankie raised her head. "I never rode a bike before so I don't know how." Her voice was low and precise; she damned him with her eyes.

"Then it's about time you learned, isn't it?" His smile made her grit her teeth. A good sign, Vince decided. After all the trouble he'd gone to, he wasn't about to let her give up and just walk away.

She didn't disappoint him. She marched over to him and grabbed the handlebars. "It's really just a matter of balance," he began. Frankie didn't say a word but she listened intently while he and Samantha offered instruction.

They wheeled the bike down the driveway and into the street. Frankie awkwardly straddled the seat, tentatively placed a foot against the pedal and pushed off.

The first and second crash made Samantha wince. She stole a glance at Vince, but his expression was unreadable. Frankie scowled fiercely, dusted off the knees of her jeans and jerked the bike upright. The third crash impelled Samantha forward instinctively, but Vince's hand closed around her arm, stopping her in midstride.

"Let her try again," he said softly.

Frankie got on the bike once more, again to no avail. Samantha wanted to go to her, to offer encouragement and maybe even a little comfort. But before she had a chance Frankie straightened abruptly, her features as ominous as a thunderhead. The bike lay jammed against the curb, one wheel spinning forlornly in the air. Samantha didn't know whether to laugh or cry.

"I can't ride that dumb thing!" she cried hotly. "Darn it, Larusso, I can't! You might as well take it back right now!"

"You know you're right," he drawled. "I should have known better."

At first Samantha couldn't identify the edge in his voice. When she did she wanted to scream with frustration. Didn't he know that sarcasm would only add fuel to a fire that was already roaring?

Frankie had stopped short, fists jammed at her sides, her eyes blazing furiously.

His gaze raked her from head to toe. "It was stupid of me to expect you to learn to ride a bike at your age. After all you're . . . how old? Eleven? Twelve?"

"Thirteen, Larusso, and you know it!"

"My mistake. I should have realized a trike would have been just the thing for a kid like you."

Samantha nearly groaned. If he'd wanted to make Frankie mad, he'd done a bang-up job. She should have realized Vince and Frankie couldn't be around each other without a contest of wills. She couldn't look away as the anger in Frankie's eyes gave way to outrage, but Vince didn't seem to notice. Or perhaps he just didn't care.

His smile was taunting. "Maybe if I get it back right away, they'll trade it for a tri—"

He got no further. Frankie spun around, seized the bike and hauled it upright. Dirt sprayed from beneath the rear tire as she rammed the pedals down.

Only this time she didn't falter—and she didn't fall.

Samantha stared after her. "Hey," she said faintly. "She's doing it. She's riding it!"

"Yeah," he said softly. "She sure is."

Samantha wasn't sure which gave her the most pleasure, the satisfaction that laced his tone or the sheer pleasure she experienced just looking at him.

He drew her gaze like a magnet. Unlike her and Frankie, he wore no coat. His stance was supremely masculine, legs splayed apart, arms folded across his chest as he stared out after Frankie. The worn, faded denim of his jeans bonded against his thighs like a second skin. The wind played havoc with the dark shiny strands of hair lying on his forehead.

Her mouth grew dry. The rugged, earthy aura that clung to him kindled a melting heat in places she had no business thinking about.

It was the sound of skidding tires that rattled her out of her daze. Frankie braked to a quick halt, her hair flying, her cheeks ruddy with cold. And she was smiling…a smile that seemed to reach out and grab hold of Samantha's heart.

"You see? You did it, Frankie. I knew you could!" She ran forward and gave her a fierce impulsive hug.

A lazy half smile played around Vince's mouth. "Nice going, kid."

One minute Frankie was grinning, dark eyes shining like a child's at Christmas. The next her smile had withered, and her triumph along with it, like a cloud creeping over the sun. She slid off the bike and took an inordinate amount of time easing the kickstand in place.

Concerned, Samantha glanced at Vince. He shook his head slightly, as puzzled as she.

She laid a hand on her shoulder. "Frankie? What is it?"

Eyes downcast, the girl kicked at a pebble in the driveway. "I can't pay you for it, Larusso." Her voice was so low they had to strain to hear. "I don't have any money."

He shrugged. "I got it at a second-hand store, Frankie." A faint light appeared in his eyes. "And I got an extremely good deal on it when I told the owner it was for a worthy cause."

Frankie stiffened. Oh, Lord, Samantha groaned. Frankie thought Vince was hitting below the belt.

Vince realized it, too. He exhaled slowly, struggling for a hard-won patience. "I wasn't poking fun at you," he stated quietly. "And I don't expect anything for the bike, either."

Frankie's eyes remained cloudy. "But I owe you for it. And my mother won't take money she didn't work for, so I know what she'll say—"

"Then let's do this. I don't know what you and Samantha have planned for the next few Saturdays, but maybe you could wash my car every once in a while depending on the weather. I wouldn't mind bringing it over when the two of you are finished." Was he looking for excuses to see Samantha? He was and he didn't mind admitting it.

Samantha nodded quickly when he glanced at her for approval.

Frankie bit her lip. This was something she hadn't bargained on, but it wasn't the work that made her pause. It was knowing that Larusso would undoubtedly stick around—and not because of her, she decided disgustedly. She was no dummy. She'd seen the way he and Miss Taylor looked at each other.

She stared longingly at the bike. So what if it wasn't new? Joey would care, but she didn't. She liked the wind on her face, the feel of rushing and leaving everything behind It was almost like flying.

She liked the bike. She didn't like Larusso. And he was still an arrogant bastard... *Bite your tongue,* another voice in her head warned. She could almost see Mama shaking her finger and fiercely scolding for daring to even think such a nasty word.

She sighed. It was bad enough having to put up with him when she reported in for probation once a month. Now she'd have to look at his ugly face a lot more! The possibility was enough to make her puke.... She was immediately ashamed. That was another word Mama didn't like.

But refusing never entered her mind. "Sounds fair enough," she shrugged.

Vince cleared his throat. "One other thing, Frankie. I also want you to stay out of trouble." *And above all,* he amended silently, *don't hurt Samantha.*

Samantha let out her breath, relieved and happy for Frankie. If nothing else, the next few months would prove interesting. Vince had been more than reasonable, but for a minute she wasn't sure of Frankie's reaction. It vaulted through her mind that Frankie and Vince were like a pair of seasoned warriors, advancing and retreating, always on the alert against each other. She quickly suppressed the urge to grin. Watching the two of them in action certainly kept her on her toes. What, she asked herself good-naturedly, would she do if the two of them ever chose to gang up on her instead...?

Since Vince's car was behind Samantha's, they reloaded the bike into his trunk and drove Frankie home. Until the moment when he parked before her building, neither adult had considered where Frankie could store the bike.

Frankie hooked a hand on the front seats. "I know," she said eagerly. "There's a storeroom on the first floor that nobody ever uses. The landlord gave Mrs. Talarico the key a long time ago since she lives right next to it. I bet she'll let me put it in there at night. She likes me."

Samantha's gaze slid helplessly to Vince. She nearly burst out laughing when she caught his eye. His dubious expression fairly shouted, *She does, does she.*

But all he said was, "Let's go check with her first."

Samantha stayed in the car while they went inside. It wasn't long before they emerged again and removed the bike. Frankie started to wheel it toward the building, stopped and said something to Vince over her shoulder. Samantha couldn't hear the exchange, but there was an odd half smile flirting on his lips as he slid back inside.

"You're looking pretty smug," she teased.

"Not smug. Just...pleasantly surprised."

"Do I dare ask why?"

He glanced down at the keys in his hand before transferring his gaze to her. "She said thanks."

Samantha looked puzzled for a moment. "You didn't expect her to?"

"Not really."

She retorted indignantly, "Come on, Larusso. Can't you admit she's not such a bad kid? You saw how much she liked the bike. But she wasn't going to take it because she couldn't pay you for it! Doesn't that tell you she has some scruples after all?"

His smile ebbed. He tapped his fingers against the steering wheel and grimaced. "I'll admit if she wanted to convince us she was a diligent, upstanding little citizen, she pushed all the right buttons. But aren't you forgetting this is still the very same girl who got caught with her hand in the till?"

He must have been reading her mind. Samantha wished she could deny the same question hadn't crossed her mind half a dozen times already. Nor could she discount his other point—the possibility that Frankie was being manipulative.

Maybe she was being a fool, and a blind one at that. But someone had to believe in Frankie. She couldn't lose faith, not yet.

"If that's what you think," she said softly, "then why did you do it? Why did you get her that bike?"

Vince was silent. He couldn't prevent the sudden bleakness that seeped into his soul. Now there was a question, a very good question indeed. Maybe it had something to do with the fact that when he was growing up, he and Tony had never had a bike that was truly their own.

Only ones they'd stolen.

But he could never tell that to Samantha. He knew intuitively she would never understand. She would be shocked. Horrified. Maybe even condemning. And he didn't think he could stand to see her look at him like that.

"I don't know," he murmured. His derisive smile was directed solely at himself. "I just don't know."

But Samantha did. He cared about Frankie. Whether he knew it or not, he cared. And all at once it didn't matter how many times they had locked horns over Frankie in the past few weeks, or how many times that might happen in the future.

Because in some strange, indefinable way, she had never felt as close to anyone as she felt to Vince right now.

She surprised them both by leaning across the seat.

"Say what you will, Larusso." Her hand was curled around his nape. He liked the feel of her fingers, gently stroking. "But I know you're not as hard as you seem to think." Her lips touched the raspy hardness of his cheek; he thought he felt her smile. "I could even fall for a guy like you," she whispered.

His heart twisted. A burning ache closed his throat, making speech impossible. *Then fall,* he urged silently. *Fall as hard and as fast as I'm falling . . .*

He wanted her too much to even think about stopping her. But God help her if she did . . .

Because he wasn't the man she thought.

CHAPTER EIGHT

"DAMN!" Samantha slammed the door to the medicine cabinet more forcefully than necessary and added a few more choice expletives. Her only desire right now was to lay her hands on two little aspirin, but it appeared she might have been wishing for the moon and the stars. She knew Lou usually kept a bottle in her desk, but Lou and the rest of the office staff had gone home. Raiding the medicine cabinet in the teachers' lounge had been a last resort but she'd come up empty-handed there as well.

She closed the door to the teachers' lounge and paused for a moment, trying to will away the throbbing in her temples. It was, she decided wearily, little wonder that her head was splitting. She had had not one, but two very distressing interviews today. The first had been with eighth-grader Allison Stiles, the second with Allison's mother.

She could put neither out of her mind.

Finally she glanced at her watch. It was well after six, time to head home like everyone else. With a frustrated sigh, she turned and plodded back toward her office. Moments later she skirted Lou's desk, then drew a startled gasp when a shadowy figure detached itself from the wall just outside her office and began walking toward her. There was something vaguely familiar about those broad shoulders, that long, almost lazy stride...

"Vince! How did you get in? The doors are usually locked at five." A jolt of pure pleasure shot through her. Despite her headache, a slow smile inched across her lips. "Or have you taken up breaking and entering in your spare time?"

Vince experienced an odd twinge. Whether it was guilt or something else, he couldn't be sure. *Lady,* he thought, *if you only knew...*

"The janitor spotted me at the doors and let me in." He opened the door to her office and motioned for her to precede him. "I stopped at your place but you weren't there. It wasn't hard to figure out where you were, so I decided it was time to rescue you from this dungeon." His tone was light, but the next instant his brows rose a fraction. "I also noticed your car was in your garage. I take it you intended to walk home tonight?"

Samantha stopped in the midst of opening the drawer where her purse was stowed. She nodded slowly.

"It's been dark for over an hour." His look was as pointed as his tone. "You shouldn't walk home alone when it's this late."

She smiled weakly and dropped her purse on the desktop. "I guess the time just got away from me."

"Then it's a good thing I showed up to give you a ride home, isn't it?" He paused long enough to slip his hands into his pockets. "In fact, maybe we could stop off somewhere for dinner first."

An unwilling smile tugged at her lips. On one hand, he thought nothing of taking it for granted that she would accept a ride home. On the other hand, she hadn't missed the note of cautious hope in his voice. She found his uncharacteristic uncertainty endearing. Very endearing, in fact. Still...

Her smile faded. "Right now my most pressing need is two aspirin for the worst headache I've had in ages," she told him honestly. "I'm afraid food trails a distant second."

Vince said nothing for a moment. Instead he scanned her face. Lord, she was pretty. Even in the dim light, her eyes were a deep velvety blue, clear and pure. But she did look tired and a little tense.

"Maybe I could drop you off at home, get something takeout and bring it back." He found himself counting the seconds. He didn't want her to refuse. Damn, but he didn't.

"That sounds great," she said at last. Her smile took his breath away. "In fact," she went on airily, "I've decided you're regular Sir Galahad."

Sir Galahad? Far from it, Vince decided. He smiled derisively as he held her coat while she slipped into it.

Half an hour later she was sitting cross-legged on the living room floor, dressed in a pair of faded pink sweats and savoring the last bite of the hot pastrami sandwich Vince had brought back from the deli on the corner. Vince, who had taken a spot on the end of the sofa, was only halfway through with his.

Dropping her napkin onto her plate, she glanced up and caught his eye. "I guess I was hungrier than I thought," she said with a sheepish half grin.

"Obviously," he murmured dryly.

Samantha rose to her feet, her plate in hand. "Ready for some coffee?"

"Anytime you are."

By the time she returned with their coffee, he was finished with his sandwich. He had pulled off his tie and unbuttoned the top button of his shirt, revealing a triangle patch of hair-roughened skin. All at once her body was seized with an unsettling heat. Their eyes met as she handed him his cup.

"How's the headache?" he asked.

"Better." She lowered herself to the floor to resume her previous spot.

"But not gone?"

She shook her head.

"Where's it hurt?"

She gestured toward the back of her head and neck.

"Come here and we'll see if we can't do something about it." He surprised her by pointing to the spot on the carpet in front of him.

Samantha took a fraction of a second to consider, then scooted to the place he'd indicated. One strong hand came down on the flannel layering her shoulders. The other gently pushed aside her hair, baring the back of her neck to his gaze.

For the space of a heartbeat—and then another— Vince held himself very still. He stared at the honey-gold fuzz sprinkled across her nape. He knew if he touched it, he would find it baby-soft and fine. Her skin looked just as touchable, as smooth as cream. And while he stared, he fought the nearly uncontrollable urge to lower his head, to nuzzle and explore with his lips that enchantingly tiny hollow that sloped into her nape. Yet she looked so vulnerable, her head bent, her nape so slender and exposed, that he felt he'd be taking unfair advantage.

He focused on the ribbed edging of her sweatshirt. His thumb joined its mate at the base of her neck. He began to stroke slowly down her neck and back up again.

"You know," he chided gently, "you really shouldn't take your job home with you so much."

Samantha had just begun to relax under the flowing motion of his fingertips. "Is that what you think?" she heard herself say.

"Am I wrong?"

She tilted her head slightly to allow him better access to her neck. Now that she thought about it, she could see where he was coming from. First there was Frankie, and now Allison. "I guess not," she admitted.

"Please tell me this doesn't have anything to do with Frankie," he said lightly.

Samantha smiled slightly. "You're off the hook, counselor."

"Thank heaven for small favors," he murmured dryly. There was a small pause. "Another irate parent?"

Her smile faded. She drew her legs up to her chest and wrapped her arms around her knees. "That's not the half of it," she said with a grimace.

She went on to tell him how Allison Stiles's mother had phoned early this morning, pleading with her to talk to Allison.

"It seems Allison ran away this weekend—for the second time in the last month. She was only gone for one night both times before her mother managed to find her at a friend's. Only this time Allison refused to go home with her mother, but she refused to tell her mother why she wouldn't go home. Or why she ran away. In fact she threatened to run away again unless her mother would let her stay with an aunt here in town."

Vince frowned. "Is that where she is now?"

Samantha nodded. "I was really surprised when her mother phoned this morning. Allison was an office runner last year so I got to know her pretty well. She's an excellent student, sweet and bubbly. Her parents are divorced and her dad lives somewhere back east. But I could tell by the way she talked about her mother that she and her mother were pretty close, which is why I was so surprised to learn she'd run away."

Vince set to work on the tight muscles of her shoulders. "There must have been a reason."

"There was," she stated quietly. "It took a lot of coaxing, but Allison finally told me why she ran away. Her mother remarried last summer, and it seems her stepfather is a rather demonstrative man. Allison said she's never really liked the way he always hugs and kisses her." Samantha's eyes darkened. "Several months ago he started touching her in places he had no business touching her. She said she always managed to pull away, but she was afraid to tell her mother. Then last Thursday, the night before she ran away, he came into her bedroom when her mother wasn't home."

A low exclamation broke from Vince's lips. "Good God! Don't tell me he—"

"Her mother came home earlier than expected, so nothing happened," Samantha clarified quickly. "At least that's what Allison said, and I'm inclined to believe her. But he frightened her half to death and that's when she ran away the second time."

His hands stilled on her shoulders. "What did her mother have to say?"

Samantha's sigh held a trace of weariness. "It came as a shock naturally. First she said Allison was making a big deal out of nothing, that her husband was just an extremely affectionate man. Then she decided Allison made up the whole thing just to get attention."

"You don't think that's possible?"

Samantha's chin firmed. "No. Frankly, I don't. Allison just isn't that type of child, Vince, and deep down,

I think her mother knows it. She wasn't pleased when I told her I thought it was wise for Allison to stay with her aunt for the time being. She was even less pleased when I told her I was obliged by law to report Allison's claim to the police and juvenile authorities. She started ranting and raving, accusing me of meddling where I had no business. She didn't leave until shortly before you arrived."

Samantha fell silent, mulling for a few seconds. "Maybe I do bring my job home more than I should. But when something like this happens, it's hard not to."

Vince's fingers ceased their soothing, monotonous motion. "Not that I'm trying to change the subject, but how do you feel?"

Samantha half turned before him, flexed each shoulder and gave him a slow, melting smile that made him burn with the fiery need to haul her into his arms, sample those delectable lips to see if they tasted as sweet as he knew they would.

Why he didn't, he had no idea. But it had something—everything—to do with the air of fresh innocence that clung to her.

"You have the magic touch, Larusso. Something tells me you're a handy guy to have around."

"I aim to please," he murmured, eyes warm and avid on her upturned face. Disappointment shot through her when he rose to his feet.

She took the hand he offered and let him pull her to her feet. "You're always in a hurry to leave. I must be doing something that scares you off." She was only half joking.

He shrugged into his coat. "If that were the case, I wouldn't ask if you're busy tomorrow night."

She glanced up at him as they crossed to the front door. Her eyes had taken on a decided gleam. "Why, Larusso, are you asking me for a date?"

"Smart lady." His tone was low and sexy, but his eyes were alight with humor. "I'll show you a real good time, too. Nothing but nonstop action."

"That sounds—" she pretended to consider "—dangerous."

He ran his finger down the tip of her nose. "Does it? I promise you'll be able to keep your eye on me at all times."

The husky note in his voice thrilled her. "In that case, I accept."

"Good. Don't dress too fancy, though. What you've got on right now will do just fine."

She blinked, convinced he wasn't serious. But she soon discovered he was...

Twenty-four hours later she was once again inside Al's gym, the last place she'd expected to find herself. Oddly it seemed right somehow that Vince bring her back here. She wasn't as frightened as she'd been that first time; she wasn't as shocked by the young boys that filtered past her. And whenever Vince's gaze chanced to meet hers, she had the strangest sensation she'd passed some kind of test.

She sat near the top row of the bleachers in the gymnasium, elbows propped on her knees, her chin cupped in her hands. Her head swiveled back and forth as she watched the action on the court. And as Vince had promised, it was nonstop. Vince played side by side with the boys, shouting and yelling both praise and ridicule along with the rest of them.

Samantha was more convinced than ever that he cared about these poor unfortunate kids—and cared deeply.

Two hours later he climbed into the driver's seat of his car next to her. He made no move to start the engine; instead he angled his body toward hers and fixed her with a wry gaze. "You've been smiling ever since we finished the game," he commented. "Do I get to know why?"

"Oh, I don't know," she said lightly. "Maybe it's because while you were in the shower one of the boys told me I was the only woman he's ever seen you bring to the gym."

"I see," he returned dryly. "And I suppose that's given you a big head, eh?"

She pretended to be affronted. "Of course not! I'm a saint, remember? My halo won't fit!" He laughed, and she went on, "Remember the day we climbed all those stairs at Frankie's apartment?"

His eyes gleamed in the darkness. "How could I forget? You were doing a lot of huffing and puffing."

"And you weren't." She gave him a playful swat on the arm. "But I was right after all. You *do* stay in shape by chasing after a lot of juveniles."

The sound of his laughter mingled with hers. He started the engine and pulled away from the curb. Silence drifted between them during the ride to her house, but it was an altogether comfortable silence. It lasted until they mounted the steps of her back porch and stood just outside the door.

Vince saw that her expression had turned rather pensive. "What's on your mind?" he asked curiously.

The bite of the night wind made her shiver. She drew her coat more closely around her. "I was just thinking about those boys at the gym. How some of them appear so much older than what they are. How they try to be that way, by acting so tough and worldly."

That's because they are, he almost said.

Samantha's breath emerged as a long sigh. Her lips carried a faint smile. "I remember when I was a kid, I couldn't wait until I was older. I couldn't wait to get my driver's license, to go out on my first date, to finish high school. Then later I couldn't wait to finish college and be out on my own."

Vince said nothing. When he was a kid, he had seldom thought beyond the end of the next day. He'd known nothing at all of hope and faith.

But that was something he couldn't say to Samantha. Not now. Not yet. Maybe not ever. He couldn't shake the feeling that Samantha, with her unblemished childhood, wouldn't understand—worse yet, that she might condemn him.

The overhead porch light enclosed them in a hazy pool of light. His tone was very quiet when at last he spoke. "I'll bet now you're one of those people who'd like to turn back the clock and experience your youth all over again."

"Are you kidding? I like the present much better."

Her prompt response startled him; it pleased him much more. "Present company included?" His question reflected a lightness he was far from feeling.

Her smile deepened. "*Especially* that."

"So you're not sorry you came with me tonight?"

She shook her head and countered his query with one of her own. "Are you sorry you asked me?"

He guided a honey-gold curl behind her ear, fighting the impulse to linger and losing. The back of his knuckles skimmed her cheek. "Not a chance," he said huskily.

Samantha couldn't help it; she leaned into his caress, loving the pleasantly rough sensation of his skin against hers. His head dipped slowly.

Their eyes met and meshed. Neither of them spoke; neither moved. Her heart pounding, Samantha waited—hoping, praying—knowing he was about to kiss her and knowing she'd never wanted anything more in her life....

"Good night, Samantha."

The soft-spoken sound of his voice was jarring. Puzzled and hurt, but most of all confused, she could only watch as he disappeared down the stairs and into the shadows.

Her shoulders sagged as she finally made her way into the house. She liked Vince. More, she was extremely attracted to him.

Until that moment, she had thought he felt the same.

CHAPTER NINE

THE NEXT FEW WEEKS were both heaven and hell for Samantha.

Allison Stiles's situation remained at a stalemate pending an investigation by the juvenile authorities. Samantha was relieved that the girl was able to continue her temporary living arrangement with her aunt, though she suspected it caused friction between mother and daughter.

As far as Frankie, Lynette Marshall phoned several times to see how the Big Sister/Little Sister arrangement was working out. As she told Lynette, she was pleased with the way things were going, for she knew better than to expect miracles. To win the girl's trust overnight would have been exactly that—a miracle. Samantha didn't fool herself. Frankie still guarded her emotions very closely; she still retreated behind her wall of defensiveness and bravado. But little by little, the walls were coming down.

There was one incident that Samantha considered a turning point.

Frankie had wistfully mentioned that she had been wanting her ears pierced for quite sometime. Only a few days earlier, Samantha had noticed a half-price special at one of the department stores downtown. She stopped in at Mullins Bakery the next day to get an okay from Anna. The following Saturday, she and Frankie stood at the jewelry counter. Frankie picked out a pair of topaz studs while Samantha went in search of a clerk.

A minute later she turned around and spotted a female clerk standing next to Frankie. The instant she drew near it became apparent that all was not well.

The woman's gaze raked over Frankie's patched jeans and faded denim jacket. "You've got something in your hand, girl, I know you do!"

Samantha gasped, galvanized into action. She stepped up behind Frankie. "Excuse me," she asked coolly. "Is there a problem I can help with?"

The woman scarcely spared her a glance. "I'm handling it, thank you. In fact I was just about to call security since I think this girl slipped something into her pocket."

Samantha's eyes narrowed. "You *think?* Don't you know?"

The clerk darted her a quick, startled look, taken aback by her tone. Samantha could almost see the wheels turning in the woman's head, wondering who she was and why she was so insistent.

"Well," she demanded, "did you see this girl put something in her pocket?"

"Not exactly." The woman hedged. "But she was wandering around the jewelry department. And just look at the way she's dressed. It's obvious she isn't capable of paying for anything. Besides, I've seen her kind here before. They think they can walk in and then walk out with their hands full of—"

A slow burn simmered along Samantha's veins. She couldn't remember when she'd been so angry.

She held on to her temper, but just barely. "This girl was waiting at the jewelry counter while I hunted down a clerk who could pierce her ears, and she happens to be a friend of mine. You have no business accusing her of stealing when she hasn't done anything wrong—except be seen by a narrow-minded woman who apparently likes jumping to conclusions.''

Her hand lightly squeezed Frankie's shoulder. "Let's go, Frankie. We're walking out the same way we came in," she emphasized coldly. "With nothing. You'll excuse me if I take my business elsewhere. This isn't the kind of place I care to spend my money in...ever.''

Frankie got her ears pierced at the jewelry store around the corner.

There was a subtle change in their relationship after that. Oh, Frankie was still guarded and defensive at times, but Samantha felt she was finally beginning to open up to her. It didn't matter that Frankie was tough and hard-nosed on the outside. Inside she was very, very vulnerable.

Not so with Frankie and Vince. During her probationary meetings, the air seethed with tension. It was the same way when Frankie washed Vince's car. While her grades had shown a slight improvement, her attitude had not. One wrong word or look—whether intentional or unintentional—and they were like a pair of wolves preparing to attack. They weren't throwing words like knives as they had that very first day, but it was as if neither would let themselves relax around the other.

Then there was Vince. Scarcely a day had gone by that Samantha didn't see him; at least talk on the phone with him. She had gone to her parents in Springfield for Thanksgiving. She very nearly returned home a day early because she missed him...missed him? Who was she kidding?

She was halfway in love with him.

Yet still he hadn't touched her, except in the most casual of ways. A hand at her back, an accidental brush of their hands. Once she looked up and caught him staring at her. For a heart-stopping moment his eyes seemed to possess her. The hunger on his face made her stomach knot in purely sensual excitement. Yet the next instant his features betrayed nothing, no hint of emotion whatsoever... she nearly cried out her disappointment.

No one had ever confused her the way he did. No one had ever made her burn with yearning the way he did, even Brad. The urges he aroused in her were painfully sweet—and just plain painful. She wanted very much to be touched by Vince. Touched and held and kissed....

The second Thursday evening in December found her sliding the key into her back door. Vince stood behind her; she felt the force of his presence in every nerve of her being.

The door swung open. Slowly she turned to face him, fighting a sudden sensation of breathlessness. "You'll come in, won't you?"

When he hesitated, she bit back her frustration. The scene was a repeat of the last three times they had been together. Their eyes met. In the moonlight, his were dark and unreadable. He shook his head, his expression regretful but determined. "I don't think so—" he began.

"I do." Samantha was just as determined. She seized his hand and pulled him inside.

Vince damned himself silently. It was getting harder and harder to be alone with her. Didn't she know that? If he had an ounce of integrity, he'd walk out and never come back. She might be hurt for a while, but she'd get over it. He'd told himself that a hundred times the past few weeks.

In the kitchen, she pulled off her coat and draped it over a chair. "Would you like coffee?"

No, he wanted to shout. What he wanted was her. Her arms clinging wildly to him. Her body arched sweetly against his. Her heart vying madly with the tempo of his own.

Even as the thought scalded his veins, a wrenching pain ripped through him. How long had he been so—so empty? Forever, it seemed. He needed someone to fill that empty space inside. But not just anyone. A woman...

A woman like Samantha.

The tumult in his heart was equaled only by the conflict in his mind. It was madness to be here. He had no *right* to be here. There were times he felt he tainted her simply by being near her. She didn't know what he was— what he'd been. He'd known precious few people like her—people who were open and honest and sincere. Was it selfish or wrong to want someone like that for himself?

He didn't know. God help him, he didn't know.

"Coffee's fine," he said finally. He gestured toward the living room. "I'll be in there."

He avoided her gaze as he passed. Samantha watched his progress into the living room, a faint crease etched between her brows. Vince seemed so quiet, almost subdued. She had the strangest sensation he was trying very hard to distance himself from her.

Pulling two cups from the cupboard, she decided she was imagining things.

A few minutes later, she advanced into the living room, a mug in each hand. She paused in the doorway, unable to stop the quiver of awareness that shot through her stomach.

He stood before the window with his back angled toward her, staring out at the darkness of the night. His stance proclaimed his masculinity in a way that couldn't be denied—and it was one she'd come to associate with him. His arms were folded over his chest, his legs spread slightly apart. His hips looked impossibly narrow. The fabric of his shirt stretched tight across his shoulders, outlining the knotted tension of biceps that appeared firm and taut. She fought the compulsion to touch him as he turned slightly. His eyes fixed on the photograph hanging on the wall. It had been taken at her parents' last summer.

It was then that the oddest thought flitted through her mind. Vince knew so much about her, even the time she'd cheated on her high-school geometry test, while she knew next to nothing about him ... Yet she felt as if she'd known him forever.

It made no sense ... it made all the sense in the world.

Her footsteps made no sound as she crossed the floor. Their fingers never touched as she handed him the cup. "What are you thinking about?" she asked softly.

Vince stared at her as emotion after emotion seeped through him, one after another, like opening a rusty valve. There was guilt and bitterness for the angry young man he had once been. A deep, burning despair for all the wasted years in his life, years that would never be recaptured no matter how much he wished it could be otherwise. And above all, fear—the fear that if Samantha ever learned the truth she would hate him.

"Nothing, really," he murmured.

Her scrutiny was faintly disconcerting. She continued to regard him, her eyes wide and unwavering.

"Is something bothering you?" she asked. "Besides me, of course," she added lightly. "My older sisters always used to say I was a nosy little pest."

His smile was slow in coming, but it was a smile nonetheless. She found herself relaxing.

Vince arched a brow. "Nosy? Or noisy?"

"Probably both," she admitted ruefully. The laugh they shared seemed to ease some of his tension. When he lifted his cup to his lips, her eyes slid absently down his throat. The shirt he wore was open at the throat, baring a patch of tanned flesh covered by a wild tangle of dark bristly hairs. Her stomach dropped at the sight; it was then that she noticed the tiny links of a chain fastened around his neck.

"Oh, how pretty!" she exclaimed. She leaned forward to inspect it more closely. The movement tentative, she lifted a hand at the same time her eyes made the return trip to his face. "May I?"

He nodded. She never noticed his reluctance.

A tiny shiver danced through her as she slid two fingers beneath the tiny silver crucifix, warm from his skin. Though it was small and simply designed, the workmanship was exquisite. "It looks rather old," she murmured. "Have you had it long?"

There was a moment's silence. "A while," he answered vaguely. "It belonged to...someone I once knew."

Her eyes flew to his face. There was something in his tone that alerted her... She probed very gently. "Someone who's gone now?"

He nodded. His features might have been etched in stone, but just for an instant, an odd expression crossed his face, an expression that might have been pain. It was so fleeting she couldn't be sure.

She eased her fingers away slowly, watching as it nestled amidst midnight-dark curls. "It must be very special," she murmured, hoping he would tell her something...anything! Even as she spoke, she groped for what little she knew about Vince. He'd told her he grew up here in Chicago, but little else. She'd paved the way a dozen times already, dropping hints, only to have him steer the conversation another direction a dozen times. He was subtle about it, so subtle someone else might never have noticed. But she was trained to seek out what wasn't said as well. And every so often, like now, she had the feeling there was something he wasn't telling her. It was as if he kept a part of himself locked away.

She waited...but she waited in vain. And he was tense, so tense. She could see it in the slight stiffening of his shoulders.

Vince stood as still and silent as a statue. A pang of guilt knifed through him. He knew what she thought—that he wore the chain for comfort. Or perhaps to honor a memory.

She didn't know it was his way of doing penance.

And he didn't know she read more in his eyes than he wanted her to see. She glimpsed an elusive sadness that came from deep inside. He looked as if the sun had gone down, never to shine again.

It was suddenly imperative that she see him smile. "You know," she chided. "Ever since we met I've been wondering how it is that some lucky woman hasn't snapped you up."

Amazingly that did the trick. His smile was fleeting, but definitely worth waiting for. "No one but you has ever been able to put up with my bedside manner. And I might ask you how you've managed to escape the noose so long.''

It was her turn to be caught off guard. She winced inwardly. At thirty years of age, her love life had become rather a sore spot. When things hadn't worked out with Brad, her parents and sisters had left her alone for a while. But once again they'd reached the stage where they never failed to drop hints about her marital status—or lack of it.

"I almost didn't," she admitted.

Vince paused, his cup halfway to his mouth. She had startled him, she realized.

"Thank you very much," she said dryly. "I'm beginning to think I look like the troll under the bridge."

"You?" His smile reappeared, along with an unmistakable light in his eyes. "Not a chance."

She feigned astonishment. "Why, Vince! Do I dare take that as a compliment?"

"You can take it any way you like, but that's how it was meant." His eyes met hers over the top of his cup. "Now tell me about this long-lost man in your life."

"There's really not much to tell," she said. But the cloudiness in her eyes belied her tone.

"Were you engaged?"

Samantha nodded, feeling just a little embarrassed. "His name was Brad. I knew him about a year before we got engaged. He was in his last year of law school and I had just finished my master's in counseling."

"What happened?"

She shrugged. "I wish I could say," she answered truthfully. "As soon as we started making wedding plans, it seemed we just couldn't agree on anything—flowers, guests, even the honeymoon. What I thought didn't seem to count at all, and I just wasn't brought up that way. If we had a problem at home, we talked about it and tried to work it out together. Brad would get mad, clam up and not say a word. I was the one who always gave in."

She ran the tip of her finger around her cup. "Six weeks before the wedding he decided he wanted to move to California and set up a private law practice with a buddy from law school. I'd just gotten a job at a youth center, but Brad assumed that I would quit. He *expected* me to quit without a second thought."

Vince studied her quietly. "You didn't want to leave your family?"

"My parents hadn't moved to Springfield yet. And that didn't bother me so much as the fact that he'd gone ahead and started making plans to move without ever consulting me. Not once did he ever ask how I felt about it. I tried to tell him, but he refused to listen. He accused me of getting in the way of his career—mine apparently didn't mean a thing. I knew then that marrying him would be a mistake."

She mulled for a moment. "If I had to point to any one thing being responsible, I guess I'd have to say Brad just wasn't willing to compromise. He was convinced that his way was always the right way—the only way."

Vince watched her closely. He didn't want to believe she was still carrying a torch for him. Damn, but he didn't. "Do you regret not marrying him?" His voice was very low.

She shook her head. "Brad wasn't the man I thought he was," she said quietly. "I regret being so blind, for not seeing him as he really was. Even at first, I was always more hurt than bitter."

Something knotted and squeezed around his heart. Her ready response surprised him—and pleased him far more. But strongest of all was the realization that he, too, was keeping a part of himself hidden from her. Frustration ate at him like acid. He tried telling himself he hadn't deceived her. He just hadn't told her. Yet wasn't that just as bad?

He didn't know. God help him, but he didn't.

"He was a fool for giving up someone as special as you." Not until the words had passed his lips did he realize he'd spoken.

"Special," she repeated. A spurt of humor flashed in her eyes. "Is that all?"

He couldn't help but respond in kind. "Fishing for another compliment, aren't you? All right then. Someone special *and* pretty. Very pretty, in fact."

"If that's what you think, then why haven't you kissed me?"

The question came from nowhere. Samantha couldn't think why she'd asked. It wasn't like her to be so forward. But it was too late to retract it, so once again she held her breath and waited....

Vince stared into eyes as blue as a summer sky, painfully aware of everything about her. Lord, that she should ask that... The uncertain question in her eyes tore him up inside. Didn't she know how he yearned to trap her lips beneath his own and taste her pure, sweet fire? He wanted to tangle his fingers into her hair and see if it was as silky and soft as he'd dreamed. He longed to bring her body full and tight against his own.

Trying to calm the raging inferno inside him, he deliberately looked away. He felt rather than saw her remove his mug and set both of them aside.

Samantha stared at him. All at once the air between them was charged with tension. Instinct told her she'd said something wrong—but what? She had no doubts about her feelings, but Vince wasn't so easy to read. Was she wishing for something that wasn't there?

She wet her lips, praying he wouldn't see her nervousness. "Vince." His name was a mere breath of sound. "I...I really thought we had something rather special. I mean—we get along so well, when we're not arguing about Frankie, that is." Her attempt at a smile fell miserably flat. She cringed inside when she saw his jaw bunch.

Suddenly it all came out in a rush. "I...I like you, Vince. And I didn't think these past few weeks were leading toward a casual friendship...I've been hoping they weren't! But I'm beginning to wonder if you feel the same way and...oh, I know it makes no sense, but sometimes it's almost as if you're afraid of me!"

Afraid? God, if anything, it should have been the other way around. Vince thought of that afternoon at the gym. The memory of that day was like a sliver under his skin. Samantha had been appalled when he'd told her about Danny Rodriguez. What would she say if she knew he'd once been a member of the same gang?

Then there was tonight. What she'd said about her fiancé only reinforced what he already knew. He was a hundred times worse than Brad. Compromise was a concept he'd never understood. As a kid, he grabbed on tight to whatever he could and to hell with anyone else.

"I'm not afraid of you, Samantha." He forced himself to look at her, then wished he hadn't when he saw the silent plea in her eyes.

"Then why haven't you kissed me? Why, Vince?"

"It's not because I haven't wanted to." There was something low, something roughly urgent in his tone, something that made hope take flight inside her.

She took a step forward. Her eyes clung to his. "Then tell me why. I—I just want to understand." She felt like a teenager who had yet to experience her first kiss and wanted desperately to know what it was like.

His gaze dropped to her mouth. He wanted to reach out and slide his fingers over her lips, to see for himself if they were as smooth and velvety as they looked. But something held him back, some vague nagging feeling that if he touched her, she would somehow change.

And she wanted him to explain? He despaired bitterly. She possessed a purity that unnerved him. Conversely he wanted to reach out and seize some of that goodness for his own. How the hell could he explain what he didn't understand himself?

He gave a curt, abortive gesture. "We're very different." His tone reflected his frustration.

"Are we?" He stood motionless as she took another tentative step forward, her gaze never wavering from his tension-filled features. His lips were pressed tightly together, as if he were determined not to show any emotion.

And indeed he was. "We are," he said curtly. "Trust me." She was so close he could smell the fresh lemony scent of her shampoo. It was sweet agony not to drag her into his arms, kiss the breath from her until nothing else existed.

They stood toe-to-toe. She angled her head back slightly, her eyes level with his rigid jawline. She knew that if she raised a hand, she'd find his face rough with five-o'clock shadow. "If that's what you believe," she said softly, "then why are you here?"

Because he couldn't stay away, he wanted to shout. The thought was like fire in his soul. Samantha was everything he'd ever wanted, but couldn't have. He cursed himself for wanting her; cursed her for being so damned irresistible.

Samantha's heart pounded like a trip-hammer. Holding her breath, she shyly raised her arms. Before she could touch him, long fingers shackled her wrists. She stared for a moment in silent fascination. His hands had always captivated her. They were so strong and wonderfully masculine, big but not at all fleshy. A generous sprinkling of hair netted the wide backs. His fingers were lean and strong looking.

Her eyes shifted to his face. What she saw made her heart trip wildly. He had stiffened visibly when she attempted to touch him. No sign of a smile softened the hard line of his lips. His expression was stark and hungry, his eyes burning deep into hers. He was all tough hard male, and something wholly female within her responded.

Another time, another place and she might not have believed her daring. But right now there was a vague sense of unreality floating all around her, and it was almost as if she watched herself from another stage.

"Tell me if I'm wrong," she heard herself whisper. "But I don't believe we're so different after all." She swallowed dryly. "I want you to kiss me, Vince, just this once. And I think you want it, too."

They stared at each other, locked in the moment, locked in each other.

It was too much. *She* was too much. His hands slipped to her shoulders, drawing her near even as his mind urged caution. She was as tempting as sin, he thought dimly. But she was his, if only he dared to reach out and hold her... Her lips hovered just beneath his. Beckoning. Enticing.

And all at once Vince wasn't thinking of why this shouldn't be happening—he wasn't thinking at all.

With a groan he caught her to him. Inside his head a warning bell went off. He didn't care. *He didn't care.* His control shattered. His mouth came down on hers. Urgent. Fierce and tender all at once. Joy and triumph surged through his veins unlike anything he'd ever known. He loved the tiny little gasp of surprise she made before melting against him in a way that made his knees turn to water. He loved the way her hands locked convulsively around his shoulders just as much.

Most of all, he loved the taste of lips eager and warm and willing. She met and matched his fervency with a wild sweet will of her own.

And indeed Samantha withheld nothing. The pressure of their mouths deepened to an intimacy that robbed her of breath. She was achingly conscious of the heat and hardness of his body against hers. Her hands glided along the fluid lines of his back, relishing in the feel of muscle and bone.

Vince, she thought helplessly. *Oh, Vince.* Her heart plunged into a wild frenzy, for this was what she had wanted . . . all she had *ever* wanted. This breathless feeling of closeness, the richness of feeling herself so much a part of him.

The kiss lessened subtly, little by little, until at last his mouth slid with slow heat to the tiny pulsebeat throbbing in her throat. Her fingers embedded themselves in the midnight darkness of his hair. They stayed like that for an endless moment while he waited for the heated rush inside him to subside. At last he felt her smile against his temple. He raised his head and looked at her.

Her eyes shone with the light of a thousand suns, a light that filled every corner of his heart. "That wasn't so bad, was it?"

The huskiness of her voice sent tiny shivers along his nerve endings. "God, Samantha." His forehead came to rest against hers. He was loath to release her from the protective binding of his arms. "You're...unbelievable," was all he could think to say.

She drew back slightly, slender brows drawn in a playful frown. "Is that good or bad?"

His laugh was shaky. "How about if I let you decide?" He lowered his head again and she met him halfway. More than halfway.

This kiss was gentler, with none of the pent-up fervor that marked the first kiss. A potent sense of déjà vu passed over him as she wound her arms around his neck. He'd held her and kissed her like this a hundred times in his dreams...no, not dreams. Fantasies.

He couldn't forget that he was the kid from the wrong side of the tracks, the side of town she scarcely knew existed. When he was growing up, she was the kind of girl who was always beyond reach.

She was the woman he'd always wanted...the woman he could never have.

But she was in his arms, and nothing—nothing!—had ever felt so right.

It was a long time later before he regretfully drew back. "I really should say good-night, Samantha."

Her eyes opened slowly. The pleasure glowing on her features made him want to shout for joy. "Already?"

His lips rediscovered the corner of her mouth. "We both have to work tomorrow." He paused. "Do you and Frankie have any plans this weekend?"

"We're going to a movie tomorrow night. Sunday we planned to go ice-skating, if the weather holds up." The area had been hit with a frigid cold front the past few days that the weatherman predicted would be around for a while. "Which means," she added, "that on Saturday I'm going to have to get started on my Christmas shopping."

"I don't suppose you'd care for some company." He tucked a stray hair behind her ear, fighting the impulse to linger and losing. His thumb stroked the downy curve of her cheek.

She felt as if she were glowing from the inside. "Only if it's yours."

She would have walked with him to his car, but he wouldn't let her past the back porch, insisting there was no point in her going out in the cold. His kiss was brief and fleeting. If he kissed her the way he wanted, he'd never be able to leave.

Halfway to his car, he paused and looked back. One look at her forlorn expression and he vaulted back up the wooden steps. Framing her face with his hands, he kissed her once. Twice. Again and again, each longer and more lingering than the last.

"Now that's more like it, Larusso," she said when at last he allowed them to draw breath.

He laughed. "God, I've unleashed a monster."

She wrinkled her nose. "Complaints already?"

"Not at all," he said mildly, then grinned. His avid gaze swept the length of her. "At least with you I don't get a crick in my neck."

"Aha. You get a crick in your neck with your other women?"

He ran the tip of his finger down her nose. "There are no other women." His tone was teasing. The heated message in his eyes spoke only to her.

"Well," she murmured happily, "it's nice to know I've got something to recommend me." One last kiss and he was gone.

She stayed outside, shivering until she saw the tail-lights of his car disappear around the corner. Her last thought was that kissing Vince was just as wonderful and thrilling as she'd known it would be.

She was still smiling when she drifted off to sleep.

CHAPTER TEN

FRANKIE STARED in dismay at the nearly full plate Mama had just removed from the table. "Mama." Her voice was very small. "You didn't eat much again. Shouldn't you be eating more? Mrs. Talarico says—"

"Bah!" Mama rolled her eyes. "You two worry too much about nothing. I'm not hungry just now, *cara*. That's all."

She hadn't been hungry the night before, or the night before that, either. Was that normal? Frankie decided she would ask Mrs. Talarico the next time she saw her.

"You were coughing again last night, too." Frankie's tone had turned half pleading, half accusing.

For a moment Mama looked very tired. She watched Mama wipe her hands on a dish towel. Something tight seemed to wrap around Frankie's chest. All of a sudden it hurt to breathe. Mama looked so—so old! And the eyes so like her own no longer sparkled like tiny black diamonds the way they used to. When had that happened?

These past few weeks, it was as if Mama were slipping away from her, sliding through her very fingers. Mama seemed like a shadow of herself. She was worried about her, Frankie realized. She couldn't rid herself of the nagging fear that if Mama didn't take better care of herself, something terrible would happen.

She carried her plate to the sink. "Didn't you take the cough medicine I got for you last week?"

Mama sighed. "Yes, Francesca, I did." As if on cue, she began to cough—a dry, heaving cough that seemed to come from deep inside.

Frankie was at her side in an instant. "Where is it, Mama? Maybe you should take some—"

Mama shook her head and pressed her handkerchief to her mouth. "There is no more," she rasped when she was finally able to speak again. Spying the warning signs on her daughter's face, she said sternly, "Do not go out and buy more, Francesca. I do not want you spending the money you make baby-sitting on medicine for me."

Frankie bit her lip. "Isn't there a free clinic over on Division Street? Maybe you should go see a doctor there—"

She got no further. Mama drew herself up proudly. "I will not!" For an instant, her eyes contained some of their usual spark. "There are others far more in need than I. Besides, the cough will pass. It always has before."

Frankie's chin drooped. "I just wanted to help," she muttered.

Mama's expression softened. "You do far more than you know. You are always so strong and so brave, *cara*. I hope you know how proud you make me." She hugged her fiercely.

Frankie clung to her, her eyes stinging, her throat so clogged she couldn't speak. *Oh, Mama,* she cried silently, *if you only knew...you wouldn't be proud of me at all.*

Her eyes were dry by the time Mama was ready to leave for her evening job. Mama came back into the kitchen where she had just washed the last of the dishes. "Have fun at the movie tonight, eh?"

Frankie's nod was absent. She slipped a plate into the dish strainer. "You like her, don't you? Samantha, I mean."

Mama slipped an arm into her coat. "Yes," she said simply. "I do. She cares about you, *cara*. I see it in her eyes. And I do not worry about you so much when you are with her."

Frankie swallowed a pang. She was just a little ashamed to admit her only reason for getting into the Big Sister/Little Sister program was to please Mama. But somewhere along the line, that had changed. Samantha was . . . well, all right. They'd done some neat things together—like the picnic. Remembering it made her feel all funny and warm inside. And there was the day they had sat at her kitchen table taking Oreo cookies apart and eating the frosting first—the way all kids did, according to Samantha. Yeah, she thought with a smile, Samantha wasn't so bad after all.

Her smile slipped away when Mama pulled up the collar of her coat, muttering under her breath about the cold snap. She stopped when she saw Frankie watching her.

Mama smiled and pinched her cheek. "Someday, *cara,* we will go where it is warm and the sun always shines." She kissed Frankie's cheek and left.

She'd been gone only a few minutes before a knock at the door sounded. Thinking it was Samantha, Frankie nearly threw it open. She made a face and changed her mind at the last minute. "Who is it?" she called. Why she bothered, she didn't know, because every time she did it she was reminded of Larusso. He was the *last* person she wanted to think about.

An indignant male voice answered. "Who d'ya think it is?"

Joey. She opened the door and beckoned him inside. He sauntered in, a cocky grin on his features. "Hi, ya, kid. I saw your mother leave so I thought I'd show off my new leather bomber." He spun around and struck a Michael Jackson pose, hands angled high in the air, pelvis and knee jutting forward.

Frankie closed the door and eyed his black leather jacket. "It's nice," she said shortly.

"Nice! Is that all you can say? Man, you know how much this set me back? Four big ones!"

Her eyes widened. "Four hundred dollars? Where did you get that kind of money?"

"I ripped off a couple of car stereos from the school parking lot." His eyes gleamed. "You should have heard Pete. 'You're just like me,' he said. 'You catch on fast.' Plus he gave me a nice little bonus." Looking very smug, Joey blew on his knuckles and rubbed them against his jacket.

Frankie wasn't smiling. "How come you didn't take them to Phil's?"

"Pete gives me a better price. That's why I've been doing some thinking. Hanging around with Pete is beginning to pay off, just the way I figured it would. So I thought I'd get a few of my buddies together and pull off a few jobs. Then I could send some more business Pete's way and we'd all divvy up the profits. Then when I tell Pete I set up the whole thing, he'll realize he's got a perfect gem right in his back pocket." He rubbed his hands together.

Frankie suddenly felt very cold. "You want to be just like him, don't you?" she asked quietly.

Joey's grin was sly. "Yeah. And who better to learn from than a pro like Pete."

"Sounds to me like you're just using him."

"So? You're using Mary Poppins, too."

"I am not!"

Amused by her indignant outrage, he spread his hands wide. "Hey it's all right by me." A slow smile spread across his face. "If the ride's free, you're a fool not to take it."

"That's not the way it is, Joey Bennett, so you can just take it back right now!"

He rolled his eyes. "Hey, no sweat. I take it back. All right? Now let's get back to business. How come you've been laying so low lately?"

She understood immediately; she wished she didn't, and that was something she *didn't* understand.

Joey grimaced. "As if I couldn't guess. Mary Poppins again."

His sarcasm made her stiffen. "I pawned a gold necklace at Phil's two weeks ago," she said hotly. "And it just so happens I was with Samantha when I stole it." Inside she winced. God, it sounded as if she were bragging! But things had been rather lean lately. Most of the stores had tightened security because of Christmas, and she had to watch herself in school now.

But that gold necklace... She'd been trying hard to forget she'd ever laid a hand on that darned necklace. Worse, she couldn't forget how staunchly Samantha defended her when the clerk accused her of having something in her hand. The only truth to that whole episode was that she didn't have the necklace in her hand....

It was hidden in the sleeve of her coat.

Joey was grinning again. His satisfaction made Frankie want to squirm even more. "Now that's more like it. Next time, though, bring the goodies to me."

She frowned. "Why?"

"Because I can go through Pete. He'll give you a bigger cut than Phil."

Frankie hesitated. She didn't think she liked Pete. On the other hand, if she got a better price from him, she'd be foolish not to take it.

Her uncertainty must have shown. "Hey, would I give you a bum steer?" Joey laid a hand on her shoulder. "We need to get you back into action, Frankie. How about a little warm-up right now to get you back on track?"

She hesitated, angry at Joey, angry at Samantha. Most of all she was angry with herself, for it seemed she couldn't win either way. If she went with Samantha, Joey wouldn't like it. If she went with Joey, she'd feel like she let Samantha down, though she didn't have the foggiest idea why. She'd known Joey a lot longer than Samantha.

For an instant she almost hated Samantha. Before she'd started doing things with Samantha, she hadn't had to make so darned many decisions. But it was the choices that were the problem, she realized. Somehow she always felt that if she said yes to Samantha, she was turning her back on Joey; it was the same way if she went along with Joey and refused Samantha. Darn it anyway! How could a simple yes or no be so...so mixed up and confusing?

She stuffed her hands into the pockets of her jeans. "I can't," she said finally. "We're going to a movie tonight."

"We?"

Her eyes slid away. "Me and Samantha."

His jaw closed with a snap. He didn't bother to hide his annoyance. "Seems like you're always with her these days."

Frankie's head shot up. "And you're always with Pete!"

Joey sent her a scathing look. "Yeah, well, at least Pete doesn't mind putting a little spare change in my pocket." He started toward the door. "Maybe we'll see you around, Frankie." The door slammed shut.

Frankie remained where she was, a lonely little figure in the tiny living room, a huge lump in her throat.

This was the second time she and Joey had argued over Samantha, she realized miserably. Still another time he'd left in a huff when she got mad because he ridiculed her bike. The heck of it was she still wasn't sure what to think about Samantha. And she couldn't even talk to Joey about it anymore! It made her feel awful, because she'd always been able to talk to Joey about anything.

Joey was...different somehow, she decided tiredly. He just wasn't the same anymore.

It never occurred to her that she was the one who was changing.

SATURDAY MORNING found Samantha hastily making up her Christmas list. It wasn't hard to come up with gift ideas for her mother, sisters, nieces and nephews. This year she had added two more to her list. Frankie's gift was nearly finished, stowed safely in a corner of her closet. Since Vince was going shopping with her today, his would have to wait, though she had yet to figure out what to get him.

Her father's gift usually presented a problem. He didn't need clothes. He had every kind of tool imaginable. But for once Samantha wasn't at a loss for an idea. Her father had an antique pocket watch he had inherited from his grandfather. He had always talked about getting a chain for it but somehow it always got put off. It hadn't been keeping good time lately so he'd taken it in to a jeweler for repair.

What he didn't know was that Samantha's mother had already picked it up. Samantha had asked her mother to send it to her; she planned to buy a chain for it and have it attached.

With that thought in mind, she reached for the jewelry box on her dresser. Only before she could open it, something caught her eye.

The latch was open.

A slight frown etched its way between her brows. Surely she hadn't left it like that. Her mind delved backward. The last time she'd opened it was late yesterday afternoon, when the pocket watch had arrived from her mother. She had left the watch in the small manila envelope and placed it on the bottom drawer. She recalled pushing the latch closed and hearing it catch....

She shoved the lid open and began to rummage through the contents. Once. Twice. Again.

It was no use. The pocket watch wasn't there.

She stared numbly at the jumbled array of necklaces and earrings spread out on her dresser. Her mind was racing. She hadn't misplaced it. She distinctly remembered putting it in the jewelry box. Nor had her house been burgled last night. Nothing else was missing, and she'd have known if someone had broken in. Besides, she'd had the pocket watch less than a day! How on earth could it have disappeared...?

A sickening coil of dread tightened her stomach. It seemed the question was not how... but who.

"Oh, no," she whispered. She didn't want to believe it—it *hurt* to believe it. But all at once Vince's words winged through her mind with shattering clarity.

They check the place out—maybe ask for a drink of water or to use the bathroom—to see if there's anything of value around.

She had forgotten her driving gloves last night. She and Frankie had stopped back here on the way to the movie. While she had been hunting through her front closet, Frankie had asked to use the bathroom.

Her fist came down on the dresser. *Dammit, Frankie,* she screamed silently, *how could you be so stupid?*

At precisely that moment the doorbell rang. Vince! His timing couldn't have been worse. She smoothed her slacks and moved to answer it, her mind frantically debating. If she told Vince about the pocket watch, he would be furious. There had been no major flare-ups between him and Frankie lately, but he didn't need more ammunition where the girl was concerned. Yet she knew she would feel guilty if she kept it from him—she felt guilty right now!

The point was moot. His gaze sharpened the instant he glimpsed her pale features. He caught her hand and pulled her close even before the door clicked shut behind him.

"Hey," he said softly. "Are you okay?"

"I'm fine." The smile she mustered was as weak as her response. She tried to pull away but his grip on her fingers tightened. He tugged her closer.

He scanned her face as if he had all the time in the world. "Samantha," he chided gently. "Didn't anyone ever tell you you're a terrible liar?" A finger came up to trace the fragile skin below her eyes. "Those big baby blues don't hide a thing."

She grimaced. It was silly to think she could keep anything from him. "Read like a book, do I?"

"Fortunately, yes." He pulled her into the living room and down beside him on the sofa. "Tell me what's wrong. Maybe I can help."

She fought what surely would have been a hysterical laugh had she let it escape. Was there a delicate way to put this? *Vince, I'm afraid you were right after all. Frankie* is *the little thief you told me all along.*

A faint bitterness crept through her. If Vince threw it back in her face, she didn't think she could stand it. Yet she was well aware she had no choice but to tell him her suspicions.

"I think," she stated very quietly, "it's already too late."

Watching his changing expressions was almost comical. She could almost see the wheels turning in his head. She knew the exact moment comprehension dawned.

His smile of encouragement withered away. Already there was a storm building in his eyes. He swore under his breath. "Tell me I'm wrong," he muttered. "Tell me this isn't about Frankie."

Samantha winced. "I wish I could." Her voice very low, she told him about the missing pocket watch. When she finished, she held her breath and waited for the outburst she was certain was imminent.

His silence was nerve grating.

She ventured a glance at him, searching for telltale signs of his anger. Oddly she found none. He was staring off across the room, his face shut down from all expression.

Her frustration mounted. Damn! Why didn't he say something—anything! This horrible silence was worse than if he'd shouted.

It was she who spoke first. "Well?" Her smile held no mirth. "Aren't you going to say I told you so?"

He looked at her then. "Is that what you expect?"

"No...yes! Oh, God, I don't know!" His utter calm was infuriating. She was suddenly far less composed than Vince. She jumped up and began to pace. "I can't believe she did this to me. I wish there was another explanation but there just isn't! Frankie is the only one who's been here since the watch came yesterday!"

Vince sympathized completely. She was angry and frustrated and disappointed—and so was he. He was holding on to his temper, but only by a hair. And only for Samantha's sake. "What are you going to do?" he asked.

"Do?" She stopped and stared at him blankly.

"It seems to me that you have two choices. You can tell her you know she took it. Or you can let it ride and see what happens."

"That would just be compounding the problem! She might take it as free license to do whatever she wants. She'd think she can walk all over me!"

Bravo. Vince silently applauded.

Samantha dropped into a chair and leaned her head back wearily. "I don't know what I'll do," she muttered. "All I know right now is that I have to try to get that watch back."

"Let's go then." He rose and came to stand before her.

She blinked. "You know what she'd do with it?"

He pulled her up from the chair. "I have a pretty good idea," he said with a grimace. "It's not hard to find a pawnshop to peddle stolen goods, and there are several in and around Frankie's neighborhood. But we'd better hurry. My guess is that she'll get rid of it as soon as she can."

Their first stop was at Frankie's; no one was home. Samantha's heart sank. Vince was right, she thought heavily. Frankie had wasted no time trying to sell the watch.

An hour later, she wasn't so sure. So far they had checked with three pawnshops. All claimed they had no pocket watch fitting the description of her father's. Samantha also brought along a picture of Frankie from last year's school yearbook. Nor did they recall seeing Frankie.

Vince insisted they check another one just around the corner called Phil's. Samantha said nothing when they walked inside, though she was sure the effort would prove futile. The shop was empty except for a burly man with a cigarette dangling from his lips. He looked up from behind the cluttered counter when they walked in. "Need any help?" he called out.

Vince walked over and placed his hands flat on the counter. "We're looking for an antique gold pocket watch that might have been brought in this morning," he said pleasantly.

Samantha spoke up. "It's rather ornate, patterned with leaves. And it has the initials *L. T.* engraved on the inside."

The man shrugged. "Don't have none like that."

"Are you sure?" Vince's voice took on an edge. "This one would have been brought in by a skinny, dark-haired girl. Her name is Frankie Lombardi."

"Never heard of her," he denied flatly.

An easy smile played around Vince's lips. "That's too bad," he murmured.

The man's eyes narrowed. "You a cop?" he demanded.

Vince didn't back down from the man's glare. "Unfortunately, no. But the watch happens to belong to the lady here." There was a deliberate pause. "It also happens to be stolen property."

The other man dragged the cigarette from his mouth. "You threatening me?"

"Not at all." Vince's tone was silky smooth. "All we want is the pocket watch."

"I'll pay double what you gave Frankie for it," Samantha put in desperately. The man behind the counter gave her the creeps. He looked as if he'd like to jump across straight for Vince's throat.

"I said I don't have it," he said rudely. He dragged a box from beneath the counter and dropped it in front of them. "See for yourself."

She glanced down at the half-dozen pocket watches in the dirty box. None of them were her father's. "It's not there," she said dejectedly. "Let's go, Vince." Her hand slid into the crook of his arm.

Vince gave the other man a long look and dropped a business card on the counter. "I'd appreciate it if you'd call me at this number if it comes in."

The minute they were outside he turned to her. His expression was as grim as his tone. "He may not have your pocket watch—" he nodded toward the pawnshop "—but whether he admits it or not, he knows Frankie. My guess is that this is where she unloads her stash."

Samantha barely heard. She was looking over his shoulder, her eyes were trained on two figures standing near the entrance to an alleyway. She stared at the back of the smaller of the two. The denim jacket and jaunty tilt of the head was unmistakable. The other figure looked vaguely familiar as well. . . .

Vince veered sharply to follow the direction of her gaze. He swore hotly. "There she is! And dammit, I think that's Joey Bennett she's with!"

Samantha nearly groaned. Oh, Lord, of all the luck! Frankie's companion registered too late. If she'd recognized Joey a second earlier, Vince wouldn't have noticed her preoccupation.

"Don't jump to conclusions. Maybe it's not what you think—"

She never got any farther. By the time she caught up with him, he'd covered half the distance between them and the unsuspecting pair that had just turned into the alleyway.

One glimpse of his tight features sent a flutter of alarm up her spine. He looked as if he were wired and ready to explode. Damn! She didn't want him confronting Frankie when he was so angry.

Frankie was the first to spot them. Her eyes rounded. Her jaw sagged. Any other time and Samantha might have laughed at her stupefied expression. Now she only wanted to moan and bury her head in her hands.

Joey turned at the exact moment Vince stepped up beside him. "You're Joey Bennett, aren't you?"

Vince towered over the boy by half a head, but Joey raked the older man with a gaze meant to insult rather than inspect. "Who wants to know?" he drawled.

"Vince Larusso." He smiled, not a nice smile at all. "I'm with Juvenile Corrections."

Joey's lips twisted into a cocky grin. "Larusso, huh? Say, I know who you are." He glanced at Frankie, who had retreated several paces behind him. "You're Frankie's probation officer."

"That's right." For all its softness, Vince's tone sent chills up Samantha's spine. "And since Frankie here seems to be rather forgetful, I'd like to remind you she isn't supposed to be anywhere near you."

Joey's face reflected a reckless defiance. "Am I supposed to be scared or something? Well, listen up, Larusso. You and the rest of the gang down at Juvie Hall can go straight to hell 'cause nobody tells me what to do."

Samantha cringed. Poor Frankie looked as if she didn't care if the earth swallowed her whole.

She could only watch helplessly as two pairs of eyes locked in grisly combat. The exchange that followed was fast and furious. She felt like a spectator at a boxing match. Curses spewed from Joey's mouth, shockingly graphic.

Then it was Vince's turn. His language as blistering as the boy's, he warned Joey to stay away from Frankie— or else. Listening to him—to both of them, Samantha experienced a kind of dazed numbness. Her head began to whirl. She sensed a ruthless harshness in Vince that was totally foreign to her. He looked—and sounded—as if he would gladly tear the boy apart. It was as if his cool civil exterior had been stripped away, exposing a cold-blooded side of him she had never dreamed existed—or perhaps she had blinded herself. Stricken, she couldn't tear her eyes from his profile, stark and relentless and piercing. All she could think was that if this is what he was like when pushed, she never wanted to make an enemy of him.

She had no conscious memory of stepping between the two, but suddenly there she was. Frankie was nowhere around. It was odd, because she didn't remember seeing her leave.

"Stop it," she commanded, only she didn't know if the words were defiant or pathetic. "Both of you...stop it right now."

Joey leveled one last fulminating glance at Vince and stalked off. Her hands were shaking so that she had to clasp them together in front of her. Vince was a watery blur in front of her. She blinked rapidly to try to bring him into focus but it was no use.

"I want to go home," she whispered. To her everlasting shame, her voice broke. "Please, Vince, just...take me home."

CHAPTER ELEVEN

NOT A WORD was spoken the entire way home.

But in his mind Vince kept up a scathing commentary that was ten times worse than what he'd directed at Joey—and it was aimed solely at himself.

The taste of self-disgust was bitter, so bitter he felt he would choke on it. He wasn't proud that Joey had succeeded in ripping the lid off his temper. It was as if he'd been plunged back in time where it took little provocation to make him see red. The angry young rebel he thought had died and been buried along with Tony had resurfaced.

His stomach knotted with dread. He fought the gut-wrenching fear that he'd just made the worst mistake of his life, a mistake that might well have cost him the best thing that had ever happened to him....

Samantha.

He couldn't forget her expression just before she stepped between him and Joey. Her horrified features burned through his consciousness over and over. She had looked at him as if she didn't know him—as if he were a stranger.

It was all his fault.

Her fingers curled around the door handle the instant he pulled into her driveway. She shoved open the door even before the car had rolled to a halt. Vince jammed his foot on the brakes and yanked the keys from the ignition. He was right behind her as she fled up the back porch.

"Samantha!"

She ignored him. Her hands were shaking so badly she dropped her keys twice while attempting to fit the key into the lock. It was Vince who pulled the keys from nerveless fingers and opened the door. She would have bolted inside if he hadn't grabbed her and pulled her back flush against his chest.

Her hands closed around his forearms; she tried to tear his hands from her but somehow he succeeded in turning her around. Too much had happened in a few hours. She was shaken to the core, her thoughts wild and disjointed. Suddenly she was pounding against his chest and babbling, only half-aware of what she was saying.

"Don't!" she cried. "Don't touch me! I—I don't want you anywhere near me, do you hear? I need to think and I can't do it with you around, so please just . . . just go away and leave me alone!"

The silence that followed was like a bomb blast. Vince's hands fell away like a puppet whose strings had been cut. A flicker of something that might have been pain flitted across his features, so fleeting she couldn't be sure. It didn't occur to her until then that she might have hurt him . . . Trapped in a haze of conflicting emotions, her gaze remained riveted to his, held there by a force she couldn't control.

Time hung suspended. "I can't," he said hoarsely. "I would if I could, but so help me, I can't."

The ragged tremor in his voice cut like a knife. Hearing it, something inside her came apart. How she came to be in his arms, she never knew.

She sagged against him. Her arms found their way around his waist and she clung to him. "Vince," she choked. "I'm sorry. I shouldn't have said that...I didn't mean to hurt you, I swear. I just wasn't thinking—"

"I know." And God help him, he did. His eyes squeezed shut as he struggled with himself. For so long now he had guarded his feelings so closely, holding them deep inside to shield against further pain. He'd always found it hard to admit he was wrong. It was harder still to vocalize what he felt.

In the past hour he'd experienced just about every emotion possible. Rage. Frustration. Hurt. Shame. A vulnerability so deep it scared the living daylights out of him. But what he felt right now was beyond anything he'd ever known before.

He rested his chin on her shining hair, savoring her warmth and the pleasurable weight of her body against his. He didn't question the need that drove him to pull her closer still, so close he fancied he could feel the drumming rhythm of her heart melding with his own. Whether this was right or wrong, he didn't know. He didn't care. He knew only that to deny this deep-seated need was to deny his very self.

His hand stroked over her hair. "Samantha. Back there with Joey and Frankie—" the unevenness of his tone betrayed his uncertainty "—I'm sorry you had to be there to see all that. I didn't mean for it to happen, I swear. The last thing I wanted was to upset you." The movement of his fingers stilled. He held his breath and waited.

Samantha didn't know what to say. Hadn't she always known he possessed an underlying hardness? Like a shadow, she couldn't touch it, but it was there.

When she finally spoke, her voice was muffled against his throat. "You gave me a start," she admitted, then faltered. "I guess I never knew you could be so... intimidating."

Vince sensed her uncertainty, saw it in her face when he tilted her chin to his. He wondered if she knew he was feeling just as uncertain.

He searched her face as if he hadn't seen her for years. "I was afraid I'd scared you away," he admitted.

His tone was so low she could scarcely hear. There was a guarded tension in his features, a kind of hurt vulnerability that touched her deeply. Suddenly she was just relieved that it was all over.

"I don't scare that easily, Larusso," she said with a tremulous smile.

It was a smile that tied him in knots. She was so sweet, so damned accepting. What would she say if she knew the truth? He was seized by a gut-wrenching fear. He'd never be able to stand the look in her eyes—he had no doubt she would cringe in horror and disgust.

The thought was like a crushing blow to the heart.

"Samantha," he said slowly. "We're so—so different, you and I." Was it an excuse? Or a plea for understanding? He didn't know.

"Are we? Somehow I don't think so, Vince."

"It's true."

His gaze flitted away. She saw his Adam's apple bob; she could feel the knotted tension in his grip. Vince was usually so blunt and direct. Once again she had the feeling there was something he wasn't telling her. It hurt knowing that he wouldn't share it with her. She could only pray that, in time, he would feel secure enough in her to realize that he could tell her anything.

"Hey," she chided gently. "You know we really ought to decide if we're going in or out. Unless you're prepared to pay my heating bill."

A tiny, sheepish smile tugged at his lips as he realized they were still standing in the doorway. He let her pull him inside.

She hastily decided to put off her shopping. She suspected neither of them was in the mood for it. Instead she made hot cocoa, which they took into the living room.

They had both finished when Samantha brought up the subject they had both avoided for the past hour. They sat together on the end of the sofa, their hands entwined, resting lightly on the solid length of his thigh. The mood was quiet and intimate. She hated to ruin it, yet she knew she must.

"Vince." She spoke his name quietly. "We need to talk about Frankie."

The sudden pall was deathly. Vince turned his head to stare at her, the tension of the moment mirrored between them.

"Do we?" His tone was very quiet, his lips ominously thin. "After this morning, I'm not sure there's anything left to say."

She silently despaired as she sensed something inside him grow as hard and brittle as glass. Nonetheless, she managed to meet his gaze evenly. "I want to know what you intend to do about this morning."

"About Frankie taking your pocket watch? Or being with Joey?"

She winced at his tone. "Both."

His jaw locked tight. "She knows the score, Samantha. She knew she was supposed to stay out of trouble. She knew she had to stay the hell away from Joey!"

Her breath caught in her throat. "Vince," she said shakily. "You can't possibly be thinking of having her removed from her home! My God, that would be the worst thing in the world for her!''

He shot to his feet and began to pace like a caged animal. ''Maybe then she'd realize this is no game we're playing!''

Samantha struggled not to lose her temper. She didn't quite succeed. ''You're always willing to believe the worst about her, aren't you? In fact, you're downright eager.''

''If I am, she gave me plenty of reason today alone! She's headed for trouble, Samantha. Big trouble! And if she doesn't stay the hell away from Joey Bennett, she'll probably find it even sooner than I think.''

''She's just a little mixed up, Vince. Is that so terrible?''

Vince wanted to throw his hands in the air. Bitterness vied with a burning frustration. How could he tell her that those were the worst kind, because they slipped into your heart without you knowing it?

And they were the ones it hurt to lose.

''You can say that after she stole your father's pocket watch? How can you be so blind?''

He delivered the words with stinging impact; she felt every one like a hooked barb. But if she didn't stand up for Frankie, who would?

She held his gaze unflinchingly. ''It was a mistake, Vince.''

He made a sound of impatience. ''And how many mistakes will it take before you see what she is?'' Feet braced slightly apart, he faced her in the posture that was oh-so-familiar by now. They were separated by the width of the room, yet the distance between them seemed far greater.

An unseen hand seemed to close around her heart and squeeze. She stared at the jutting angle of his jaw, wondering why he was so inflexible. So demanding and unyielding. She didn't understand him, she thought sadly.

She wondered if she ever would.

Vince had once expressed the belief that Frankie had probably been stealing long before she was ever caught. More than ever, Samantha wished she could believe otherwise. But for a long time now, a vague, nagging doubt swirled in her brain whenever she thought of Frankie's "take." She just couldn't rid herself of the feeling that something didn't quite fit.

Her voice was very quiet when she finally spoke. "You think Frankie's never stopped stealing, don't you? That the two of us have made no difference at all."

"How can you even ask that after today?" His disgusted tone said it all.

She gave him a long, measuring look. "Then tell me something. What's she doing with the money she gets? Haven't you ever wondered about that?"

"Frankly, no. There are dozens of different things she could spend it on!"

Samantha's chin lifted. Vince might be stubborn, but so was she! "Like what? Think about it, Vince! What's she spending it on? And have you ever taken a good look at what she wears? She's obviously not buying clothes for herself! And she's too young to even think about putting money down on a car or anything like that."

He gestured impatiently. "Drugs is the first thing that comes to mi—"

"No! I don't believe that. And I don't think you do, either!"

Hands on his hips, he stared at her in mute frustration for a second. Finally he dropped his hands to his sides. "Even if I don't, that doesn't change a thing! Stealing is a crime and there are no two ways about it!"

"No? I'm not so sure, Vince."

His eyes narrowed. "What are you getting at?"

Samantha took a deep breath. "I—I'm not sure," she admitted. "But what if she gave that money to her mother?"

"And what if she didn't? Maybe she bought a stereo for her room. She could be buying tapes. Magazines. For crying out loud, what does it matter? She's being deliberately defiant. She's still seeing Joey Bennett and she's still stealing. As far as I'm concerned, that's all I need to know!"

Samantha's shoulders sagged. There would be no convincing him. That was patently obvious.

Her gaze met his, silently pleading. "Can't you give her the benefit of the doubt? Can't you give her just one more chance? I think she can change, Vince. But I don't think she can do it alone."

His reply was heated and instantaneous. "But *she* has to make the effort, Samantha! It's something she has to do for herself and I honestly don't think she wants to."

That was Vince, typically blunt. In an anguished kind of way, she appreciated what he was trying to say—that it was impossible to instill values into a closed mind. In that, he was right. But Samantha knew she'd never forgive herself if she abandoned Frankie right now... because now was when she really needed someone to believe in her.

"Just let me talk to her," she urged. "Please, Vince. I honestly think we can put all this behind her."

His thoughts were just a little self-deprecating. There were times he couldn't help but like Frankie. She had a lot of spunk and determination. Like Samantha, he'd actually begun to think she could change . . . which only proved what a fool he was.

"What about Joey?" he demanded. "Am I supposed to let that slide, too? I'm not a fool, Samantha. I know today isn't the first time she's seen Joey since she was put on probation."

Samantha caught her breath. She hated keeping it from him, but she knew she didn't dare tell him about the day she'd caught Frankie with Joey outside her building.

The pitch of her voice was very low. "I know it's not fair for me to ask this of you, but can't you bend the rules just once?"

The pleading in Samantha's eyes cut him to the quick. He cursed both himself and her, for already he felt himself weakening.

"Hell," he muttered. "I don't like the idea of you being anywhere near her, let alone continuing as her Big Sister. That's what you intend to do, isn't it?"

It was on the tip of her tongue to argue that *he* seemed dead set against her. But whether he knew it or not, he cared about Frankie. Otherwise, he wouldn't have been so angry with Joey.

"I can't turn my back on her now, Vince." Her eyes reflected her resolve. "She needs to know that someone has faith in her."

"You said it yourself," he reminded her grimly. "She'll think she can walk all over you."

God, how she hated the finality in his tone. "You think I'm expecting too much, don't you?" If she sounded hurt, she couldn't help it.

"Too much? You're asking for a miracle." His mouth thinned ominously when he caught her expression. "Don't look at me like that. I know you think there's a sweet loving girl somewhere inside Frankie. Hell, I was beginning to think maybe you were right—that I was wrong about her after all! But she's shown her true colors and she's waving them like a red flag! You trusted her and look how she repaid you!'' He shook his head. ''I've seen this happen too many times to believe in miracles. She's headed for trouble—big trouble.''

For the longest time Samantha said nothing. On one plane of thought, his words struck a note of truth in her consciousness. On another, all she could think was how much alike Frankie and Vince really were. They shared the same strength, the same unyielding backbone. Both wore their toughness like a protective shell, shielding them from anything that might hurt them. Yet she suspected neither of them would ever admit it.

Oh, yes, she thought again. They were so much alike it nearly broke her heart. She wondered bleakly if she could ever reach either of them...but she had to try. She *had* to.

She rose and crossed the room. With a bravado she was far from feeling, she touched his forearm. Beneath her fingertips, his muscles were rigid and tense. At her touch, he tightened further, as if in protest.

Doggedly she kept her hand where it was, though all at once she was trembling inside. She had the curious feeling that the outcome of this moment was somehow crucial. ''Then help me,'' she whispered. ''Help me...to help Frankie.''

Help me. Such simple words that demanded so much...perhaps more than he had to give. *Don't do this to me!* he wanted to shout. He felt like the scum of the earth, while she looked like an angel, her eyes were wide and blue and so damned trusting he wanted to cry out in shame. Vince silently cursed the fate that had brought the two of them together...the sinner and the saint. God, but that was rich. He'd have laughed if he weren't crying inside.

Her hand slid tentatively down his arm and stole into his. He stared transfixed as she slowly weaved their fingers together. Against his, her hand looked small and fragile. The contrast between their skin was striking, hers so fair and unblemished. But his was stained crimson with the blood of his brother....

Her voice seemed to come from far away. "Frankie needs someone to believe in her. And right now I need you to believe in me, too."

With her eyes she traced the contours of his mouth. So stern. So harshly beautiful. Unable to help herself, she lifted their clasped hands and rubbed her cheek kitten-like against the back of his hand.

Her eyes clung to his. "Please," she whispered. "I need to know that you're with me—and not against me."

He might have been etched in stone. He wondered if she knew just how much this was tearing him up inside. He knew she probably thought he really didn't give a damn about Frankie. He did, but concern for Samantha overrode all else.

The edge in his voice revealed his frustration. "I don't want you to end up hurt."

She pressed her lips against his knuckles. "That won't happen," she whispered.

He swallowed. The feel of her lips against his skin unraveled a flurry of emotion. Tenderness. Desire. A surge of protectiveness so fierce it was frightening.

His fingers slowly uncurled. He shaped her cheek against his palm. "I hope to God I'm wrong about Frankie," he said intensely. "But what if I'm not? What if she stumbles and falls? You'll blame yourself, Samantha. I know you will."

The fiercely possessive look in his eyes thrilled her. Staring into his chiseled features, she relived that poignantly sweet moment when he'd first kissed her. She wanted him to hold her again, she thought achingly. She wanted to feel his warmth surround her, his lips warm and demanding, taking as well as seeking.

She edged closer, so close their bodies brushed from chest to thigh. She stared up at him, not caring that her heart was in her eyes. When she spoke their lips almost touched. "If I do, will you be there to pick *me* up?"

Her shaky smile, as much as the words themselves, took his breath away. "Yes." The word was a fervent whisper. "God, yes."

All at once she was engulfed in his arms. Their bodies clung together with a strength that bordered on desperation, saying all that words could not. When their lips finally met, the kiss they shared was a tender, healing caress, so unbearably gentle it brought tears to her eyes. If anything, the tumult of the day made the moment all the more heartrending . . . all the more precious.

His lips seemed reluctant to leave the parted softness of hers. He kissed her again and again until finally he rested his forehead against hers.

"Samantha." Her name was half laugh, half groan. "Why do you put up with me?"

She smiled, her senses filled with the vibrant promise of his body against hers. "It can't be your bedside manner," she teased, snuggling closer as one lean hand charted the small hollow at the base of her spine. "Maybe it's because I don't get a crick in my neck when you kiss me."

One dark brow hiked imperiously upward. "I know for a fact that's an excellent reason. Only I thought you kissed me."

"Oh, it was definitely the other way around. You kissed me." She looped her arms around his neck, loving the laughter that lit his eyes to pure gold. "Of course, I'd be happy to oblige...."

"Please do."

Those were the last words either spoke for a very long time.

Much later that night a renegade thought slipped into her mind, a nagging doubt she'd managed to sidestep while Vince was here. He had agreed to let her talk to Frankie, but she feared his reasons had little to do with Frankie. He had agreed solely for her sake.

The realization was like a sliver in her skin. Vince was a sensitive, caring man; this she believed with every fiber in her being. But it only made it harder to comprehend his attitude toward Frankie. With her he was so rigid and uncompromising.

Uncompromising. The word was jarring, for it reminded her of Brad. And all at once she couldn't deny that there were times Vince was every bit as stubborn as Brad. Brad would never admit to a mistake—never.

Had she fallen for a man who was all wrong for her... again?

Or was she overreacting? Reading more into Vince's hard-line stance than was actually there?

She didn't know. She could only rely on her instinct—and instinct told her there was a very good reason Vince was convinced Frankie was headed down a one-way path of self-destruction. She chafed inside, wondering what it could possibly be . . . but the only one with the answer was Vince.

And Vince wasn't talking.

CHAPTER TWELVE

THE SITUATION with Frankie was just as frustrating. Sunday dawned sunny and cold and windless, the sky was a clear unbroken shade of indigo.

It was a perfect day for ice-skating.

As she had a dozen times already that morning, Samantha scowled and let the curtain fall away from the window. She was sorely tempted to call off her "date" with Frankie. After yesterday's disastrous encounter, Frankie surely wouldn't expect her to keep it.

It was that very reason that finally spurred her into action. Frankie might have written her off, but Samantha had no intention of abandoning her just yet, though Frankie probably expected it.

Ten minutes later she walked out her back door, a pair of ice skates looped over each shoulder—and a small package tucked inside the pocket of her coat.

A short time later, she knocked on the door of Frankie and Anna's apartment. It was quiet for so long she thought no one was home. She was just about to turn away when the door was pulled slightly ajar. Dark eyes peered cautiously over the chain.

Samantha summoned a smile and stepped forward. "Hello, Mrs. Lombardi. Is Frankie ready yet?"

Anna fumbled with the chain, then finally opened the door wide. She was smiling but her expression was puzzled.

"Frankie and I were going to go ice-skating this afternoon." How she managed to sound so matter-of-fact, she didn't know. "Did she forget to tell you?"

"*Sì*. She did, or I would not have sent her down to the market. You come in and wait, no? She will be back soon."

Samantha peered over her shoulder and saw a pillow and rumpled afghan on the sofa. Frankie had mentioned several weeks ago that Anna had been down with a bout of the flu. Was she still sick? "If you're not feeling well," she said quickly, "Frankie and I can always make it another day."

"But you are here and Francesca would be so disappointed." Anna seized her hand and pulled her inside. "Besides," she insisted, "I am f—"

Without warning she succumbed to a paroxysm of coughing. Samantha was at her side immediately. Her arm around her shoulders, she guided her the few steps toward the sofa. The cough seemed dragged from deep inside her, racking her entire body as she struggled for breath. Unable to stand by helplessly, Samantha bolted into the kitchen for some water.

By the time she returned, the spasm was over. Anna straightened, a sheepish smile on her lips as she accepted the glass of water. "You baby me," she murmured. "I am not used to this."

Samantha sat down beside her, a worried frown etched between her brows. "Are you okay?"

"I am fine." Anna leaned back against the cushions. "I am," she insisted as she spied Samantha's skepticism. "It is my asthma acting up again. It is always worse in the winter."

Samantha eyed her closely, reminded of the day Frankie told her about her mother's asthma. The harsh raspiness of her breathing was certainly indicative of an asthma attack. But it bothered her that Anna was so pale. Her skin had an unhealthy pallor. She looked frail enough to blow away with the next breeze. Still, her hand hadn't felt overly warm...

"Frankie told me you've been sick the past few weeks."

"It was just a touch of the flu. And I feel better now." She leaned over and patted Samantha's hand. "You are as bad as my Francesca. You both worry too much."

Her breathing was no longer as choppy, but Samantha remained troubled. "Mrs. Lombardi," she said slowly. "Frankie told me you dislike doctors, but maybe it wouldn't hurt for you to see one. He might be able to give you something for your asthma."

"Rest is usually all I need." Anna seemed determined to pass off the episode lightly.

Samantha was not. "Working two jobs doesn't leave much time for rest." She paused, her lips tightening. It hadn't been difficult to figure out that the cost factor was at least partially to blame for Anna's reluctance to visit a doctor. "I don't suppose either job offers any health insurance."

Anna's smile faded. Her gaze fell. "No," she admitted. "And I am still trying to catch up in my rent, you see..."

"I know." Samantha touched her shoulder gently, sparing her the explanation. Like Frankie, Anna possessed no small amount of pride.

Their situation had preyed on her mind often these past few weeks. Anna's health problem was just another added burden to a load that was already far too heavy. Was it possible Anna didn't know there might be some other alternatives that could make life far easier?

She watched as Anna plucked a handkerchief from her pocket and held it to her mouth for a moment. She spoke very gently. "Please don't think I'm being nosy, Mrs. Lombardi. But I can't help but wonder if you shouldn't talk to a state caseworker. You might qualify for some type of—"

Anna's head shot up. Her eyes rounded. "Welfare!" she gasped.

Samantha stopped, suddenly recalling what Frankie had said the day Vince had given her the bike. *My mother won't take money she didn't work for.*

"It wouldn't have to be permanent," she clarified quickly. "Maybe just until you start feeling better so you don't have to struggle so to make ends meet. You'd have medical benefits, too." She glanced around. "In fact, you might even qualify for government subsidized housing, or some kind of assistance with your rent—"

Anna made a strangled sound. Stunned, Samantha broke off abruptly. The look in Anna's eyes was one of blind, sheer panic. Her breath grew ragged and jerky. As Samantha looked on, she shook her head wildly and erupted into a stream of rapid-fire Italian.

She slid her arm around the other woman, frantically wondering what she'd said to provoke this reaction.

Cold clammy fingers clung to hers. "No. No government! No papers! They will find out . . . !"

Samantha balked. Apparently Anna had an irrational fear of government agencies. But why? She had lived in this country for years already. Even as she soothed the woman, her mind groped for what little Frankie had told her about her mother. But she could think of no reason why Anna should be so panicked.

"Anna. Anna, please look at me." She caught her chin in her hand and turned her face. "I didn't mean to upset you, I swear. I'm only trying to help, honestly."

Her stricken expression began to fade. But just as Samantha began to relax, two huge tears welled in her eyes. Without a second thought, she slid her arms around the other woman's thin shoulders and pulled her shaking body close.

Anna couldn't help it. For so long now, she'd been so afraid. So guilty. Most of all, so *alone*. Padre Antonio was gone. There was no one to talk to. No one who understood her fears... But she had felt something for Samantha right from the start, a closeness she didn't understand but couldn't deny. She knew instinctively that she could trust Samantha with the secret she had guarded so well and so long.

"Anna, what's wrong? Why are you crying? Has something happened? Frankie's okay, isn't she?"

Her tone was so gentle, almost more than Anna could take. "*Sì*. She is all right. It is me, you see." Anna knew she was babbling but she couldn't help it. "I—I have done something terrible and I am so afraid that someone will find out and send me back to Italy...."

"Send you back!" Samantha was totally bewildered. "Of course that won't happen. Why, you've been here for years already. And Frankie told me you married an American G.I."

Anna choked back a sob. "Francesca does not know," she blurted. "Paulo and I...we were never married."

Samantha sucked in a breath. "But I thought... Frankie told me her father ran off when she was just a baby."

Anna's shoulders drooped further. Her eyes flitted away. "That is what I told her," she confided, her voice very low. "But there is much that Francesca does not know." Something came apart inside her. There was no help for it and suddenly it was all pouring out, like water through a sieve.

Stunned, Samantha could only listen. It seemed the orphanage where Anna had been placed after her parents died was operated by a group of nuns. Samantha had no trouble picturing the sheltered existence Anna had spent during her teenage years there. She had stayed on to help the staff until funding problems forced them to let her go. Naive, on her own for the first time in her life, desperately needing to feel loved, she had fallen hard and fast for an American G.I. attached to the U.S. Embassy in Rome. As Anna recalled wistfully, everything was perfect.

"When he told me he would marry me, I remember thinking—how lucky I am! My mama would have been so happy knowing that Paulo's grandparents were Italian. But then Paulo was suddenly transferred to Chicago before we could be married. We had no money for me to travel so soon, but before he left, he was able to get all the papers I needed so I could come later."

"So you planned to marry once you joined him here in Chicago?"

Anna nodded. A faint distress crept into her features. Seeing it, Samantha gently encouraged her. "What happened then?"

Anna found she couldn't look at her. "After he left I found out I was—to have a child." Her voice was scarcely audible.

Samantha leaned forward. "He didn't know until after you arrived here?"

She nodded, eyes downcast. "I remember he was angry—so angry."

Listening to her, Samantha was filled with a fury that made her see red. She had no trouble envisioning a cocky, swaggering G.I. seducing an innocent young girl with stars in her eyes. No doubt Frankie's father had been solely after a good time. He clearly hadn't planned on getting snagged with a wife *and* child. Maybe he had never even planned on marrying Anna in the first place.

Anna shuddered, her body cold with the chill of remembrance. "But then he told me the baby changed nothing. We could marry as soon as I found a job and a place to live."

She fell silent. Over and over her bony fingers plucked at the handkerchief in her hands. Watching her, Samantha felt an icy prickle ease up her spine.

"That's when he deserted you, isn't it?"

"Yes," she whispered. Her voice raw, she went on to tell how there was no money to find him, how she knew nothing at all about his family. Even the Army didn't know where he was since he'd gone AWOL. Anna didn't want to return to Italy; she wanted her child to be born an American. When she had been really desperate for help, she had gone to the parish church—and Padre Antonio. Samantha remembered the day Frankie had mentioned his name. No wonder Anna had been so upset when the priest died.

There was more.

"They warned me at the embassy in Rome that if I did not marry Paulo, I must return to Italy," Anna went on. "But I did not want to go back. I wanted my child to be born an American." What followed came in jagged bursts and phrases. "But Paulo was gone...I was afraid to apply for another visa...I knew they would think I lied about marrying Paulo just so that I could come into the country...."

Samantha balked. At first her mind refused to grasp her implication. Then comprehension dawned with shattering clarity. All at once she realized...

Anna Lombardi had remained in this country illegally.

Everything clicked at once. The reason for Anna's earlier panic was suddenly crystal clear; her wariness the day Samantha had broached the Big Sister/Little Sister program. She recalled Anna's reluctance to fill out the application and undergo the interview with Lynette Marshall. Samantha had thought then that Anna seemed afraid—and she was! No wonder Anna had never sought any kind of subsidized housing or assistance. She was afraid of being deported!

Through a haze she heard her voice again. "I am so ashamed," she whispered. Her voice caught painfully. "And I am such a coward! What if my Francesca should find out the truth? What would she think of me?"

Samantha had never felt so helpless. The anguish in those dark liquid eyes cut like a knife. Her heart bled for this woman whose lifelong struggle was still not over. Samantha wished with all her heart that she could tell Anna her fears were groundless. But she couldn't, and so she sought to comfort her in the only way she knew how.

Her hand stole out to cover Anna's. She could feel her trembling. "Anna," she said gently. "Don't talk that way—don't even think it! You are not a terrible person. You're not a coward! You're a very strong woman and you've done what you had to, for yourself and for Frankie. There's no shame in that—no guilt in trying to protect someone you love." Her tone grew very soft.

"Frankie loves you, Anna. And I don't think there's anything that could ever change that."

Anna's fingers clung to hers. "You will not tell? Especially Francesca. I could not bear it if she knew—"

Samantha shook her head.

Anna released a sigh. Oddly, she felt relieved that her terrible secret was out. She wanted very much to believe Samantha, but all at once what had happened in the past no longer mattered. What mattered was Francesca.

Her eyes darkened. "I am so glad that Francesca has someone like you," she said haltingly. She hesitated, praying she could find the right words.

"I know she is sometimes reckless—she has her papa's temper—but she is not bad. I know with all my heart that she is a good girl." Her eyes turned beseeching. "Will you help her to stay this way? Please?"

Her features were taut and strained, her expression desperately pleading. Even if Samantha had wanted to refuse, she couldn't have.

Her fingers squeezed Anna's. "I will," she promised softly.

"Thank you," Anna whispered. Her lips parted in a quivering smile that was both sad and hopeful, a smile that tore Samantha's heart.

Without a second thought, Samantha leaned over and hugged her. Neither needed words to express what was most in their hearts; the way they held each other spoke eloquently. Nor did it matter that they had known each other but a short time. The bond they shared was one that transcended the boundaries of time. When they drew back, there was a suspiciously moist sheen in both their eyes.

Anna got up, smiling tremulously. "I had better go dry my eyes before Francesca comes back. She always knows when I have been crying."

She disappeared into the bathroom, while Samantha reached for her purse to dig out a tissue. It appeared she wasn't much better. At that precise moment the door burst open.

"Mama?" called a voice. "I'm back."

Frankie bounded inside, her thin arms clutching a grocery sack. She didn't see Samantha until she shoved the door shut with her foot.

She froze. Her smile vanished. She regarded Samantha with all the welcome of a venomous snake.

Samantha rose to her feet. "Hello, Frankie," she said calmly.

Frankie scowled. "Where's Mama?"

Samantha inclined her head toward the bathroom. She had no trouble interpreting the mute betrayal in the girl's eyes. Frankie thought she had come and told her mother about the pocket watch.

She crossed the few steps to where the girl stood. "Why don't we put these away so your mother won't have to do it?" she suggested. "As soon as we're done we can leave to go ice-skating." She reached for the sack, her eyes silently conveying a warning message of her own.

Frankie's mouth opened. Samantha sensed she was about to argue but Anna chose that moment to emerge from the bathroom.

"Francesca! You are back! Did you know you forgot to tell me that today was the day you and Samantha planned to go ice-skating?" she gently scolded. "You two go now. I will get those—"

Samantha already had her by the arm and was steering her toward the sofa. She wouldn't have thought it possible, but Anna looked more exhausted than when she'd arrived. "Frankie and I can get it done in half the time," she said firmly. "We still have plenty of time to skate so why don't you take advantage of the quiet and take a nap?"

Frankie looked ready to argue but she meekly agreed when Anna insisted. Ten minutes later they were on their way to the outdoor skating arena.

So far Frankie had yet to say a word. The way she sat huddled against the passenger door was a painful reminder of their first outing together. And to think she'd been convinced they had come so far since then! Samantha fought a feeling of hopeless frustration. Would it always be like this? One step forward, two steps back?

She had already decided to take her cues from Frankie. If the subject of her father's pocket watch came up, it would have to be initiated by Frankie. Judging from the girl's shuttered expression, Samantha decided Frankie expected her to pounce like a cat upon a mouse the instant they were alone. But Samantha didn't want to pressure Frankie into confessing; if she wanted to, fine. If not, she would simply have to believe the right time would come eventually. It was a question of faith. Frankie's course of action would be dictated by one thing. Either Frankie trusted her... or she didn't.

Vince would have thought her a fool—and maybe she was. It was certainly a gamble, but she prayed that Frankie wouldn't fail her.

And indeed Frankie's conscience was reading her the riot act. She hadn't expected Samantha to take her skating today. She hadn't expected to see her again period! Unfortunately Samantha had been constantly on her mind. She kept seeing that horrible scene yesterday in front of Phil's, over and over until she wanted to scream.

Frankie knew stealing Samantha's pocket watch was wrong. As always, she'd told herself she was doing it for Mama. Joey had been really steamed when she refused to hock it. Yet she couldn't, even for Mama. And even Frankie couldn't explain why. She hadn't felt like this all those other times she stole. Why now?

Maybe it had something to do with the way Samantha had looked yesterday. So crushed and disappointed. Most of all, so hurt Frankie just wanted to wither up and die.

Outside the city whizzed by. She guessed vaguely that they were heading north along the lake. Samantha pointed out Buckingham Fountain and Soldier Field, but Frankie scarcely heard. She didn't know when she'd felt so miserable.

She sat motionless when the car rolled to a halt. "Here we are," Samantha announced cheerfully. "Looks pretty crowded, doesn't it? I'll bet the warming house is full all day long."

Frankie neither agreed nor disagreed. All at once she remembered the day they had first planned the outing. They'd been sitting in a booth at McDonald's having a Coke. Samantha was telling her how she'd gotten even with her older sister Beth once for calling her a brat— she'd put toothpicks in the sandwich Beth took to school that day. Then Samantha started blowing bubbles in her Coke with her straw. And pretty soon, she'd been doing it, too. They sat there grinning at each other like a couple of fools, but neither one of them cared.

It was on the way home when Samantha mentioned that the city's park district flooded some of the meadows and athletic fields for skating when the weather turned cold enough. She even had a spare pair of ice skates... It was then that they decided the first chance they had, they would go.

A huge lump lodged in Frankie's throat. And now, here they were, only—only it was all spoiled! And she had no one to blame but herself...

She followed Samantha to a bench where they sat down to put on their skates. They were a little big but she'd brought along an extra pair of socks. She said nothing while Samantha showed her how to lace up the skates.

Samantha took their shoes back to the car. Frankie squinted into the cold bright sunshine. A slow curl of smoke drifted from the chimney of the warming house. A couple of teenagers emerged, hand in hand. Out on the ice, a little girl swirled across the glasslike surface, bright red pompoms tied to her laces, her hair flying like a banner behind her. There were people everywhere. Talking. Laughing. Looking as if they were having the time of their lives.

She spotted Samantha heading back and scowled. Darn it, Frankie thought furiously. Why wasn't Samantha mad at her? She had every right to be—for crying out loud, she'd *stolen* from her. So why didn't she just point her finger and shout at her? Frankie could handle that. She could fight back then and it would be so much easier than trying to pretend that everything was all right when she'd never been more miserable in her life!

She lurched to her feet and almost lost her balance in the process. Samantha's arm shot out to steady her. Frankie was sorely tempted to jerk her arm away when she noticed Samantha held a small gaily wrapped package. Geez, she thought scathingly. Joey was right. Samantha was nothing but a goody-two-shoes like Mary Poppins.

Samantha's heart sank when she glimpsed Frankie's closed features. So, she thought helplessly. The old Frankie was back and this time with a vengeance.

The girl's eyes fixed suspiciously on the package. She shivered against the icy bite of the wind and shoved her hands into the pockets of her coat. She was suddenly glad Samantha had told her to wear another sweatshirt beneath her denim jacket. "What's that?" she asked gruffly.

Samantha's smile nearly faltered. Somehow she kept it in place. "Actually," she said lightly, "I planned to give you this for Christmas. But I finished it early and...well, with this cold snap we're having I thought you might like it now."

Frankie stared at the package as if it might bite. A dull red flush crept into her cheeks. Her gaze flitted quickly away and then back again.

Samantha held it out and chided her gently. "*You're* supposed to open it, Frankie. Not me."

Frankie bit her lip. "I will," she muttered. "First I gotta give you something." She dug into her jeans pocket for a second, then grabbed Samantha's gloved hand and shoved something inside it.

Samantha slowly uncurled her fingers. The sunlight caught the glint of something shiny and gold....

Her father's pocket watch.

Frankie confined her attention to the tips of her ice skates. "I'm sorry I stole it. And I'm sorry if I caused you any trouble yesterday with Larusso."

Samantha remained silent for a moment, overcome with a dozen tremulous emotions. "Why, Frankie? Why didn't you sell this at the pawnshop yesterday?"

Frankie shifted uncomfortably. "Joey said I was turning into a sissy but I—I just couldn't." She gulped and raised her head. Looking Samantha straight in the eye was the hardest thing she had ever done. But Samantha didn't look angry or resentful, as she had feared. And suddenly Frankie knew exactly why she'd felt so guilty.

"I didn't expect to feel so bad about it." The confession seemed wrenched from deep inside her. "I started thinking if you found out I stole it, you probably wouldn't want anything to do with me. And after I saw you yesterday, I figured ... you'd never want to see me again."

Samantha went very still inside. No matter how much it hurt, she had to know... "And that bothered you? The idea of you and I not doing things together?"

Frankie swallowed. It was hard to talk around the huge lump in her throat. "Yeah," she said unevenly. "Anyway, I just wanted you to have it back. And if you'd rather just take me home now, well, that's okay, too."

The traitorous wobble in her voice sped straight to Samantha's heart. It spun through her brain that Frankie expected a flat-out rejection, but that was the last thing on Samantha's mind. Vince was convinced she was getting too involved with Frankie, and maybe she was. But she wouldn't have traded this moment—painful though it was for both of them—for anything in this world.

"Everybody makes mistakes," she said softly. "I wouldn't think much of myself if I deserted you at the first sign of trouble." She smiled. "You're stuck with me, kid. And right now I'm so darned proud of you that I—why, I could kiss you!"

Frankie's eyes widened but she didn't look too terribly displeased at the prospect. Samantha chuckled. "Why don't you open your present—" she held it out once more "—and then we'll hit the ice."

This time Frankie didn't hesitate. She ripped at the wrapping with all the finesse of a typical child at Christmas. Samantha watched as she pulled out a pair of royal-blue mittens, a stocking cap and a matching muffler.

She ran her fingers over the knitted material. "Hey," she said faintly. "You made this, didn't you? I remember you had yarn this color at your house."

Samantha nodded. The slow grin creeping across Frankie's lips made her heart turn over. "Let's just hope it all fits," she chuckled, "or it may be next Christmas before I get enough ambition to drag out my knitting needles again!"

Frankie whisked the stocking cap over her head. The bright color brought out the shiny highlights in her dark hair. Next she jammed her hands into the mittens and wiggled her fingers. "They fit just right," she announced. Last but not least she looped the muffler around her neck.

Samantha eyed the mittens. "Gloves would have been better," she said with a rueful smile. "But I'm afraid this is the extent of my knitting ability so I hope you can manage to ride your bike with those."

Frankie rubbed her mittened hands together. "I'll be lots warmer with these."

"Good. Let's go take a turn on that ice then."

Frankie's hand on her arm stopped her. "Samantha?"

Samantha was startled to find that Frankie's grin had faded. Her expression was tentative and uncertain. Samantha frowned and stepped closer.

Frankie swallowed. Her gaze slid away. In all her life, she couldn't remember a time someone had done something for her that they hadn't been forced to do. Except Mama, of course. And now Samantha. She felt like crying, but crying was for babies.

The words burned deep inside her. She knew she had to say them now or she never would.

Samantha sensed there was something Frankie wanted to tell her. She watched the muscles in her throat work convulsively, aware of her own throat growing achingly tight. "What is it?" she asked softly, hoping to make it easier for the girl.

"I just wanted to say thanks," she said haltingly. "And to tell you—" she gulped, for this was the hard part "—next to my mom I think you're the best friend I ever had."

The words spilled out in a rush. Frankie flung herself against Samantha for a quick spontaneous hug.

Samantha was still reeling when Frankie stepped back. She found herself gripped by a rush of emotion so strong she felt giddy. All she had ever wanted was for Frankie to trust her—to know and believe she wanted to help her. Vince had told her she was expecting too much of Frankie... *You're asking for a miracle,* he'd said. In that mind-splitting instant, one thought rose head and shoulders above the rest.

Maybe miracles really *did* happen.

CHAPTER THIRTEEN

THERE WAS A REAL CHANGE in their relationship after that, an acceptance by Frankie that hadn't been there before. She talked more freely and openly than Samantha had ever dreamed possible. Samantha was more convinced than ever that Frankie's tough, independent exterior masked a very vulnerable little girl.

She wished she could say that Vince felt the same.

Frankie and Vince had yet to come face-to-face since the incident in front of the pawnshop. He'd managed to hide his surprise when he found out Frankie had returned her father's pocket watch. It wasn't so much what he said...as what he didn't say that led her to believe he hadn't changed his mind about Frankie.

Samantha didn't know why it hurt so much. She only knew that it did.

As for Allison Stiles, it appeared the situation had been defused. On the last day of school before Christmas break, Allison's mother paid her a surprise visit. Though she'd been immediately on guard, Samantha discovered there was no need. Allison's mother had apologized profusely for the day she had rashly accused her of meddling. Tears stood out in the other woman's eyes as she told Samantha she had discovered that Allison's claims against her new husband were true. Her husband had finally admitted the truth.

Allison's mother had filed for divorce the very next day.

As Samantha soberly told Vince, it was a shame that Allison's mother had taken the word of her new husband against that of her daughter. But with him out of the picture, Allison was home with her mother where she belonged; their relationship might be strained for a while, but hopefully both mother and daughter would soon put it behind them.

Like the previous few weeks, Christmas shivered its way into the city. Most of the midwest remained locked tight in the grasp of an Arctic cold front. Samantha's parents had left the previous weekend to visit friends in North Dakota. They'd planned to start home the day before Christmas Eve; unfortunately a blizzard hit the state the night before and left many of the roads nearly impassable. Her mother had phoned from North Dakota with the news that they wouldn't make it back in time for Christmas after all.

As always, Samantha had planned to spend Christmas with her family. This year, though, she'd asked Vince to come with her. But the prospect of spending Christmas without her family wasn't as disappointing as it might have been were it not for Vince. In fact, so far the day had been anything but disappointing.

She poked the last bite of juicy turkey breast from her plate into her mouth. "Perfect," she sighed, pushing back her plate. "At least I can tell my mother we had turkey for dinner."

Vince smiled indulgently from across the table, his mind not on the meal they had just shared, but the woman he had just shared it with. He marveled at how his life had changed in these weeks since he'd met Samantha. She brought light into a world that had once held only darkness and shadows.

Yet he was stung with a bittersweet resignation, for the realization brought as much pain as pleasure. Samantha also made him feel emotions he wasn't certain he even *wanted* to feel again. Ever since Tony, he hadn't let himself get close to anyone... until Samantha.

He was afraid to love... even more afraid to lose.

It was inevitable, perhaps, that he should be reminded... how different the two of them were, the sinner and the saint. The thought made his gut twist. If Samantha knew the truth, would she run as far and as fast as she could?

That was his strongest fear of all.

Yet a tiny little voice relentlessly prodded him, reminding him he wronged her dearly. Samantha was not a woman to give herself lightly. She cared as much as he did. It was all there in those beautiful blue eyes that hid nothing. The same voice told him that all he'd ever wanted was within reach. For the first time in his life, he had a chance at happiness.

So why did he have the feeling everything was about to shatter wide open?

He rose from the table, trying not to grimace, shaking off the darkness invading his soul. It was Christmas. He was here with Samantha, and there was nowhere on earth he would rather be.

Together they cleared the table. Samantha had just finished running dishwater in the sink when the phone rang. Vince started in on the dishes while she talked to first her mother, then her father. She had barely hung up the receiver than it rang again. He gathered from the conversation her three sisters were together and had decided to phone. By the time she'd talked to all three, he had the dishes washed, dried and put away. He turned just as she replaced the receiver. Vince quickly spied the betraying glitter in her eyes.

"You miss them, don't you?" he asked softly.

She nodded, her smile watery. "I can't remember a Christmas we weren't all together."

Vince said nothing. For just an instant, he was consumed with a burning despair. He had *never* spent Christmas as a family. His father had never been around. His mother had always been too drunk to care. And for him and Tony, Christmas was just one more day among many.

He was totally unaware of Samantha's scrutiny, but his silence reached all the way inside her. Seeing the shadow that crept into his eyes, she sensed the bleakness of his thoughts. A lean-fingered hand had come up to finger the silver crucifix just below the base of his throat, a gesture she guessed he was totally unaware of. She recalled the other times she had seen him absently stroking the crucifix. Always...always he had been vaguely troubled, even rather distant.

It belonged to someone he once knew—someone he had cared about. The knowledge seeped through her with disturbing clarity. Not for the first time, she wondered who... She dismissed his parents. She'd sensed his youth had not been pleasant. Who then? A friend? A woman...perhaps a lover? Her heart lurched. A knife-like pain sliced through her.

All at once she wasn't sure she wanted to know.

She crossed to where he stood leaning against the counter, driven by a compelling need she couldn't deny. "I miss everyone," she said again. She splayed her hand upon his chest; its mate crept up to join it a scant half second later. She tipped her face to his. "But I like having you all to myself."

Her whispered confession sent a surge of emotion rushing through his veins, so overwhelming it nearly brought him to his knees. The sweet supple lips hovering beneath his proved more temptation than he could bear. Vince wanted nothing more than to crush her to him; instead his hands settled lightly on her waist. He drew her unresisting body full and tight against his own, then lowered his head and kissed her breathlessly parted lips, putting all the tenderness he felt for her into the slow, sweet melding of their mouths. He reveled in the tiny sigh of pleasure she gave, the way her breath swirled and mingled warmly with his own.

Her hands slid up to curl around his shoulders. Her eyes were shining when at last he raised his head. "You know," she teased, "it occurred to me you might have ordered up that snowstorm so you wouldn't have to meet my parents."

She loved his lazy, slow-growing smile. "Your father might have demanded to know my intentions."

"And what are they?"

His eyes glowed warm and golden. "Thoroughly unmentionable."

"That sounds...interesting."

His laugh was low and sexy. "Doesn't it, now."

This time their kiss quickly caught fire. Deep in her belly, a sensation of heavy warmth unfolded. She sensed the hunger in his kiss. She felt the yearning in the arms that held her, a yearning that met and matched her own. It was impossible not to notice, given the intimacy of their embrace. She could feel all of him against her; feminine softness sweetly cradled all that was full and bold and potently male. Yet even as her body strained against his, there was a subtle softening of his mouth on hers. The delight she felt was near-painful. She nearly cried out in protest.

All along she had cautioned herself against becoming involved in a relationship that paralleled her last in a way that was far too close for comfort. Vince was so staunch, so unwavering in his beliefs. His refusal to give Frankie the benefit of the doubt was the prime example. Oh, yes, she understood her reasons for holding back.

But she sensed the same reluctance in Vince—and she didn't understand *his* reasons. For so long now, she'd had the feeling he was fighting against wanting her. And it was at moments like this when she fervently wished she had the power to see into his heart.

They were both gasping when he released her mouth. He lingered, grazing her cheek, her temple, the curve of her jaw before finally resting his forehead against hers. She caught his shoulders, struggling for breath, confused, frustrated . . . and so full of wanting she thought she might burst.

Long moments later Vince drew back. The merest hint of a smile played upon his lips. "Why aren't you pestering me for your present yet?"

She smiled up at him, knowing her heart was in her eyes and not caring. "Why aren't you pestering me for yours?" Her voice was as shaky as she felt inside.

It was on the tip of his tongue to counter that by the simple virtue of being here with him, she bestowed a gift that was priceless. His arms were filled with her warmth and sweetness, his heart filled with emotions he had thought far beyond his capacity to ever feel.

He ran the tip of his finger down her nose, pulled her into the living room and gently pushed her down to her knees before the tiny Christmas tree in the corner. "Stay right there," he instructed.

He strode from the living room. Samantha blinked in surprise when she heard her back door open. It closed scant seconds later. Again his footsteps echoed across the kitchen floor.

"Close your eyes," he commanded from the doorway.

"Why do I have to close my eyes?" she laughingly protested. "It's supposed to be wrapped, Larusso."

He chuckled. "I'd have a hard time wrapping this particular present," he said by way of explanation. "Now do as you're told, Samantha. Close your eyes."

She sighed and complied, hands on her denim-clad knees. She couldn't stop smiling as she heard him advance toward her.

"Now you can look."

Her eyes flew open. Her smile turned to a gasp at the sight of a wiggling small brown furry body, tongue lolling and tail wagging madly. "A puppy!" she exclaimed.

"A puppy that's half grown," he clarified. "He's six months old, though, so he won't get much bigger." Vince lowered himself to the floor next to her. "Well? Are you ready to brain me for getting you a dog?" He smiled crookedly. "To tell you the truth, I racked my brain trying to figure out what to get you. I admit it was a snap decision, though. One of the guys at the office mentioned last week they still had the runt of the litter. His name is Butch, by the way."

Samantha reached out and cuddled the small bundle of fur against her cheek. "What kind of dog is he?"

His lips twitched. "Pure mutt, according to Walt. I told him I wasn't sure you would even want a dog, but he'll take him back if that's the case. But he's house-trained already and used to staying in a portable dog kennel at night and when he's left alone. That should save a lot of worrying when you're at work—" he darted a cautiously optimistic look at her through his lashes "—if you decide to keep him."

Her smile was beaming. He watched as the puppy lapped her cheek. "Of course I'll keep him. He's ador-able!" Her eyes began to dance with an unholy light. "Only I never dreamed that you'd get me a puppy." Her smile was transformed into a full-blown laugh. Once started, she found she couldn't stop. She buried her face in the puppy's fur, her shoulders heaving with mirth.

Vince frowned, puzzled at her reaction. "You just said you wanted to keep him."

"Oh, I do." Samantha was laughing so hard she was crying. She thrust the puppy at Vince. "Here, hold him while I get your present—and I do mean *hold* him." She disappeared up the stairway.

He understood her warning when she reappeared. He could only stare in amazement at the fluffy white-and-yellow kitten in her hands. Around its neck was a bright red ribbon.

The dog bolted from Vince's lap and began to yap fu-riously, jumping from side to side on all fours in front of Samantha. The kitten hissed and leaped from her arms, scurrying across the room and vaulting gracefully onto the back of the sofa. Butch raced madly in front of it, from one end to the other.

Samantha struggled hard to keep a straight face. "At the risk of sounding rather familiar, I'm afraid I didn't know what to get you. When the girls' P.E. teacher mentioned she had some kittens she was trying to find a home for, I thought I'd found the perfect gift for an apartment dweller. As Shirley pointed out, this kitten is cute and affectionate and here's the clincher—she's already box-trained.''

Vince's shoulders heaved with silent mirth. "God, I don't believe it. A dog and a cat...why, they're perpetual enemies." He shook his head and began to laugh helplessly.

Samantha just smiled. She watched the kitten lick its paw and prance daintily across the back of the sofa to sit at the other end. Butch growled and took up his vigil at the other end as well.

Ten minutes later neither animal had moved. Vince lay stretched out on the floor, leaning back against a big overstuffed pillow. Samantha lay curled in his arms, her head on his shoulder. They both looked on in amusement when the kitten padded across the back of the sofa. Butch bared his teeth and stayed where he was, eyes trained on the feline.

Samantha chuckled. "Those two remind me of you and Frankie."

"Thank you very much," Vince pronounced dryly. "I'm the one with the big teeth, I suppose."

"No," she retorted playfully, "that's the wolf." It was easy to joke now, but even though Vince knew Frankie had returned her father's pocket watch, Frankie was the one subject she and Vince had studiously avoided lately.

She walked her fingers across the broad landscape of his chest. "What are you going to name the kitten?"

Vince smiled. "Rover."

She sputtered. "Rover! That's a dog's name...Vince, you can't name a cat Rover."

"I just did." His grin made her heart turn over. She couldn't look away as he slowly weaved his fingers through hers. The contrast between their skin was striking, his so dark, hers so fair. Deep inside, a fluttering curl of awareness unfolded. He brought their clasped hands to his lips, barely skimming the inside of her wrist. Light as his touch was, the feel of his lips against her skin kindled a poignant surge of longing.

Oh, Vince, she thought achingly. *Why can't it always be like this?* She wanted to capture the peace and contentment of this day and hold it close forever. Yet life was never that easy, she realized with a resignation that verged on bittersweet. *Love* was never easy.

She gave a deep, weary sigh and sat up. Her gaze flickered to the front window, where darkness prepared to drop its murky veil. Even as she watched, huge puffy snowflakes began to sift from the leaden gray sky.

"It's snowing," she murmured absently. She didn't know why, but all at once a snatch of something Frankie had once said whispered through her brain.

Mama doesn't like winter. She likes it when the sun shines and it's warm.

Vince sensed the exact moment her mood changed. He sat up as well and slid his hands beneath the fall of her hair. Gently stroking her nape, he had no trouble recognizing the distress in her eyes for what it was.

"I recognize that look," he said gently. "Why so blue all of a sudden?"

Samantha focused on smoothing a fold in her jeans. For the longest time she said nothing. When at last she spoke, her tone was very quiet. "I was just thinking about Anna." *And Frankie,* she added silently.

His fingers on her nape went still. "Anna Lombardi?"

She nodded. She braved a glance at his face. There was a guarded tension in his features as he held her gaze; after a moment, it seemed to ease.

"She hasn't been well lately and...well, I'm a little concerned about her. Her cough was one of the first things I noticed when I met her," she went on. "Frankie mentioned a few days ago that sometimes Anna coughs so hard she can scarcely breathe. She had a bad case of bronchitis in the fall and now she's just getting over the flu. I don't think working so much is helping her any, though Anna keeps insisting it's her asthma." Her eyes grew troubled. "It's difficult for most kids to grasp when someone is really ill, especially when the person won't admit it. Maybe it wouldn't worry me so much except I know that Frankie's worried, too."

Vince frowned. "Hasn't she seen a doctor?"

Samantha was already shaking her head. "I tried to convince her she should but she has no medical insurance, Vince. She's also very proud," she added quietly. "Frankie told me one of their neighbors tried to get Anna to go to the free clinic, but Anna seems to think there are other people far more in need than she."

As she had for the past week and a half, Samantha found herself seized by a feeling of inadequacy. She had racked her brain over and over but she had yet to figure out a solution. There had to be a way for Anna to get the help she needed without risking her secret—there just had to. It was on the tip of her tongue to blurt out the rest of Anna's dilemma, yet her promise to Anna tore at her conscience.

"Maybe you should talk to her again," he suggested.

Samantha linked her arms around her knees and rested her chin on her knees. "You think I should?"

"It can't hurt, can it? Besides, if she's anything like Frankie, she won't hesitate to tell you if she thinks you're butting in where you have no business."

Samantha felt her mood begin to lighten. Just talking about it had made her feel better. Her mouth relaxed into a grin. "Watch it, buster," she warned playfully. "That's my Little Sister you're talking about there."

Vince opened his mouth to laughingly retort that was one fact he wasn't likely to forget. "You know—" he began.

He never got any further. The chime of the doorbell sent both their gazes swinging toward the front door. His brows shot up as he glanced at Samantha. "Adding to the guest list, are we?"

"It's probably just the other man in my life," she teased.

"I thought *I* was the only man in your life," he complained, pulling her to her feet.

"Conceited, aren't you?" she threw over her shoulder, striding away from him. She was still smiling when she pulled open the door.

A blast of stinging cold preceded her gasp. A small, slight figure stood on the doorstep. Huge dark eyes stared unblinkingly back at her. For an instant Samantha stared numbly at Frankie, thinking dazedly that she looked like an iceberg ready to topple over with the next gust of wind. Snowflakes clung to her short dark hair, even the tips of her eyelashes. Frost glazed her muffler, which was wrapped around her nose and mouth, obscuring half her face.

"Frankie!" Galvanized into action, Samantha cried out sharply and reached for her even as the girl stumbled inside. It was Vince who slammed the door shut.

Samantha tore at the muffler. "My God, Frankie, what's wrong? Why aren't you home? You're not dressed for weather like this—you shouldn't even be outside when it's so cold!"

White-faced and numb, Frankie regarded her dully. Her lips opened as if to speak; then she pressed them together and began to shiver.

Vince had caught her firmly around the shoulders and was already guiding her across the floor. "Let her catch her breath," he said grimly. "And get her a blanket. She looks half-frozen."

Samantha bolted. Fear nourished her flight into the hallway. Her hands shaking, she grabbed a blanket from the linen closet. All she could think was that something was very, very wrong or Frankie wouldn't be here.

In the living room Vince had peeled away Frankie's coat. He dropped down to his knees before her, seized one of Frankie's hands and massaged it gently between both of his own, muttering under his breath at her chilled flesh. Her expression alarmed him. It was vague and distant. He felt a deep shudder shake her body as Samantha draped the blanket over her shoulders, yet he sensed Frankie was scarcely aware of her chilled, sodden state.

Samantha knelt down beside him and set to work on Frankie's ice-encrusted shoelaces. They were frozen together, so finally she jerked them off. Her socks followed in quick succession. Snow littered the carpet but she paid no heed, grabbing a towel and briskly rubbing Frankie's bare feet.

Vince glanced at Samantha. "Her skin doesn't look frostbitten," he said in a low voice. "I think she'll be okay once she's warm and dry."

Frankie shivered. "I lost my hat," she said plaintively. Her voice was high-pitched and quavery, sounding nothing at all like Frankie. Her gaze touched briefly on Samantha then slid away, as if in shame. "I didn't mean to but I...I lost my hat." Her face crumpled. Her voice wavered. Seeing her like this, his stomach twisted inside him.

Samantha's frantic gaze sought his and telegraphed a silent question. Vince sensed she was in little better shape than Frankie.

"Frankie." He spoke with calm deliberation. "Did you walk here? All the way from home?"

She shook her head.

He gently coaxed her. "From where then?"

The muscles of her throat worked spasmodically as she fought to speak. "The hospital."

The hospital. Samantha's heart began to pound in thick, dull strokes. Her mind veered straight to Anna; she hovered on the fringe of panic. "Oh, no," she whispered in horror. "Please, no..."

Vince scarcely heard. His entire being was concentrated on Frankie. She gazed at him imploringly, wordlessly beseeching, her expression so wounded and bruised some nameless fear gripped his heart.

"Why were you at the hospital, Frankie?"

Her lips trembled. "Mama," she said hoarsely.

"What happened, Frankie?" He encouraged her gently, reaching for her other hand and kneading her cold flesh. "I know you're still cold but we'll have you warmed up in a jiffy. Just take a deep breath and start at the beginning...take it slow now, that's the way...."

Her voice came in jagged bursts.

"After dinner Mama said she didn't feel so good. She went in the bedroom to lay down. After a while I heard her coughing...." Cold, clammy fingers clung tightly to his. Vince couldn't have let go even if he wanted to.

"...but she couldn't seem to stop! I went in to help her...her skin was this funny color...I ran downstairs for Mrs. Talarico but she wasn't home...one of the other neighbors called 911 . . . I ran back upstairs and Mama was lying on the floor.''

She cringed visibly. "She just lay there . . . she wasn't coughing anymore but she didn't move. . . ." She choked on a half sob. "I thought she was dead . . . then I heard her making this strange sound I never heard before. . . ."

Watching her, listening to her, Vince experienced a wave of battering remembrance. The ragged edge in her voice tied his heart in knots. It was impossible for him to remain unmoved, for he knew exactly how Frankie had felt.

He watched Samantha slide onto the sofa next to the girl. "The paramedics took her to the hospital?"

Frankie nodded. Her eyes clung to Samantha's. "They said they couldn't help her there at home . . . I—I didn't know what to do. Mama doesn't like hospitals . . . but she couldn't talk. . . ."

Samantha slipped an arm around her shoulders. "Shh," she soothed. "You did the right thing, Frankie. You got help for your mother and that's the important thing."

"But maybe I shouldn't have left her there! Only they took her back into this big room and they wouldn't let me go with her. I waited and waited but nobody came," she said in a tear-choked voice. "Nobody would tell me if she was okay! I asked the lady at the desk and she told me to go sit down again."

The thought of Frankie sitting in a hospital, alone and terrified and frightened to death for her mother, caused a suffocating tightness in Samantha's chest. "Honey, why didn't you let me know? You shouldn't have had to be there all alone—''

"I was gonna call you, but I didn't have any money." Her tone took on a note of hysteria. "Darn it, I didn't even have a quarter!"

And so she had walked here instead. Samantha squeezed her shoulders and opened her mouth, but it was Vince who took the words from her lips.

"Don't worry," he said quietly. "We'll get you back there as soon as you get into some dry clothes."

Less than an hour later they were back at the hospital. The gaily decorated Christmas tree just inside the entrance seemed almost obscene. At the front desk they learned that Anna had been moved to the Intensive Care Unit on the third floor.

The atmosphere in the elevator was tense and heavy. Although Samantha was grateful for Vince's presence, she was centered wholly on trying to comfort a badly shaken Frankie.

She didn't notice the change that came over Vince almost from the second they entered the hospital.

They stopped before the nurses' station. Samantha stepped forward. "I understand Anna Lombardi is on this floor," she said to the ward clerk behind the long counter. She put her arm around Frankie. "This is her daughter. We'd like to see if she can see her mother."

The woman hesitated. Something flashed across the woman's face as she glanced at Frankie. Pity? Samantha began to pray. *Please, no.*

"We weren't aware there was any family," she said with a frown. "Hold on and let me check." She moved back to confer with a nurse just beyond a curtained area.

She returned after a moment. Her gaze swept over Samantha and Vince. "Are all of you together?"

"We're friends of the family," Samantha stated quickly.

The clerk smiled briefly at Frankie but spoke to the two adults. "Dr. Morgan would like to speak to her first," she explained. "Then she can go see her mother."

They were led to a small waiting room down the hall. Vince took the chair near the door. Frankie dropped onto the edge of a love seat and jammed her fists between her knees, as if she were poised to bolt out the door any second. Samantha eased down next to her and laid a hand over the girl's knuckles. Her skin was cold and clammy. She murmured to her softly, scarcely aware of what she was saying.

Vince never even heard. The room was stuffy and hot, yet he was so cold he felt he'd never again be warm. He should have known better, he realized with a sickening sense of certainty. But he'd thought he could handle it. But all at once he felt himself plunged backward...

The passage of time might have been hours instead of years. Memories crowded into his mind, memories he couldn't escape. The long sterile corridor, faceless figures in white gliding all around, like ghosts in a graveyard. An ominous pall hung in the air. Now, as before, the antiseptic smell made his stomach heave.

His breathing came fast, then slow, then fast again. He recalled with vivid, gut-twisting clarity every minute he'd spent cloistered in a tiny hospital room... waiting. Wondering. Praying that Tony would live... raging inside because he already knew he would die.

Death was the one thing he and Tony couldn't fight. The one thing they couldn't steal from or cheat.

He was on his feet before he knew it. Startled, Samantha jerked her head around. Her eyes widened when she saw that his skin was a pasty shade of white.

"Vince! What's the matter?"

He waved her down when she started to rise. "I'll be all right," he muttered. "I just need a little air."

He was gone before she could say another word. There was little chance to speculate about his ashen features because a tall white-coated figure appeared in the doorway.

"You two are here to see Anna Lombardi?"

Samantha was already on her feet. "Yes," she said quickly. "I'm Samantha Taylor, a friend of the family. This is Frankie, Anna's daughter. You must be Dr. Morgan."

"That's right." He briefly clasped her hand, his gaze traveling between her and Frankie. "Are there any other close relatives?"

"No." Samantha resumed her seat next to Frankie, sliding her arm protectively around her shoulders as Dr. Morgan took the chair Vince had vacated.

Frankie looked up at him. "Mama," she said unevenly. "Is she okay?"

He paused. For a fraction of a second, he said nothing. Samantha took quiet note of his expression, regretful but compassionate. Her arm tightened around Frankie; she felt as if a giant hand had reached out and grabbed hold of her heart. And in that moment, she knew what Dr. Morgan was going to say, even before he said it. . . .

"Had your mother been sick long?" He posed the question very gently.

"She had the flu a while ago. Then her asthma started acting up and she coughed a lot more than usual." Frankie's voice was as thin as a reed. "That's all it is, isn't it? Her asthma?"

Dr. Morgan shook his head. Samantha listened with aching heart as he began to speak.

"She has a severe case of postinfluenza pneumonia that's spread to both lungs, undoubtedly a complication of the flu.... If it had been caught in the early stages we might have been able to halt its progression and clear it up. Unfortunately a pulmonary weakness like asthma doesn't help...she's also severely anemic and extremely undernourished, so there was little resistance to infection...battling pneumonia in both lungs was simply too much for her in her weakened condition. All of these put together, I'm afraid, contributed to respiratory failure...when she collapsed there was a loss of oxygen to the brain...I'm afraid there's no hope for recovery at this stage...."

Time stood still. It took a second for the words to sink in. Samantha knew the instant Frankie understood. Her body gave a tiny jerk. The next second she tore from her grasp and lurched to her feet.

"I want to see her!" she cried.

Dr. Morgan got to his feet. "You understand," he said gently, "she isn't conscious. She won't know you're there."

"I don't care! I—I want to see her!"

So strong, Samantha thought achingly. So determined even though she was battered and bruised inside. She watched her step toward Dr. Morgan, her narrow shoulders stiff with pride.

She faltered just outside the door. Her eyes swung back to Samantha. "Will you come with me?" she asked, her voice very small. "Please?"

Samantha glanced at the doctor for approval. He tipped his head in silent assent. They stepped into the Intensive Care Unit, Frankie between them. He showed them to Anna's room and quietly withdrew.

There was a wide glazed window on the outside wall of the room. Samantha gave Frankie's shoulder an encouraging squeeze. "Would you like to go in alone and see your mother? I can wait right here—" she indicated the window "—that way I'll be able to see if you need me."

Frankie swallowed. Dark, betrayingly moist eyes searched her face. "You won't leave?"

Samantha's heart wrenched. Never in her life would she forget the sound of that pathetic little voice. "I'll be right here," she promised.

Through eyes that stung, she watched Frankie enter her mother's room.

Neither of them knew just how wrong Dr. Morgan was when he predicted Anna would never know that Frankie was with her.

THE ROOM WAS QUIET and hushed, yet every corner was filled with shimmering light. Anna couldn't move. She couldn't speak. She couldn't even open her eyes, yet she could see the golden light that burned as bright as a flame.

A hand touched hers. "Mama?" whispered a tiny voice. "I'm here, Mama."

A smile filled her heart. Anna knew, with some strange sense never before possessed, that she wasn't alone anymore. She knew also that she had merely been waiting, biding her time until Francesca could be with her....

Frankie squeezed her fingers. And Anna tried, through the power of her mind and will, to squeeze back.

"I love you, Mama."

And I love you, too, cara.

"You'll get better, Mama. You'll get better and then you can come home again."

A twinge of regret drifted through her. It was hard, leaving Francesca, and yet she knew, with that same strange sense of destiny, that Francesca would not be alone. Even now, she could feel the presence of one who loved Francesca almost as much as she....

A curious peace descended. The bitter chill seeped from her bones. She felt as if a tremendous weight had been lifted from her body. The crushing pain in her chest was gone; it no longer hurt to breathe. The absence of pain kindled a blessed feeling of joyous relief.

In the corner, a radiant circle of light appeared, like glistening beams of the sun. Deep within, a shadowy figure beckoned. The beams came closer, flooding her with heat and light... She smiled. She was being lifted, floating high and free to a place where the sun shone forever bright and warm. Never again would she be cold....

She called back one last message. *You will be all right, cara. Be strong and brave, and remember I am with you always.*

Frankie straightened abruptly. She clutched at Mama's fingers frantically. She was afraid if she let go, Mama would slip away.

The grip on her fingers grew slack.

"Mama," she screamed. *"Mama!"*

This time Mama didn't hear.

CHAPTER FOURTEEN

THERE WERE NO TEARS. No jagged sobs of grief. Only a heartrending silence that pierced Samantha's chest like a rusty blade. A short time later, the three of them left the hospital—Frankie, Samantha and Vince.

At her house, Samantha led Frankie into the spare room next to her bedroom. Neither Frankie nor Vince questioned her when she stated her intention to take Frankie home with her for the night. Yet why should they? she acknowledged with a rare twist of cynicism. What else could Frankie have done? The girl had no one now. No one at all...

But that wasn't quite right, Samantha vowed fiercely. Frankie had *her* ... only she was afraid Frankie didn't know it yet.

The thought lingered while she left the girl alone to wash and dress in an extra pair of warm flannel pajamas. A few minutes later, she rapped lightly on the door and stepped inside. Her heart caught at the picture Frankie presented. She stood lonely and forlorn in the center of the room.

Samantha turned down the bedspread and fluffed the pillow. Straightening, she beckoned to the girl. "It's all yours," she said briskly.

Frankie slipped into bed. Samantha pulled the covers over her. After a fractional hesitation, she sat on the edge of the bed. The gesture tentative, she smoothed tumbled dark strands of silk from Frankie's forehead.

"Are you okay?" she asked softly.

Frankie's nod was nearly imperceptible. She stared at Samantha, yet Samantha had the oddest sensation that the girl looked right through her. The frown between her brows deepened. Frankie's eyes were so blank and dull, she almost hated to leave her alone. Her reaction wasn't at all what Samantha had expected.

"Would you like me to stay with you for a while, Frankie?"

Again that tiny shake of her head. "I just want to go to sleep." This was the first Frankie had spoken since they left the hospital. She sounded so tired, so utterly bone weary that Samantha decided perhaps sleep was the best medicine after all.

"Let me know if you change your mind, okay? And it doesn't matter what time it is, either. My room's right next door, but I'll be downstairs for a little while." She bent and pressed a kiss on her forehead. "Good night, Frankie. I'll see you in the morning."

Her expression was troubled as she made her way downstairs. A lamp glowed dimly in a corner of the living room. Vince was on the sofa, bent over and scratching behind the dog's ears. The kitten was perched atop the rocking chair. Though Butch sat placidly at Vince's feet, his eyes were trained on the kitten.

Samantha sighed, a deep rush of air that seemed to take everything from deep inside her. Frankie hadn't even seen the dog and cat yet. And it seemed a lifetime had gone by since she and Vince had laughed at Butch and Rover.

The sound alerted Vince to her presence. He had no trouble deciphering the shadows in her eyes. He rose and crossed to where she stood, then pulled her into his arms. For a long moment, they simply clung to each other, each taking comfort in the other's presence.

Finally Samantha drew back. She peered up at him. "Vince," she said quietly. "I doubt if Frankie's mother left a will. Since there's no other family, won't that make her a ward of the court?"

He nodded. "Eventually her custody will be decided by the State."

Her fingers curled unintentionally into the hardness of his arms. Almost from the moment Anna had died, her mind had been filled with a deep overwhelming concern—what would happen to Frankie now that her mother was gone?

Samantha already knew what she *wanted* to happen; she had to caution herself to keep from blurting everything out all at once. But she wasn't sure what Vince would say... but this wasn't the time for an argument.

"I don't want Frankie to be pushed into some kind of juvenile facility—or be left with some stranger," she said quietly. "Is there a way you can help me get temporary custody of Frankie for the time being?"

She held her breath. He didn't fight her, thank heaven. Indeed, his expression was rather worried as he nodded. "I'll see what I can do first thing in the morning." He glanced up the stairs. "How is she?"

Samantha grimaced. "Typically Frankie, I'm afraid. She's not giving me much to go on." Her eyes darkened. "Did you notice how withdrawn she was in the car? And just now I wanted to stay with her, but I got the impression she just wanted to be left alone." Samantha battled a feeling of helplessness. "She's reacting so much differently than I would have expected—"

"You thought she'd scream and rage? Deny it or strike out at everyone around her?"

She stared at him, stunned by his perception. "Yes," she said slowly. "She loved her mother very much, Vince. At the very least I thought she'd cry her eyes out."

Never, he thought. It wasn't Frankie's way to show her pain. It hadn't been *his* way, yet he wasn't sure he could explain.

Instead he shook his head. "Maybe it's better this way."

"Is it? She's not as tough as she thinks she is, Vince. For that matter, neither are you. She hurts and bleeds just like the rest of us." There was a heartbeat of silence. "Just like you."

Just that quickly, in the instant between one breath and the next, everything changed. Her eyes locked on his face, wide and unwavering. And Vince cursed himself silently as he realized she was no longer thinking of Frankie.... She was thinking of him, the way he'd behaved at the hospital. No doubt she thought him foolish and weak.

The taste of self-loathing was bitter in his mouth. "I suppose I owe you an explanation."

If anything, the probing look in her eyes intensified. He felt she was reaching clear inside him, where no one had ever been before, and he couldn't stand it. He retreated several steps and turned his back to her.

Silence mounted between them, as thick and heavy as the night.

When she finally spoke, her words weren't at all what he expected. "You don't owe me anything, Vince. But did you think I wouldn't notice the way you looked when you tore out of the waiting room? Did you think I wouldn't *care?* At first I thought maybe it was just a bad reaction to the hospital setting. I know some people find it difficult to cope with being surrounded by sick people. But that's not what happened, is it?''

The words hung between them. His shoulders and back were so rigidly tense, he looked as if he would snap with the slightest movement. Just when she was certain he didn't intend to answer, she heard his voice, low and strained.

"You don't want to know, Samantha. Believe me—" he swallowed "—you don't.''

In the muted light, his profile was bleak and stark. His jaw was bunched and knotted. He looked as if he were fighting some fierce inner battle.

As indeed he was. At his side, his hand curled into a fist. But it wasn't Samantha he was angry at. He could never be angry with her. She was all that he wanted—all that he needed. It was wrong to touch her—to want her the way he did—wrong to believe he could escape what he was. He should never have laid a hand on her.

Now it was too late.

Samantha slowly edged closer. Her hand lifted to touch him, but she abruptly checked the move. "You can tell me anything,'' she said quietly. Her eyes searched his. "Don't you know that?''

His eyes squeezed shut. He spoke on a tense breath of air. "I can't,'' he said almost desperately. "My God, Samantha, you don't know what you're asking. There are things you don't know about me—''

"Then tell me,'' she pleaded. "Please, Vince . . . just talk to me.''

Fear gathered in the pit of his stomach; fear and a tight heavy coil of dread. His eyes flicked open. His body gave an involuntary jerk as he beheld her standing before him . . . so sweet. So innocent. So pure he wanted to scream with the pain it caused.

The silence was never-ending. With every second, every heartbeat, she could feel him pulling away from her. Retreating further and further into himself.

And she couldn't let him do that. To himself. To her. To the two of them.

Samantha was suddenly trembling. This moment was crucial. She knew it beyond the shadow of a doubt. If Vince turned away from her now, all that lay between them meant nothing.

She swallowed, her gaze endlessly dark and searching. "Don't shut me out, Vince. Do you think I don't know there's something you're not telling me? Whatever it is, you don't have to hide from it any longer. You don't have to hide it from *me*."

He expelled a harsh breath of hair. "You don't understand." His tone was harsh, but hidden in the low roughness of his voice were a million layers of hurt. "This isn't a game of truth or dare. I don't want you to hate me. I—I don't want to lose you!"

Her denial was swift and adamant. "That won't happen. I could never hate you, Vince, never!"

She started to reach up to touch his face. A hand like a vise came up and locked around her wrist, thwarting her cold.

"Remember that day with Joey outside the pawnshop? You looked at me as if you didn't know me—as if I were a stranger. And maybe that's all I am to you— a stranger!"

His eyes bored into hers, creating a brittle tension that was nearly unbearable for them both.

He was angry, she realized numbly. Yet she sensed his anger wasn't directed at her, but himself. She swallowed, lifting her chin bravely. "It's true I don't know what you've been. But I know who you are."

She was so calm, so serene, so damned accepting. "So you're saying the past doesn't matter? If that's true, why this inquisition? Why can't you just let it the hell go?"

Something quickened in her eyes, some emotion too fragile for him to name. "You're the one who doesn't understand," she whispered. "You said you didn't want to hurt me. But there's a part of yourself you've kept locked away from me. And what hurts is knowing that you refuse to share it with me."

He stiffened. His hand fell away from her wrist. He would have turned away but she wouldn't let him. Her hands closed around his forearms, but it was the depth of emotion reflected in her tone that kept him rooted in place.

"I know there's something you're not telling me, Vince. And maybe it's my fault that you felt you couldn't tell me." She gave a tiny shake of her head. "Because I'm just beginning to understand how blind I've been . . . all along I've thought there had to be a reason you were so dead-set against Frankie. You kept telling me not to expect too much from her, that she would probably go from bad to worse. At first I thought it was because of your job, from seeing so many kids like her. But it's more than that, isn't it?"

Stricken, he could only stare at her. She read more in his face than he wanted her to see. But there wasn't a damn thing he could do about it except pray helplessly. Samantha was the one good thing that had come into his life. It was almost as if he could see her slipping away from him forever . . .

"That day you took me down to Al's gym. You had a special kind of rapport with those kids—you understood them so completely! And I remember you talked about the cycle they faced ... The bureaucracy's answer to the juvenile crime problem—pulling a kid out of his home, giving a few pretty speeches and then sticking them right back into the very same situation that created the problem in the first place."

There was a heated rush of silence. Her gaze never wavered from his. "You knew," she said softly, "because that's what happened to you. You were once just like those kids, weren't you?"

The truth was like acid burning into his soul. "No," he whispered. "I wasn't just like them. I was worse ... *worse.*"

Vince knew then that his moment of truth had finally arrived. Yet maybe Samantha was right, he decided wearily. Maybe it was past time he stopped running.

He said nothing when she pushed him down on the edge of the sofa. Then, slowly, his voice taut and strained, he began to talk. And talk. It wasn't long before the fragmented pieces in Samantha's mind began piecing themselves together and taking shape.

The picture portrayed was not a happy one. Like Frankie, Vince's father had run out on his family at an early age. His mother found solace in a bottle—or the company of other men. There was no one who really cared....

Except his older brother Tony.

"Tony and I grew up like every other kid around," he said heavily. "You either joined the neighborhood gang or you risked becoming a target. You came out swinging or you just gave up. The only way to stay on top was to *be* on top—and if you quit fighting you tumbled right back to the bottom of the heap. You looked out for yourself because no one else was about to do it for you."

Samantha had no trouble envisioning Vince as a boy. She had only to think of the hard young faces gathered outside Al's gym. They treated the world with careless disregard because that's how the world treated them.

Then suddenly he stopped. Samantha stole a glance at him and saw his fingers absently stroking the silver crucifix around his throat. A prickly feeling of foreboding crept over her. All at once a horrible notion flew into her mind.

Her fingers closed around his, halting the monotonous movement of his fingers.

Vince glanced down in surprise. Beneath her fingers, beneath his, he belatedly registered the smooth feel of metal. He was stunned to realize he held Tony's silver crucifix beneath his thumb and forefinger.

Samantha drew a deep breath and forced her gaze up to his. "You always do that," she whispered, "when something is on your mind." Her lips formed a tremulous smile. "At least that's my theory."

Still he said nothing. The silence was nerve grating.

Her smile withered. She spoke before she lost her nerve.

"You said once that this belonged to someone you once knew, someone you cared about, someone who was gone now. Who, Vince? Was it Tony?"

A look of fleeting anguish crossed his features. When he nodded, she almost hated herself for asking, for putting that look on his face.

Her heart began to bleed. "How?" she whispered. "How did he die?"

She didn't try to stop him when he got to his feet. Careful, concise footsteps carried him toward the window. All the muscles in his face seemed to be locked, his features wiped clean from all expression. Even his voice was stripped of any feeling whatsoever.

"I was fifteen when it happened. Tony was sixteen. We were out one night, just Tony and I. It was late, we were a long way from home and it started raining. I got this bright idea to make it a quick trip home. So I stole this car, a souped-up shiny Mustang, and talked him into taking it for a joy ride.

"I was hooked. It was new. It was fast. I wanted to take the damn thing and just keep on driving forever, but Tony wanted to call it a night. One more spin, I said. One more spin and this time I'd let him drive. Just one more spin..."

He began to falter. At his sides, his hands knotted. His knuckles turned white. Something caught in her chest, something that made her hurt as she knew he was hurting.

"Tony took this highway out of the city. I remember going around this curve. We were both laughing.... Just a little faster, he kept saying. *Just a little faster—*"

He broke off. Lines of pain scored his cheeks, his expression so acute she nearly cried out. She watched him clench his fists, saw him battle for control and win. But within his carefully blank features was a world of pain as vivid as a bloodstain.

His voice sounded hoarse and unnatural. "All of a sudden everything went dark. I found out later we smashed into a telephone pole. I remember waking up inside the car... I couldn't move...."

Samantha gave a faint choked whimper. "You were hurt...?"

He shook his head. "A few scrapes and bruises, that's all. But Tony..." He swallowed. "It was so dark... so quiet...I remember screaming for him, over and over..."

His voice grew thinner and thinner. "He never answered..."

His lips parted. No sound came out. Samantha forced her voice past the clogged lump in her throat and said the words she was sure he couldn't say. "Tony was dead—"

"No," he said woodenly. "Not yet. He was critical, in a coma." He stared sightlessly ahead. "I sat in a hospital room for two weeks and watched him die little by little. If I hadn't stolen that car the accident would never have happened." His voice was as raw as he felt inside. "And I knew that I'd killed my brother as surely as if I'd—"

"No. No, Vince!" The agony on his face cut her to ribbons. The cry tore from deep inside her as she launched herself against him. Her arms wrapped around him from behind. "Don't say that. Don't even think it. It wasn't your fault, Vince, it wasn't!"

Vince froze. His throat tightened oddly. She pressed herself against him, her grip so strong and fierce he was stunned. It was as if she sought to take all his pain into herself.

He eased around so that he faced her. A little shock went through him as he saw she was silently crying. At the sight, a fist seemed to knot in his chest.

"Oh, God." He caught her face in his hands. With the pads of his thumbs, he skimmed the wetness from her cheeks, his touch immeasurably gentle. At the feel of her tears, moist and hot against his skin, something inside him came apart.

"Don't," he pleaded. "Please don't. You see now why I didn't want you to find out the truth? If I hadn't been so reckless, so rebellious...so damned selfish...! I'm not worth your tears, Samantha. I'm not..."

The catch in his voice made her want to cry all over again. Something he'd once proclaimed lightly winged into her mind...*honesty sometimes commands a high price.* She hadn't understood then, but she did now. Just as she understood that he wore Tony's chain not in comfort or remembrance, but to punish himself.

Her fingers against his lips stifled the flow of words. "You're wrong," she told him raggedly. "It's time you stopped blaming yourself. Tony's death was terrible, yes! But it wasn't your fault. It was an accident!"

"But I'm not the man you thought." The admission came at no small price. "I lied, Samantha. I cheated. I stole. I've done so many things I'm ashamed of, things I could never begin to tell you."

Her eyes were swimming again. "It doesn't matter what you were, what you did all those years ago. What matters is what you are *now*. Oh, don't you see, Vince? You were strong enough to turn yourself around. What happened doesn't make you less of a man—" she stared at him beseechingly "—it makes you *more* of a man."

The heartfelt emotion in her tone made his eyes sting. He dragged her into his arms and clung to her, his desperate embrace saying all that words could not.

It was a long time later when he finally drew back. Samantha was relieved to note that some of the bleakness had left his features. She reached up instinctively, needing suddenly to touch him, to ease the faint lines etched into his forehead.

Vince snared her fingers before she could reach him. He brought her hand to his mouth and pressed a kiss into her palm. His gaze never wavered from hers. "I don't deserve you," he said unsteadily.

Her palm shaped his cheek. She inhaled deeply, loving the warm pulse of his breath on her skin, loving the raspy hardness of his cheek beneath her fingertips . . . loving him.

She gave a shaky, breathless little laugh. "You won't get rid of me so easily, Larusso."

His head lowered even as hers began a slight, upward ascent. The kiss they shared was slow and sweet. Neither one had heard the soft rustle of clothing on the stairway behind them a long time earlier.

And neither one saw the shadow that slipped just as quietly back up the stairs.

CHAPTER FIFTEEN

FRANKIE WOKE sluggishly the next morning. Her mind still netted with sleep, she registered the vague sensation that something wasn't right. The room was too bright, the bed too warm, the pillow too hard. Another part of her urged her to turn over and go back to sleep, because something awful had happened. If she were asleep she wouldn't have to remember...

Mama was dead.

The knowledge ripped through her, gouging like a knife. She came awake instantly, her body stiffening. She tried desperately not to think of it, but the burning remembrance gripped her mind and refused to let go. She remembered the shattering instant when Mama's last bit of strength drained from her fingertips.

Frankie clutched the pillow to her chest and rolled on her side, drawing up her knees. She held herself perfectly still. She was afraid that if she moved, everything inside would explode. Every muscle in her body rigid, she recalled Joey's little sister Linda confiding how she'd cried herself to sleep one night when their mother wasn't home. Linda said that in the morning, her eyes were so swollen and puffy from crying that they hurt.

Tears had never been an outlet for Frankie. But her eyes were so dry right now that they burned, which made no sense to her. Linda said it hurt to cry... how could it hurt *not* to cry?

That was how Samantha found her when she peered into the room a few minutes later—dark eyes wide open and unblinking, curled up into a tight ball, huddled beneath the covers.

"Frankie?" She rapped softly on the door to give her some warning. "Can I come in?"

There was no response, no sign that the girl had even heard. Samantha tightened the sash of her robe and gave a silent sigh of despair. Her slippered feet made no sound as she crossed the floor. The mattress dipped as she sat down.

Acting on instinct alone, she gently smoothed a shiny dark swirl of hair on Frankie's temple. The girl stiffened, but Samantha doggedly let her hand slide down her back. Frankie looked so young, so vulnerable and defenseless right now. She gently rubbed the tightness in Frankie's shoulder, the motion absent and monotonous. It seemed ages before she finally felt her begin to relax.

"Did you sleep okay last night?"

She felt rather than saw her shrug.

"I looked in on you before I went to bed," she went on. "Were you awake then?"

Another shrug.

Samantha studied her quietly. Frankie's eyes were focused on the far wall, her expression dull and carefully blank. Her lack of spirit tugged at Samantha's heart. This was so unlike Frankie's usual fire. Why couldn't she cry or rage or scream? Anything was better than this terrible silence—anything!

Something hopped up on the bed beside her—Butch, she saw. She turned to scold the dog but before she could say a word, he'd leaped across her lap and thrust a cold nose under Frankie's hand where it lay curled limply on the sheet. Poor Frankie started abruptly. She blinked as if she couldn't believe her eyes, then sat up and pushed her tumbled hair from her forehead.

Samantha smiled at her wide-eyed amazement. "He's a Christmas present from Vince. His name is Butch."

Butch had plopped his rear right smack dab in front of Frankie. His tail swished madly back and forth.

She reached out to scratch behind his fuzzy ears. "Butch," she murmured. "It fits him."

Samantha experienced a pang. This was the first time Frankie had spoken of her own volition since she'd emerged from Anna's hospital room last night.

"Want to hear something funny? Vince gave me this dog, and I got him a kitten for Christmas—only he named him Rover!"

Frankie didn't laugh; she didn't even smile. But just before she bent over Butch, something flickered in her eyes that might have been amusement.

Samantha hesitated, feeling her way very carefully.

"Frankie," she said quietly. "I know this isn't the best time, but there's something we need to get settled fairly soon."

Frankie raised her head. Dark, suspicious eyes pinned her unwaveringly.

Her tone was as gentle as possible. "I know what happened to your mother was unexpected. But both of you told me the two of you had no other family, so I'm assuming she never made arrangements for a guardian—"

"Guardian!" Frankie's heart lurched. "What's that?"

"Someone to take care of you. Someone for you to live with."

"Mama never did anything like that." Frankie's stomach was churning. Why did Samantha want to know? she wondered. Was she trying to tell her she was going to have to live at Juvenile Hall? A wrenching pain tore through her. Why was this happening? she thought wildly. Wasn't it enough that Mama was *dead?*

She heard Samantha through a haze. "The juvenile authorities will have to be made aware of your situation then." Only snatches of phrases made it through the dull buzzing in her head. *Judge...ward of the court...foster home.*

Something inside her snapped.

She shot off the bed like an arrow. Eyes blazing, she whirled to face Samantha. "I don't care what some dumb old judge says! He can't tell me what to do. He can't make me do anything I don't want to! I—I'll run away first before I let them send me to Juvenile Hall— and I won't go live with some stranger, either!"

Her outburst caught Samantha wholly off guard. She'd wanted some sparks; she'd gotten fireworks instead. Well, she thought dryly, at least this was better than indifference.

Yet the sight of pajama-clad Frankie, standing in the middle of the floor in her bare feet, the dog clutched against her chest, kindled a poignant ache deep in Samantha's soul. Her throat clogged tight with the threat of tears. Never had she seen the girl so defiant; never had she been more vulnerable.

She longed to reach out and hug her fiercely, urge her to let loose of the storm in her heart and have done with it. She was half-afraid Frankie might push her away, but in the end that was exactly what she did. She wrapped her arms around the girl and pulled her close, dog and all. Frankie was rigid against her but she paid no heed.

Nor did she care that her voice was thick with tears. "I don't want that, either," she whispered above her head. "That's why I asked Vince to help me make arrangements so you can stay here with me. He phoned just a few minutes ago to let me know he talked with a social worker already and there shouldn't be any problem. In fact, the social worker is coming over tomorrow to get things in order."

She felt the tension begin to seep from Frankie's body, a kind of silent concurrence. She squeezed Frankie's shoulder as she eased back. "I know how hard this is on you, Frankie. I know you loved your mother very much so I know how you feel."

Frankie went very still. She couldn't help the bitter resentment that crept through her. Samantha couldn't possibly know how she felt. It wasn't *her* mother who had died.

One glimpse of her frozen expression was all it took. Samantha battled a helpless dejection. Frankie's withdrawal was almost tangible. It was as if she could see the girl closing herself in . . . and shutting her out.

Samantha forced a calm she was far from feeling. "I wish I knew what to say," she told her very quietly. "I wish there were some magic formula that could wipe away all the pain you feel right now."

She gave Frankie's slight form one last hug. Frankie might not want it, but it was what she needed. "It'll get easier, honey, you'll see," she whispered. "Just remember I'm here to take care of you now, okay?"

The door clicked quietly shut behind her. For the longest time, Frankie remained motionless, a forlorn little figure in the center of the room.

It'll get easier, she said. *Just remember I'm here to take care of you now.*

Frankie wanted to believe Samantha, but she wasn't sure she dared. Sure, she had worried about Mama when she was sick. So had Mrs. Talarico. But she'd never thought Mama would *die*. She had always believed Mama would get better. Not once had she thought she'd wake up one morning to find Mama gone. Not once had she ever considered how it might be without Mama.

Now she knew. It was as if there were a huge hole inside her, a hole that would never go away.

Her shoulders slumped. Maybe, she thought tiredly, it was better not to let herself care about Samantha too much. Maybe then it wouldn't hurt so much when Samantha went away, too....

SAMANTHA WAS GLAD the schools were closed for Christmas vacation. She hoped the next week and a half would give Frankie the opportunity to let go of some of her grief.

But Frankie had little to say throughout the day. She stayed home that morning while Samantha saw to the funeral arrangements. Half of the afternoon she napped in her room. Samantha curbed her disappointment, reminding herself that sleep was nature's way of healing the body—and the mind's way of detaching itself from reality.

She couldn't stop herself from thinking a good long cry was what Frankie really needed.

Vince stopped by later that evening. "Where's Frankie?" he asked, stripping off his coat as he glanced around the living room.

Samantha put a finger to her lips and gestured toward the ceiling. "Sleeping."

Thick black brows shot up. "It's barely eight o'clock! And there's no school tomorrow."

Another time and Samantha might have laughed at his incredulity. Instead her makeshift smile gave her away.

Vince caught her hand. "You're still worried about her."

She let him pull her down beside him on the couch. "I can't help it," she admitted. "She's so listless and apathetic."

He slipped an arm around her and urged her head onto his shoulder. "It's going to take some time for her to get over this."

"I know." She swallowed, both anxious for and dreading what she was about to reveal next. "Vince, when the social worker comes tomorrow—"

"I wouldn't worry about it if I were you. You'll get the green light, no holds barred. When I talked to Paula today she said they'd kill to have more foster parents like you, so—"

"I don't want to be Frankie's foster parent, Vince."

There was a lengthy pause. Samantha found she couldn't look at him.

"Come again," he said slowly.

Her fingers slowly uncurled on his chest. She pushed herself back slightly so she could see him. Meeting his gaze just then was one of the hardest things she'd ever had to do in her entire life.

Somehow she found the courage to look him straight in the eye. "I don't want to be Frankie's foster parent," she said again. There was a heartbeat of silence. "I want to adopt her."

His withdrawal was as complete—and even more painful—than Frankie's had been earlier that morning. He shoved himself up from the chair and began to pace the length of the room. Back and forth, back and forth until she wanted to scream aloud in frustration.

He stopped directly before her. "How much thought have you given this?" he demanded.

She laced her hands around her knees and regarded him, her expression as unyielding as his. "I don't have to think about it, Vince. It's right for Frankie—"

"And what about you? What about what's right for you? What if you're just feeling sorry for her?" He gave her a long penetrating look.

Samantha shook her head. If anything, Frankie's outburst that morning only crystallized her intention. "I'd be lying if I said I didn't feel sorry for her." Her heart twisted as she remembered how Frankie had screamed for her mother in that final, awful moment.... No one who saw her—no one who heard that heartbreaking plea could remain unmoved.

"It's not pity she needs, but love." Her gaze met his squarely. "I can give her that, Vince."

He dropped onto his knees before her and seized her hands. "You think I'm being harsh and unfeeling, don't you?"

His voice cut like a knife. "I don't want to," she said helplessly.

There was a note of pleading in his voice she'd never heard before. "I just don't want you to rush blindly into something like this. There's a lot more at stake here than when you became her Big Sister. Frankie's not a kid who's grown up in a stable, well-adjusted environment like you did. She can be..." He hesitated, grappling for the right word.

"Difficult at times." Samantha smiled slightly.

"Exactly. And we're not talking about having her around for a day here, a day there. We're talking day in, day out, seven days a week."

His concern touched her deeply, and yet all her being right now was geared toward Frankie. Frankie's touch-me-not facade didn't matter, for it was just that—a facade. Deep down, Samantha knew that Frankie was hurting as she never had before.

"I'm not sure I can explain," she said slowly. "You've been telling me all along I was too involved—and you're probably right. Maybe I *did* let myself get too close to her." There was a brief pause. "But I don't think I could live with myself if I abandoned her now—and that's exactly how I would feel."

"And what if it doesn't work out? What if you adopt her and then find out you can't handle her? What then? How do you think that will affect Frankie? You'll both end up hurt."

When at last he spoke again, his tone was very low. "I know you won't like it, but why don't you just let things ride for a while?" She opened her mouth to protest; his grip on her hands tightened.

"Don't jump to the wrong conclusion," he said quickly. "All I'm saying is that maybe you should continue with the foster care arrangement for a while. That way Frankie can still live here with you. If things work out, you can go ahead with the adoption proceedings."

Samantha smothered a pang of disappointment. *If things work out,* he said. But she heard another message entirely. What he meant was if Frankie *behaved*.

She jerked her hands away and refused to meet his eyes. Wounded pride dictated her silence. Something inside wouldn't let her admit he was right. And an argument was the last thing she wanted. Dammit, she thought wildly, why did he have to sound so—so damned reasonable!

Vince took one look at her pale features and knew he'd blundered. Her look of anxious distress stabbed him. In some distant corner of his mind, he realized how badly he was handling this.

He got to his feet and plowed his fingers through his hair. Samantha tried hard to ignore it, but the gesture made him seem curiously vulnerable.

"Look," he said at last. "I'm sorry. I'm sorry that I can't tell you what you want to hear. But I can't just sit back and keep my mouth shut while you get hurt. I'm only doing this because I care about you, Samantha."

Care. Even as he said the words, Vince knew that didn't even begin to describe his feelings for her. He ached with the need to hold her, to claim her for his own, to love her with heart and mind and body. He wanted nothing more than to reveal all that was most in his heart to say. *He loved her.* The words burned fitfully inside him, but now was not the time.

He battled a bitter despair. His struggle to overcome the memory of Tony's death had been long and hard. Now it was finally behind them. But with the closing of one door, another opened.

Samantha's feelings about Frankie had been strong right from the start. He had grown to accept that Frankie was a part of her life—and now it appeared that role would be expanded even further. Somehow, he was going to have to resolve his doubts about Frankie. He had to. Indeed, he had no choice.

Because he didn't want to lose Samantha. Not now, not ever.

He was scarcely aware of pulling Samantha up before him. A finger beneath her chin demanded that she look at him. His tongue felt clumsy as he struggled to find his voice again. "It's only because I care about you," he said again. "Tell me that you know that."

The rough thread of need in his voice sped straight to her heart. She rubbed her cheek against his shoulder, loving the feel of muscle and bone. "Oh, Vince," she whispered tremulously. "I do, honestly." She drew a deep, painful breath. "You're probably right about the foster care. I'll try it and see what happens. But I—I don't want to keep secrets from Frankie right now."

He frowned, his eyes searching hers.

"I want her to know that I want to adopt her. Now, more than ever, she needs to know there's someone on her side, someone she can depend on."

He nodded, drawing her nearer. She lifted her mouth but even as he lost himself in the heady warmth of her kiss, a tingle of unease shivered down his spine. He couldn't shake the feeling that where Frankie was concerned, things might get a whole lot worse before they got better.

In that, he was right.

SAMANTHA was under no delusions. It was like a pebble in her shoe knowing that Vince had reservations about her decision to adopt Frankie. She phoned Lynette Marshall several days later to let her know all that had transpired. She also told her of her plans to adopt Frankie.

She hadn't counted on Lynette expressing the very same doubts as Vince. But when she did, it only solidified Samantha's resolve even further.

The following Saturday at breakfast, she broached the subject with Frankie.

"Frankie," she said very carefully, "how would you feel about living here permanently?"

Frankie frowned questioningly.

She laid her hand over Frankie's where it rested on the tabletop. "I hope this doesn't come as too big a surprise to you, but what I'm trying to say is this—" her laugh was breathless "—honey, I'd like to adopt you!"

Silence followed her pronouncement. The girl regarded her unblinkingly.

A cold knot of dread began to tighten in her stomach. "Did you hear what I said, honey?"

Frankie's gaze slid back to her plate. "I heard," she muttered.

Samantha fought an unfamiliar dryness in her throat. "I was hoping this foster care could be sort of a trial run. You know, to make sure this is what we both want...." Her voice trailed off. Oh, Lord, she thought jerkily. Did that sound as hollow and cold-blooded as she feared it did?

Frankie said nothing. She merely pushed her scrambled eggs around with her fork.

Samantha began grasping at straws. "I don't want to take your mother's place, Frankie. I wouldn't dream of even trying! In fact, I thought it might be a little like the two of us being Big Sister and Little Sister, only a lot more often."

The silence stretched out so long Samantha wanted to shrivel up and die. Just when she thought she couldn't stand it any longer, Frankie shrugged. "It wouldn't be so bad, I guess."

It wouldn't be so bad. Samantha fought a hysterical laugh. Was that all she had to say? Her lukewarm response was nearly as bad as none at all!

There was a terrible pain in the region of her heart. How she kept her voice from shaking she never knew. "Honey, I realize this past week has been hard on you.

It's never easy to lose someone you love. But I know how you feel—''

Frankie leaped to her feet so forcefully her chair crashed to the floor with a resounding bang. To Samantha, it was like a shot being fired.

"You *don't* know!" Frankie shouted. "How could you? It wasn't your mother who died, or even your father. It was mine, Samantha—*mine!*"

Her outburst stunned both of them. Time stood still while they stared at each other in shocked, frozen silence. Frankie couldn't tear her eyes away from Samantha's stricken expression.

Oh, God, Frankie thought sickly. She wanted to apologize—she *knew* she should tell Samantha she was sorry. But the words stuck in her throat, and in the end, it was Samantha who recovered first.

"Frankie," she said in a voice thick with strain, "could you take Butch and put him out in the backyard?"

Frankie practically bolted from the room.

That episode lingered in both their minds for days afterward. The next month wasn't easy for any of them, including Vince. Samantha knew beyond a doubt that she loved him—she was almost certain he felt the same. But the atmosphere was strained; they had no choice but to put their relationship on hold until the situation with Frankie was resolved. Vince was the most important thing in her life, but Frankie was just as important, though in a different way. There were times she felt torn in two, divided cleanly in half. Her greatest fear was that she could only have one of them…at the expense of the other.

It didn't help that the cold front that had settled over the region showed no signs of moving on; many of the students at school were apparently tired of being cooped up inside and were taking it out on their nearest neighbor. Samantha lost count of the students sent to her office for engaging in petty squabbles.

Nor was there any surcease on the home front. Frankie was like a seesaw—there were spurts of temper, then bouts of silence where she was sullen and withdrawn. Vince was on the warpath because her grades were once again slipping. Samantha tried to talk to her about it, but Frankie made no pretense of listening. Samantha realized the girl was unleashing her anger and bitterness over losing her mother, but knowing the reason didn't make it any easier to cope with her moods.

But Frankie was just as torn.

Samantha had promised it would get easier. When, Frankie wondered for the hundredth time. *When?*

She tried not to think of Mama. It made her stomach feel all funny and twisted inside. But no matter how hard she tried, she just couldn't forget . . .

She was angry at God for taking Mama and leaving her alone. She felt cheated and picked on. Or was this God's way of punishing her for stealing?

She didn't know. She didn't know what to believe. She didn't know how to act. Mama had always told her she was so strong and brave but that wasn't how she felt! She was trying so hard to do what Mama wanted, but she felt so—so out of control! She hated the way she acted toward Samantha but she just couldn't help it. There were times she wanted to shake her fists high in the air and demand that Mama come back where she belonged. Other times she wanted to curl up in a little ball and cry her eyes out.

She felt so confused. So lost and scared sometimes.

She felt that way more than ever since Christmas vacation had ended. God, but she hated going back to school! Mrs. Carruthers, the old bat, announced to her math class that Mama had died. Now everybody stared at her. She heard them whispering when they thought she wasn't looking. Hardly anybody ever talked to her anymore. And when she walked into class, everyone stopped talking. The room got real quiet. The first time it happened her face burned for hours. Now she just wanted to blow up and tell every last one of the kids in class—and Mrs. Carruthers—to take a hike and never come back.

The last Friday in January was no different. The bell clanged noisily, signaling it was time to change class for the last period of the day. Frankie walked toward Mrs. Carruthers's room, trying to ignore the cold lump of dread wedged deep in her chest. With every step, the lump got bigger and bigger until it was almost as if she couldn't breathe. She paused in the doorway, garnering the courage to step inside.

One by one the voices dropped away and grew silent. Even the group of boys at the blackboard turned to look at her.

There was a clean break inside Frankie. Not caring who saw her, she slammed her fist against the locker next to her and spun around. She began to walk blindly down the hallway, gaining momentum with every footstep. A kaleidoscope of babbling voices and dingy gray walls surrounded her. Escape was her only thought.

The frigid bite of the wind made her gasp. Not until then did she realize she was standing on the wide stone steps outside the school. She quickly scuttled down the steps when the warning bell rang, glad she'd already been to her locker and had her coat along. She dropped her books on the sidewalk and hurriedly jammed her arms through the sleeves. Next she shoved her hands into her gloves, taking a deep breath of the cool, stinging air. She didn't mind the cold. At least here she could breathe and she didn't feel everyone was closing in on her.

She wouldn't go back in, she decided stubbornly. So what if she cut math class again? She'd skipped out last Wednesday but Mrs. Carruthers apparently hadn't reported it to the office. Frankie didn't know why and right now she didn't really care, either.

It was then she spotted a figure strolling away from her toward the corner. She had no trouble recognizing that jaunty swagger.

"Joey! Hey, Joey!" She gave a frantic wave when he turned. A wave of giddy relief rose inside her when he reversed his direction.

She met him halfway. He looked her over with a crooked grin. "Hey, there, Frankie. Nice jeans you got there."

For an instant the muscles in her face felt stiff. Frankie didn't have to wonder why she was so uncomfortable. Samantha had taken her shopping last weekend. Frankie had resisted at first. Some devil inside made her demand why the clothes Mama had bought her weren't good enough for Samantha. The heck of it was that it could have been fun, if she hadn't made both of them so miserable.

Frankie was just beginning to realize she had only herself to blame.

"Thanks." Her voice rather small, Frankie clutched her notebook tighter to her chest and glanced up at Joey.

His smile faded. "I...uh, I heard about your mom." There was an awkward pause. "Must be pretty tough."

Frankie's eyes stung. She blinked rapidly and looked quickly away. "Yeah," was all she said.

Joey nodded toward the school. "How come you're out so early?"

Frankie grimaced. "I cut last period."

His grin reappeared. "Atta way, kid. I thought maybe you were turning into another Mary Poppins." When he started forward, Frankie fell into step beside him. He glanced over at her. "Mrs. Talarico said you're staying with her now—Mary Poppins, that is."

Frankie didn't particularly like his emphasis on *her*. He made it sound like a dirty word. Her name is Samantha, she wanted to shout. Instead she repeated curtly, "Yeah."

"How come?" His lip curled disapprovingly.

"'Cause she wanted me to." Frankie couldn't help it. All at once she felt as if she were betraying Samantha. "It's better than going to live with somebody I don't know. Besides, Samantha said she wanted to adopt me—"

"She *what?*"

Frankie's chin lifted. "She said if this foster care thing works out, she's gonna adopt me."

Joey gave a shout of laughter. "What's stopping her from doing it now?"

Frankie glanced away. "I dunno," she muttered. "But I think it's got something to do with Larusso."

His smile vanished. "Larusso. Mr. Tough Guy with the smart mouth, right?" When she nodded, his expression grew hard. "You told me once they were in real tight together."

"Tighter than ever," Frankie confirmed glumly. For a moment there was only the echo of their footsteps on the sidewalk. "I've got this funny feeling it won't be long before they get married."

He made a sound of disgust. "No wonder she hasn't gone ahead and adopted you. She probably just felt sorry for you and decided to feed you a line of bull to make you feel better. Hell, who knows why?"

Frankie ground to a halt. Her eyes were huge as she stared up at him. "But she said—"

"Forget what she said and use your head! If they get married they're gonna want a picture-perfect little family—" he rolled his eyes "—cripes, like the Brady Bunch. You think they're gonna want you in the picture? Think again, Frankie. They tried to make you into a little goody-two-shoes and it didn't work. She's just trying to let you down easy!"

Every word was like a claw, digging deeper and deeper. Oh, God, Frankie thought sickly. Joey had just voiced every gnawing little question that had been on her mind for weeks now. Mama had loved her no matter what. That was the one thing she had never doubted. But what about Samantha?

A terrible fear clutched at her insides. Her mind whirled. She had been so mean to Samantha lately! What if Joey was right? What if Samantha decided she didn't want her around after all? And then there was Vince...

Joey stared out over her head. "Hey, there's Pete." He waved his arms over his head.

Frankie scarcely noticed the sleek, powerful car that pulled up to the curb. Joey cocked his head toward the car. "You comin', Frankie?"

Frankie climbed into the back seat automatically. Everything in her mind was blurry and fuzzy. She could hear Joey and Pete talking, but nothing seemed to make any sense.

It wasn't long before the car purred smoothly to a halt. Pete said something to Joey and he laughed. She vaguely registered several items changing hands between them but she was too numb to pay much attention. A second later Joey opened the car door and beckoned her out.

Frankie joined him on the sidewalk, still clutching her notebook. Awareness returned and she noticed they were only three or four blocks away from Samantha's house. They were standing in front of the neighborhood grocery on the corner. Next to it was a liquor store.

The low-slung black car eased around the corner, out of sight. Frankie frowned. "Where's he going?"

Joey's lips curved slyly. "Didn't you hear? This is my big test." He nodded toward the liquor store. "It's onward and upward, kid. If this works out, Pete's gonna make me his right-hand man. And today's take we get to split 50/50."

Frankie's eyes widened. There was a ski hat in his hand, she saw, the kind that covered the entire head. Comprehension dawned with sickening clarity. Joey planned to rob the liquor store!

He clamped a hand to her shoulder and laughed. "You can stand just inside the door and keep an eye out for me. I'll make it worth your while, too. It'll be just like old times—"

"No!" She wrenched away from him. "Pete's using you, Joey, the way he uses all those other kids! They do all the dirty work—they take all the chances while he sits back and does nothing. He's not the one sticking his neck out here, Joey, you are!"

His eyes chilled. "So what? That's the way it is, Frankie. That's the only way to get ahead—the only way to get to be like Pete and that's what I want!"

"No...no! Joey, you don't want to be like him! It—it's not right!"

"Since when did you start caring about what's right or wrong?"

It was funny, but all of a sudden Frankie knew...she'd never really stopped caring... She tugged at his arm, pleading desperately. "Don't, Joey. Please, we can leave right now. We can just walk away and—"

He shook her off, his expression ugly. "What's it gonna be?" he demanded. "Are you in or out?"

Her heartbeat echoed dully in her head. She backed slowly away, shaking her head over and over.

Joey's lip curled disgustedly. He whirled around without a word.

It was then that Frankie truly understood. It seemed Joey had made his choice, and she had made hers.

"Goodbye, Joey," she whispered.

She turned and ran as fast as her legs would carry her.

CHAPTER SIXTEEN

"I HAD A VISIT from Mrs. Carruthers this afternoon."

Frankie carefully slid the plate she'd been drying into the cupboard. As low as her voice was, she felt Samantha's eyes drilling into her back. It was funny, she thought vaguely. All through dinner she'd had the sneaking suspicion something was wrong.

She was right...but oh, how she suddenly wished she weren't!

Slowly she turned. Half a dozen excuses sprang to her lips. One glimpse of Samantha's set expression and she decided it might be better to keep her mouth shut.

Samantha flicked the tablecloth over the table and gave a sharp tug on the nearest edge. "Mrs. Carruthers told me you cut class this afternoon—and it wasn't the first time. In case you're interested, she was prepared to excuse you once, but it looks like you intend to make a habit of it. Personally I think it was a mistake, but the only reason she didn't report it to me last week was that she felt sorry for you."

Frankie slapped the dish towel on the counter. It wasn't hard for her to summon a little indignant anger. "Did she tell you what else she did? She told everybody in the class about Mama. Now everybody stares at me. Nobody talks to me anymore and it's not just in her class! They—they make me feel like I'm some sort of freak!"

Samantha pressed a hand to her forehead. How could she explain that most of Frankie's classmates had precious little experience with death? In all likelihood, no one close to them had ever died. They probably found it frightening. Disturbing. Perhaps it was an unwelcome reminder that someday they would be forced to face the loss of their own parents.

Yet all of that was nothing compared to what Frankie had gone through, and it hurt unbearably to see her like this.

"Frankie," she said gently. "I don't think they even realize what they're doing. I'm sure they just don't know what to say to you. Maybe they think 'I'm sorry' just isn't enough, and so they say nothing. Just give them some time, honey." She stretched out a hand. "Things will get back to normal soon and—"

Frankie wrenched away when she would have touched her. "You keep saying that! And you keep telling me it'll get easier but it doesn't!"

Samantha struggled for a patience that grew ever more elusive. "And maybe," she pointed out deliberately, "it's because you won't let anyone help you. How do you think *I* feel when you refuse to talk to me? I might be able to help, Frankie. But I can't do it alone. I can't do it without some cooperation from you."

Frankie's gaze flitted away. Hot shame welled inside her. She knew Samantha was right. But there was a part of her that didn't want to let anyone close, even Samantha. And she couldn't talk about Mama yet, she just couldn't.

She wanted to explain, she really did. But all at once there was a gigantic lump in her throat. She was terrified that if she said a word, she would break down in

tears. And she had the craziest notion that once she
started to cry, she'd never stop.

Samantha was aware of the silent battle going on inside the girl. Frankie's eyes clung to Samantha's, huge
and wounded and desperately pleading. Samantha held
her breath, her angry despair turning to a budding hope.
It quickly turned to a bitter resignation as the silence
spun out endlessly.

She turned away so Frankie wouldn't see how hurt she
was. "I can't let this go unpunished, Frankie. But we'll
discuss it later after I've had a chance to cool off."

Frankie stole upstairs to her room. A few minutes later
the doorbell rang. Samantha knew it was Vince. They'd
planned to take in a movie tonight. She had hoped they
could persuade Frankie to come along.

Right now there was no point in even asking the girl.

She summoned a wan smile and swung open the front
door. One look at Vince and her smile withered.

"Where's Frankie?" He brushed past her, his face like
a thundercloud.

Samantha's heartbeat quickened. "What is it? What's
wrong?"

He reached into his coat pocket and dropped a wrinkled sheet of notebook paper into her hand. Puzzled,
Samantha lowered her gaze and smoothed the edges
while Vince began to pace. There was a barely con-
trolled, dangerous aura around him that worried her....

Frankie's name leaped out at her. It was scribbled at
the top, along with today's date.

"What time did she get home this afternoon?"

Samantha shook her head. "I'm not sure," she said
faintly. "I worked a little later than usual." Her eyes
sought his. "Vince, I don't underst—"

"I had a little visit from Joey Bennett's probation officer just before I left the office. It seems there was a liquor store robbery this afternoon, just a few blocks from here. The police found *that* outside the door on the sidewalk when they arrested Joey." He jerked his thumb at the paper, his lips thin. "Is Frankie in her room?"

Samantha nodded, feeling sick to her stomach. *Oh, God, Frankie,* she thought. *What have you done now?* "I'll get her."

But she didn't get more than a few steps. Frankie had heard every word. She stood at the foot of the stairs, her thin hand curled around the banister.

Vince spotted her at the same time. "You heard?" he asked tightly.

Frankie gave a terse nod.

Vince spoke to Samantha, his gaze trained on the girl. "Joey was armed, Samantha. He pulled out a handgun and demanded the clerk give him all the money in the till."

Frankie's body gave a little jerk. She remembered that instant in Pete's car when something changed hands between Pete and Joey. She had caught a flash of something dark and shiny. Not once had it occurred to her that it was a gun... *Joey,* she thought sickly. *Oh, Joey, how could you be so dumb!*

"He got caught?" Her voice seemed to come from very far away.

"The minute he stepped outside. The clerk tripped a silent alarm." Vince's eyes never wavered from her face. "The clerk also thought he saw a girl outside with Joey just before he came in. What I'd like to know is why you were there when you were supposed to be in school at the time this thing occurred!"

Frankie's fingers tightened on the banister to a white-knuckled grip. The silence was deathly.

"Well?" he demanded harshly. "What do you have to say for yourself? Were you there to play watchdog for Joey, to tip him off and stall anyone going inside?"

Frankie faltered. A flurry of panic gripped her mind. Her first instinct was to deny she'd even been there, but they had that darn paper that must have fallen out of her notebook when she ran!

"What do you want me to say?" she cried. "I was there, yes, but it's not what you think. I saw Joey at school and then we got a ride with Pete—"

"Pete Renfrow?"

She gave a jerky nod. Vince muttered under his breath, while Samantha looked on numbly. "Did you know about the robbery?"

Frankie swallowed. "Yes," she admitted. "But not until right before Joey was gonna go in. Pete's the one who wanted Joey to do it. I—I tried to talk him out of it—" She broke off when his lips tightened.

Her chin tipped. She felt her face grow hot. While her color was rising, so was her temper. "I did!" she said fiercely. "But he wouldn't listen so I left. I left because I didn't want to have anything to do with it!"

No one said a word.

He didn't believe her, she realized. And now Samantha had stepped up beside him. They were both staring at her. Judging her. Accusing her. Only they had no right. *He* had no right!

"You aren't supposed to be anywhere near Joey Bennett, Frankie. This is the second time you've been caught with him."

No, Samantha thought dimly. It's the third time.

Frankie said nothing. If anything, her little chin tilted higher still. "Are you gonna threaten me with Juvie Hall again 'cause I broke my probation?"

Their eyes collided. "Believe it or not," Vince stated coolly, "this has nothing to do with your probation. Joey's bad news, Frankie. When are you going to see him for what he is?"

Samantha stepped forward, unable to keep silent any longer. "Vince is right, Frankie. You know how I feel about Joey—you know how Vince feels. Apparently that doesn't matter to you, though. My God," she said shakily. "He was carrying a gun! What if he had panicked? What if he'd lost his head? Someone could have been hurt—*you* could have been hurt. You could have been killed! Joey's not the kind of friend you need!"

Frankie blinked. Now even Samantha was taking Larusso's side against her. It was too much, the two of them ganging up against her like this.

Her eyes locked on Samantha. "Why don't you just come right out and say it?" she cried hotly. "You think I'm just as bad as Joey!"

Her gaze swerved to Vince. "And what about you, Larusso? Who are you to tell me what I can and can't do? Who are you to tell me anything! You didn't want me to come and live here with Samantha, 'cause you didn't think I was good enough for her. Well, I got news for you. I heard you the night Mama died. I heard you tell Samantha about your brother—that you were a lot worse than I am. I heard you tell her you lied and cheated and stole... Maybe you're right. Maybe I'm not good enough for her. But if I'm not, *neither are you!*"

She whirled and fled up the stairs. A second later her bedroom door slammed. The sound echoed throughout the house.

For an instant Samantha was too shocked to move. But when she would have lurched up the stairs after Frankie, hard hands caught at hers. Vince spun her around to face him.

"Let her go," he said tightly. "She won't listen to you right now. She's too upset and too angry. The best thing we can do right now is leave her alone. She needs some time to cool off."

It was all Samantha could do not to snap at him and jerk away. But deep down, she knew he was right. There would be no reasoning with Frankie right now . . . right now? Her thoughts bordered on hysterical. There was no reasoning with Frankie at all this past month!

Her shoulders slumped defeatedly. Vince's hands still gripped hers. As she stared down at the taut cords of his wrists, reality gradually seeped back. She was stunned to see how pale and drawn he was. Lines of strain were etched beside his mouth.

She didn't need to wonder why. She was still reeling with the shock of discovering that Frankie had overhead his confession about Tony. Was it only a month ago? Lord, it seemed like a lifetime had passed since then.

She didn't protest when he pulled her over to the couch. He collapsed on the cushions, leaned his head back and closed his eyes. "God," he muttered. "What a mess."

Samantha said nothing for the longest time. Then, very quietly: "I want to start adoption proceedings, Vince."

The words fell with the weight of an anchor. His eyes snapped open. He stared at her as if she'd lost her mind.

Samantha clasped her hands together in her lap to still their tremor. She was half-afraid to look at him, afraid of what she might see . . . even more afraid of what she wouldn't see.

"The sooner the better, I think. That's why I intend to call the social worker first thing Monday morning."

Vince straightened slowly. One single demanding word was all he said. "Why, Samantha? *Why?*"

"I tried it your way, Vince. Now I'm going to do it mine."

He surged to his feet. "Things are no different now than they were a month ago!" he reminded her harshly. "She lashes out one minute and clams up the next. If anything, she's worse, and this episode with Joey today just proves it. She knows right from wrong—that's the one thing neither of us ever doubted. But I don't think she even *cares* anymore—and that scares the hell out of me!"

Samantha went very still inside. "You didn't believe her, did you?" Her tone was little more than a thread of sound. "When Frankie said she tried to talk Joey out of robbing that liquor store, you didn't believe her."

"You want an honest answer? No. No, I didn't."

Her eyes never left his face. "I used to wonder why you were so certain she was headed downhill," she said quietly, almost whimsically. "I know now that you have tunnel vision, Vince. Where Frankie's concerned, you see only the bad and none of the good."

"And you refuse to see what's there." There was no give in his voice.

She didn't back down from his brittle regard. "She's just like you, Vince!"

Frustration ate at him like acid. "Don't you think I know that? It took a tragedy for me to realize the path I was taking. I lost my brother, Samantha, and that's something that will haunt me forever! What will it take for Frankie to open her eyes? Another tragedy? You say I can't see Frankie for what she is, but Frankie can't see Joey for what he is. There's a difference between recklessness and courage but these kids don't know that. What if she decides to play follow the leader? You think I'm supposed to be all sweet and nice and not say a word to her. Well, 'pretty please' just doesn't cut it with kids like her!''

Samantha went cold to the tips of her fingers. "Vince, listen to yourself! You're not even thinking of *her* feelings. My God, she just lost her mother!"

His denial was swift and vehement. "I haven't forgotten. But you can make excuses for her only so long. It's one thing to play big sister to a kid like her. But it's a different game entirely when it comes to being a parent and living with her. And ever since she's been here with you, she's been defiant and resentful. She's miserable and she's making sure everyone around her is, too."

"And you just can't admit you might be wrong, can you? I can't give up on her now, Vince, don't you see that? Do you know that not once—not once!—have I seen her shed a tear since that night? She's got everything bottled up inside her and she just won't let go! Sometimes I think all she needs is a good cry!"

He slammed his palm against the wall. "Dammit, Samantha, I can't believe you're doing this. You're letting her come between us."

"No," she said quietly. "You're the one who's doing that. You, Vince. Not Frankie."

She rose to her feet. Only a few feet separated them, but the distance between them had never been greater. She wondered vaguely if he knew how it tore her apart inside to have to say this.

Her voice was wrenched from deep inside her. "I thought I understood you, Vince. But right now I feel like I'm looking at a stranger. I—I really thought you cared about Frankie...that day you bought her that bike, I remember thinking...he might not want to, but he does.... I guess I was wrong. I guess you don't give a damn about Frankie because if you did, you couldn't be so hard and rigid and demanding—and so damned uncompromising!"

She drew a deep shuddering breath. "You just can't give an inch, can you? Maybe it's because of the way you grew up. Maybe you've never been able to overcome that 'me first' mentality. But it looks to me like the only thing that matters to you is being right. Coming out on top, coming in first, getting *your* way and to hell with the other guy. And maybe—" she choked back the burning threat of tears "—you haven't changed at all."

His eyes were riveted to hers. There was no pretense between them now. Nothing but raw, brutally honest emotion. "So what are you saying? That I no longer fit into your life?" A low exclamation broke from his lips. "Dammit, Samantha, you know how I feel about you. I'd have asked you to marry me weeks ago if it weren't for all this trouble with Frankie—"

Oh, hell. *Hell!* It hadn't come out as he'd planned. He couldn't look away as her face whitened.

The silence was stifling. He dragged a hand down his face, grimly aware he'd just cut his own throat. There was a crushing sensation deep in his chest. He had the awful feeling he'd just lost the best thing that had ever happened to him.

Samantha's lungs burned from the effort it took to hold back her tears. The pain that tore through her was excruciating.

Nothing had changed, she realized bleakly. Vince was as unyielding as ever; he still thought Frankie was nothing but trouble. Tonight he had dashed all her hopes like shattered glass. The gulf between them yawned wider than ever.

From somewhere she found the strength to cross the room. Slowly, the action painstakingly resolute, she opened the door. A rush of cold air swept into the house but she was too numb to feel it.

Her lips barely moved as she spoke. "There's no point in either of us saying any more. Good night, Vince."

She managed to hold herself together until the door closed. And then the tears began to flow, slow and hot, scalding her cheeks, searing her heart. She hadn't wanted to lose either of them—not Frankie, and certainly not Vince.

She was afraid she had just lost both of them.

HOURS LATER, Samantha lay tossing and turning in her bed.

I'd have asked you to marry me weeks ago. Again and again Vince's words echoed through her mind, pouring through her heart.

He loved her. *Vince loved her.* It didn't matter that he had never said the words. It was there in every look, every burning touch. It was there in his stubborn desire to watch out for her, to protect her so fiercely, even though she had no need of it.

Would she have changed anything if she could? Would she have changed *him?* The gentle, caring side of his nature was as much a part of him as the hard-bitten man she'd seen that long-ago day with Joey, and again tonight. She had fallen in love with all that he was. Sensitive and tender. Volatile and fiery. If he were different, he would not be the man she had fallen in love with.

Along with that realization came another.

She was suddenly deeply ashamed of the bitter accusations she had flung at Vince. If he cared nothing about Frankie, he wouldn't have been so angry with her. So disappointed. So hurt.

Curious, that the very thing that had provoked their stormy exchange should lead to such comfort now. Unfortunately she had no ready answer to smooth the precarious situation with Frankie, but a fragile tendril of hope lifted her heart. If the three of them could get through this difficult time, they could get through anything. On that note, she turned over and let exhaustion pull her into a fitful slumber.

It was very early the next morning when Samantha paused before Frankie's door. She had tried to talk to the girl last night, but Frankie made no bones about wanting to be left alone. Samantha had reluctantly backed off and respected her privacy, but perhaps now was a better time after all. Maybe if she caught her sleepy and off guard, before the girl had time to throw up her defenses . . . She tapped on her door.

That same moment found Vince tucking his hand beneath his head, staring at the filmy streamers of light that crept over his bed. The covers lay knotted and twisted around the lower half of his body, silent testimony to his sleepless night.

An angry gust of wind rattled the windowpane, but Vince didn't hear. Every part of him ached. His heart. His soul. That empty spot inside him he was sure would never be filled until he'd met Samantha.

He had just spent the longest night of his life; he was cursed with a sudden vision of what the lonely nights ahead would bring. The future stretched before him, as stark and barren as his past.

It didn't have to be that way, a voice inside prodded.

His eyes squeezed shut. Frankie was right, he realized. All along he'd been fighting the feeling he wasn't good enough for Samantha. But sometimes habits died hard...God, wasn't that the truth! Maybe he needn't have fought that particular battle at all. Samantha believed in him...the same way she believed in Frankie.

For the first time he wondered how he and Tony might have turned out if they had had someone like Samantha in their lives. Someone to pick them up, dust them off and guide them back whenever they strayed on the rocky path of life.

Perhaps he wouldn't have been so hard. So rigid and demanding. So—damn the word—uncompromising!

And maybe he'd have learned how to bend long, long ago....

It was in the midst of his desolate mood that the ring of the phone intruded. There was a bitter taste in his mouth as he reached for the receiver and murmured an automatic "hello."

"Vince?"

It was Samantha. Every nerve in his body tightened. There was a note in her voice he'd never heard before.... Something was wrong. Something was very, very wrong.

His feet hit the floor. "What is it, Samantha? What's happened?"

"It's Frankie! I went in to talk to her just now and...she's gone, Vince. She's gone!"

He bolted upright. "Was her bed slept in?" he asked sharply.

"I—I think so. At least it looked like it—"

His gaze fastened on the bedside clock. "It's just past seven. The sun's just come up. I doubt she's been gone long."

"After what happened last night I wouldn't put it past her to have sneaked out in the middle of the night!" Her breath caught on a sob. "Oh, God, Vince, she's run away. I know she has! She's wearing her old clothes and she left the muffler and gloves I made for her just thrown on the bed! Her bike is gone and . . . oh, Lord, maybe I should call the police!"

"Samantha, calm down. It's too soon to jump to conclusions. Just give me a chance to find her."

"Find her!" she cried. "I don't have the slightest idea where she would have gone!"

But Vince did. Already a half-formed suspicion had taken root. He had a very good idea indeed where Frankie might have gone. Somewhere familiar. Somewhere she had always felt safe and secure.

A note of cautious excitement entered his voice. "Samantha, please. Just sit tight for an hour or two while I look for her. I promise, I'll bring her home." He hung up before she could argue or plead to come with him.

He wasn't sure he could explain the urgency inside that commanded he do this alone. When he came face-to-face with Frankie again, he wanted it to be just the two of them.

Just the two of them . . . He wasn't certain Samantha would understand his compulsion.

Oddly, he was just as certain that Frankie would.

CHAPTER SEVENTEEN

THE CAR ROLLED smoothly to a halt behind a battered, rusted pickup truck that looked as if it hadn't moved for the past twenty years. Vince pulled the keys from the ignition and stepped to the curb. He paused long enough to scan the stone-fronted town house across the street, the church spires rising on the next block.

A misty fog swirled in the air. The potholed street was still and quiet so early in the morning, the sunrise pale and watery. It wouldn't be long before the neighborhood awakened and small children drifted into the street, their mothers sitting out on the front stoop in the very same manner as their mothers before them.

In tandem with the thought, a siren screamed in the distance. Nearby a door slammed. It was then he spotted it—a handlebar jutting out from a crumbling brick corner.

Frankie's bike.

Seconds later he mounted the wide stone steps of the apartment building where Frankie had lived with her mother. At the top, he hesitated, gingerly testing the doorknob. It opened with the slightest of pressure.

The elevator still wasn't working. As he had that very first time with Samantha, Vince climbed the stairs to the fourth floor. He was stunned to find he was scared, more scared than he could remember being in a long long time, which was utterly ridiculous. Why should the prospect of facing a thirteen-year-old girl frighten him so?

Maybe it was because this particular thirteen-year-old didn't hesitate to give as good as she got. Or maybe it was because he was finding out just how hard it was to swallow his pride, the pride he'd been so convinced was his salvation all this time. Or maybe it was because it was never easy to admit to someone else that you were wrong.

Sure enough, there she was, at the far end of the hall. She sat huddled in the dusty corner, her thin arms wrapped around her legs, her knees pulled up to her chest. Her head was drooped forward, resting on her upraised knees.

His legs carried him forward. So lost in misery was she that she didn't even hear his footsteps until he halted before her. Her head slowly lifted. The anguish he glimpsed in her eyes cut like a knife blade, tearing at his gut, wounding his soul.

And Vince knew then he couldn't have been angry with her even if he tried.

The sigh she gave seemed pulled from some lonely place deep inside her. "How did you find me?"

Vince smiled slightly. "It wasn't hard."

Her gaze veered beyond him into the shadows. "Is Samantha here?"

He shook his head. There was no need to say more. The last thing he wanted to do right now was to make her feel guilty. Her eyes first widened, then narrowed when he settled his back against the wall and eased down next to her.

They were both silent for several seconds. Then Frankie turned her head slightly. "Aren't you gonna ask me why I'm here?'' She was neither annoyed nor irritated; instead she sounded incredibly weary.

Again Vince shook his head. ''Sometimes it's okay to be alone,'' he said gently. ''And other times ... well, sometimes it's not so good.''

His words had an unexpected effect. Frankie's gaze slid away. She didn't say anything, but her chin began to quiver.

For once Vince wished she would fly off the handle, rant and rave and yell at him—anything but look the way she did right now. So beaten. So defeated. So broken. So impossibly young and as old as Eve, all at the same time.

A spasm of regret seized him. Somewhere along the way he'd forgotten that she was just a kid.

He settled his wrist upon an upraised knee. ''Frankie,'' he said quietly. ''You were telling the truth last night, weren't you? About Joey, I mean. You weren't an accomplice in that robbery, were you?''

She shook her head. ''It was just the way I said. I tried to talk him out of—''

Vince held up a hand. ''You don't have to explain. I believe you.''

''You do?'' Her jaw sagged. At any other time, her expression might have struck him as humorous. But right now, he suspected neither of them felt like laughing.

Vince nodded, then grimaced. ''Look, Frankie. I know this isn't what you want to hear. But Joey's not the kind of friend you should have right now. I'd hate to see him drag you down with him. And I'm afraid that's where he's headed.''

Frankie bit her lip. ''I don't think I want to see Joey again anyway. Me and him ... well, it's just not the way it used to be. Ever since he started hanging around with

Pete Renfrow, he's...different somehow." Her jeans were ripped at the knee; she toyed with a loose thread. "Besides," she added, her voice very low. "Joey likes taking chances. He likes doin' stuff like stealing."

Vince watched her closely. "And what about you?" He hesitated, but only for an instant. "I wasn't born yesterday, Frankie. I know you were probably stealing long before you got caught."

"I was," she confirmed in a small voice. "Watches, jewelry, things like that."

"Why, Frankie?" He strived very hard to keep the censure from his voice and somehow managed to succeed. "Did you steal just to go along with Joey? So you could be like him—do the things he liked to do?"

Frankie shook her head, avoiding his gaze.

"It wasn't like that at all," he said slowly. "Was it?"

"No," she whispered. "I did it...for Mama."

A deep abiding shame tore through Vince. All at once he knew what she was going to say...even before she said it.

Her voice came haltingly. "I unloaded stuff at Phil's pawnshop. I told Mama I was baby-sitting for Joey's mom, but I gave the money to Mama because we were always so short—so she wouldn't have to work so hard. I thought maybe then she'd quit her night job. And once—once I bought her some cough medicine."

All at once he was filled with bitter self-recrimination. Samantha had tried to tell him all along that Frankie wasn't a bad kid—that there was good inside her. But he had refused to listen. He'd refused to look far enough— he hadn't looked at all! Instead, he had been oh-so-quick to judge. To accuse. God, how he despised himself in that moment!

"Samantha suspected you'd given the money to your mother," he said unsteadily. "But I . . . I'm ashamed to say I thought she was just being gullible." He swallowed. "Only I don't understand why you didn't say so—why you never defended yourself, especially when you knew what I thought of you."

"I—I don't know. I guess because I knew I'd have to stop then. The money wasn't much, but I—I know it helped." Her eyes grew tortured. "And it was better to have you think I was a little jerk than Mama. I didn't want her to find out. She thought it was just that one time. Besides, I—I didn't think you'd believe me."

It was Vince's turn to evade the touch of her eyes. In the back of his mind he wondered what Samantha would think if she saw the two of them the way they were now—shoulder to shoulder against the wall, his long legs stretched far beyond Frankie's. It came as a shock to realize his palms were sweaty. His throat was dry. Lord, but this was one of the most difficult things he'd ever done!

"I owe you an apology, Frankie. I've been hard on you. Too hard." He stopped, the hoarseness in his voice revealing the strain he was under. "I'm not sure you'll understand, but I think it's because you're so much like I was at your age. I guess I didn't want you to end up being as rebellious and reckless as I was."

There was a heartbeat of silence.

"Samantha was afraid you were running away." At last he summoned the courage to meet her eyes. "I hope to hell you weren't. Because I'd hate knowing that I'm the one who drove you to it."

"I wasn't," she said quickly, then paused. "I guess I was just running. I thought if I came here for a while, it might make me feel better about—'' to her horror, her voice began to wobble ''—about Mama being gone.''

His tone was very gentle. ''Did it help?''

Frankie didn't answer, though it wasn't because she didn't want to. All of a sudden her throat felt raw. She saw the dark, dismal hallway through a watery blur.

The glistening sheen of her eyes gave her away. Vince touched her shoulder awkwardly. ''Frankie—''

A thin hand convulsively grabbed the sleeve of his coat. She turned into him with a strangled half sob. In that split second, Vince caught a glimpse of her face. She looked defenseless and vulnerable, valiantly brave as she struggled not to cry.

Something unraveled deep inside him. He groped for a handkerchief and came up empty-handed. He hesitated but an instant. With a low mutter he circled her trembling body with his arms, hauling her up against his side and tucking her head into his shoulder.

Her fingers clenched and unclenched against him. ''I miss her,'' she said brokenly. ''I miss Mama so much.''

Her words tore at his heart. He stroked her hair, his voice as uneven as hers. ''I know, Frankie. I know.''

And suddenly he did. The emotion that rocked his soul was painfully sweet ... and just plain painful. Samantha had accused him of not caring about Frankie. But he did ... and he hadn't realized just how much until that moment. He didn't know how, or when, but somehow this scrawny little kid had inched her way into his heart.

A scalding tear wet the hollow of his throat. He felt as if it seeped clear to his heart. She cried until he was certain there couldn't possibly be a drop of emotion left in her. She cried until his eyes began to sting and a burning ache constricted his lungs. She cried until she was lying limp and exhausted against him.

"My head hurts," she sniffed at last, sounding both puzzled and forlorn.

He was sorely tempted to chuckle but didn't think he dared. Instead he probed very gently. "Other than that, are you okay?"

She expelled a long serrated breath and drew back. "You know what? It hurts to cry. But not as much as it hurts *not* to cry."

"I'll take your word for it." Vince rose to his feet, then extended his hand. "Think it's time we headed home?"

She nodded, her eyes on his outstretched hand. Vince held his breath, wondering if she would ignore it. It was more than just a gesture and they both knew it. He was asking for her trust and acceptance... and her forgiveness as well.

She shyly placed her fingers in his. A gentle tug and she was on her feet before him.

Silence drifted between them as they descended the stairs and went outside, but it wasn't an uncomfortable one. Frankie watched as he loaded her bike into the trunk of his car. He unlocked the passenger door and started to step away. Her voice stopped him.

"Hey, Larusso?"

He raised his head. Her eyes were clear and unerringly direct. He saw no shadows, no anger, no resentment.

Her gaze flitted quickly away and returned, as if she were embarrassed. When she spoke her voice still carried a betraying catch. "I... uh, I just wanted to say... you know you're all right."

For the second time in just a few short minutes, Vince felt his throat tighten. A fleeting smile touched his lips. He reached out and cuffed her gently on the chin with his closed fist. "Thanks," he said huskily. "You're not so bad yourself."

IT WAS BUTCH who announced their arrival back at Samantha's. Even before the sound of footsteps echoed on the back porch, he began to yip and race madly in circles before the door. Samantha rushed toward the kitchen and threw the door open.

Vince stepped inside. "Vince," she cried, stricken. She peered anxiously past his shoulder. "Where's Frankie? Didn't you—"

Frankie's head bobbed into view. She emerged from the direction of the garage. Near the screen door she halted, her expression uncertain as she came face-to-face with Samantha.

Samantha didn't waste another second. The words she choked out reflected her tangled emotions. "Oh, Frankie, don't you dare do anything like this again!" She seized the girl's hand and pulled her close. "You scared me half to death!"

Frankie found herself wrapped in a hug that threatened to squeeze the breath from her. She didn't mind, though; her arms slid around Samantha and she returned the hug just as fiercely.

Finally Samantha pulled back to scan Frankie's features. The girl was pale, her cheeks streaked with tears. Samantha's head jerked up. Her gaze slid accusingly to Vince, who was in the midst of helping himself to a cup of coffee.

He raised his brows in mock innocence and gave a silent shake of his head, then nodded at Frankie. "I think

Frankie has something to tell you." He turned and went into the living room, leaving them alone.

The air grew hushed and very quiet. Samantha shifted her attention to Frankie, who looked a little uncertain. She wondered vaguely if Frankie were aware she was just as scared.

Frankie shuffled her feet. "I guess it was pretty dumb running off like that. And I know I've acted like a brat lately. I—I don't even know why, except I've felt like—like I'm the only one that this ever happened to."

A tender hand smoothed the hair from her forehead. "Most children your age never have to cope with losing a parent," Samantha said gently. "And everyone reacts differently to grief."

Frankie bent to pet Butch, who was jumping at her legs, vainly trying to get her attention. She didn't look at Samantha when she spoke. "I just wanted to say I'm sorry. I know I've probably ruined everything 'cause of the way I've been acting." She stood up, hugging Butch's wriggling body to her chest. "So I guess I can't blame you if you change your mind about having me stay here with you."

Samantha's heart wrenched. She knew what Frankie was trying very hard *not* to say—that she was afraid Samantha had changed her mind about the adoption. "I'm not going to change my mind, Frankie. Everyone makes mistakes once in a while. But when we do something wrong, or something we regret, it doesn't mean that the people who love us will *stop* loving us." She raised Frankie's chin from where it was buried in Butch's neck. "Do you know what I'm trying to say?"

Frankie gulped. "I think so."

"Good. Because I plan to get the ball rolling on this adoption first thing Monday morning." Her expression became anxious again. "If you still want it, too, that is."

"I want it," she said simply. "I want it a lot." She flashed a blindingly sweet smile, the one Samantha so loved. "Is it okay if I go up and take a shower now?"

Samantha's eyes grew softer still. "Sure, honey." She watched her stride from the kitchen, still holding Butch snuggled in her arms. Everything was going to be all right, she realized giddily. She was so relieved she felt weak. But one thing still remained . . .

Facing Vince.

She was scarcely aware of her legs carrying her into the living room. Her heart was pounding so that she could scarcely think.

He stood in the middle of the room, his back to her, legs braced slightly apart in that oh-so-familiar pose. The morning *Tribune* was folded in one hand, the other stuffed in the rear pocket of his cords as he scanned the newspaper.

She paused for just a moment, feeling her heart turn over, absorbing the sheer power and wonder of his presence. She loved the way his shoulders stretched to fill his sweater as much as she loved that supremely masculine stance that bordered on arrogant.

"Vince?"

He turned slightly. She had dreaded facing him again after last night, but when he dropped the paper on the end table and extended a hand, she knew this wasn't going to be the ordeal she had feared.

Three steps brought her to his side. His fingers closed around hers, strong and sure. "Thank you for bringing Frankie back," she said softly. "Where did you find her?"

He set aside his coffee and reached for her other hand. "Outside her old apartment. It wasn't hard to figure out that's where she went." He grimaced. "I was just relieved that she didn't go any farther."

Samantha nodded. "After I was through with my panic attack," she said dryly, "I wondered if that's where she was. But you were gone so long I was beginning to think the worst. Though maybe I should be glad I wasn't there for the big showdown." She was only half joking.

His lips quirked. "You'd have been pleasantly surprised."

"Oh?"

His smile faded. "I think you were right all along when you said she just needed a good cry." He paused. "She admitted she'd been stealing for a while before she finally got caught. Jewelry and watches, stuff like that."

There was a brief silence. Sensing he wanted to say more, Samantha searched his face, puzzled at his expression. He should have been angry, yet he wasn't. Instead he appeared rather guilty. Maybe even ashamed.

"What is it?" she asked softly.

His words seemed to come with difficulty. "You were right about what she did with the money she got from pawning the items. She gave it to her mother, to make things easier for her."

Samantha wasn't surprised. She'd known all along that Frankie wasn't a bad kid—and this proved it beyond a doubt. But looking at Vince right know—knowing how he must feel—her heart began to ache.

Her fingers tightened around his. "What she did was wrong—the lying and the stealing. But somehow it just doesn't seem so bad now, because it was for all the right reasons."

"I know. God, Samantha, when she told me I kicked myself a hundred times for refusing to listen to you. She wasn't being defiant or selfish or anything like that at all. She was only trying to watch out for her mother." The undercurrent of regret lay thick and heavy.

"She did it out of love," Samantha said quietly. "It's ironic, isn't it? We were both trying so hard to teach her about principles and values."

His mouth was tight with self-disgust. "But she already knew. I sat there and listened to her, and all I could think was that I'd just learned the biggest lesson in my life—and I'd just been taught by a thirteen-year-old."

They were both quiet for several moments, each lost in reflection. Frankie had put them all through hell this past month, but at least he was beginning to understand her. Her defiance was part self-defense, part self-reliance. And perhaps her so-called resentment was really a fierce kind of pride because she was afraid she wasn't really wanted.

He gently tipped Samantha's chin to his. "It seems I have a lot to make up for where Frankie's concerned." His gaze tenderly roamed her features. "And where you're concerned, too."

"That's not true," she began.

"Oh, yes, it is." He took a deep breath, searching for the words he couldn't say last night, because they laid wide open every vulnerability inside him.

"You were right, Samantha. I've been selfish. My only excuse is that you're the best thing that ever happened to me and I didn't want to lose you. Maybe I've even been a little jealous of Frankie because I wanted to come first in your life."

His gaze captured hers. "I love you," he said, his tone very low and intense. "I've never said that to anyone before. But I feel it when I look at you. I feel it when I hold you. I feel it with every breath I take. And it scares the hell out of me to even think about how empty my life would be without you." He tugged her close, so close his lips hovered just above hers. "Marry me, Samantha. Please marry me."

His searing look robbed her of breath. His eyes were clear and bright, eyes the color of gold . . . eyes the color of love. It was all there, in the hoarseness of his voice, the yearning he couldn't hide and didn't want to.

It was a moment she would carry in her heart forever.

"Oh, Vince," she whispered achingly. "I love you, too—you don't know how much. And I want more than anything to marry you." The breathless cry tore from her lips. "But what about Frankie? I couldn't love her more if she were my own daughter—"

His fingers pressed gently against her mouth, stifling the flow of words. Inside she began to tremble. She held her breath, scarcely daring to hope, to even breathe.

Vince let a slow smile curve his lips. "You know she's never had a father. Maybe it's time she had one."

The world spun crazily. Caught fiercely in his arms, Samantha clung to him blindly. Vince closed his eyes, shaken by a rush of emotion so strong it nearly sent him to his knees. Their hearts pressed together as one, their lips met in a soul-shattering kiss that consumed them both.

Behind them there was a small cough.

They drew apart reluctantly. Samantha offered Frankie a wavering smile, while Vince merely chuckled.

"You're the first to know," he said with a grin. "We're getting married." Before Frankie had a chance to say a word, he beckoned to her.

Samantha looked on curiously when he unclasped the silver crucifix around his neck.

"Samantha gets a diamond," he said huskily, "and you get this." He held the chain suspended over his palm for a moment.

Frankie leaned closer. "Gee," she murmured. "It's really pretty."

Vince gestured for her to turn around so he could fasten it around her neck. "This belonged to my brother Tony," he murmured.

Samantha's heart constricted. Hard as she tried, she couldn't stop her vision from misting with tears. In a way she couldn't define, Tony's chain had held Vince in a curious sort of bondage all these years.

Now he was free.

Frankie faced Vince once more. Her hand fluttered up to her neck. "It's pretty," she said again. "But why are you giving it to me?"

He smiled crookedly. "Tony was always very special to me. That's why I want someone just as special to have it. But you know what makes it even better?"

Frankie shook her head.

He leaned forward and kissed her forehead. "It gets to stay in the family."

EPILOGUE

ONE WARM FALL Saturday nearly a year and a half later, Vince stood by the kitchen window. Arms folded across his chest, he gazed outside where Frankie was carefully polishing her brand-new mountain bike.

"She's going to have that bike worn out before she ever rides it."

Samantha laughed at his good-natured grumbling. "She said yesterday she refuses to ride it anywhere there's a chance of the paint getting nicked. She's really pretty darned proud of it."

The observation provoked a smile. "She has a right to be. She's mowed lawns and raked leaves till her arms were ready to fall off. And suffered through baby-sitting for the holy terrors." The holy terrors were five-year-old twins across the street—and so christened by Vince and Frankie.

They had decided to buy a bigger house in the suburbs the summer after they were married. Frankie had come along on all their house-hunting trips and had a say-so in their final choice. The move had meant attending a different high school than anticipated, but as Samantha pointed out, it was her freshman year and many of the students were in the same predicament. Frankie had made the adjustment far better than they had dared to hope. In a way, it was a new beginning for all of them.

Samantha peeked over Vince's shoulder. Frankie was now painstakingly running her rag over each spoke of the rear wheel. "Personally," she went on lightly, "I think it's a good sign. She'll probably be just as fussy and careful with her first car."

"Her first car..." She laughed at his stricken expression.

Out in the yard, Butch had set up a ruckus. He raced madly around the tree where Rover stared down aloofly. The dog and cat had had no choice but to learn to get along; when they had, they were practically inseparable. But occasionally—like now—one took exception to the other.

More than ever, the pair reminded Samantha of Vince and Frankie. Yet she wouldn't have traded these past months for anything in the world.

Oh, there had been a few hurdles. Not only had Samantha and Vince had to cope with the newness of marriage, but they'd had the added responsibility of a child as well. Vince was sometimes adamant and stubborn, and Frankie was still as outspoken and feisty as ever. They were so much alike—occasionally too much alike.

But Samantha wouldn't have changed either of them in any way.

Frankie knew that she was loved and wanted and it made all the difference in the world. Their only real scare had come several months ago when Frankie saw in the newspaper that Joey Bennett had shot and critically wounded a man during an armed robbery. He was remanded to adult court, eventually convicted and sentenced to a prison term.

Frankie was very quiet and withdrawn for over a week. Sometime later, on the day Vince came home and broke the news about Joey's sentence, tears welled in her eyes.

Samantha slid her arms around her and tucked her head into her shoulder. "Honey, I know it hurts because Joey was once your friend," she whispered. "But Frankie, when I think of how different things might have been, it scares me. I'm so glad it wasn't you."

Frankie swiped at her tears. Her wobbly little smile tore at Samantha's heart. "I know," she said unsteadily. "Only I was just thinking...maybe this wouldn't have happened at all if Jocy had somebody like you for a friend instead of Pete Renfrow."

Across the room, Samantha's gaze met that of her husband's. She knew from the poignant wistfulness on his features that he was thinking of lessons learned the hard way....

The sound of the phone ringing jarred Samantha back to the present. It was Vince who answered it. A second later he opened the screen door.

"Hey, Larusso!" he called out.

Larusso. As always, Samantha felt her heart turn over. From the start, she and Vince had made it clear that if Frankie wanted to retain Lombardi as her surname, that was fine. Either way, the choice was hers. Samantha remembered how touched—and how proud— Vince had been when she confided she wanted to change her name to Larusso.

Outside, Frankie glanced up.

Vince thumbed over his shoulder. "The phone's for you."

Frankie dropped her rag and ran into the house. Judging from the way her eyes lit up, she'd been expecting the call.

Vince wandered into the living room and dropped down beside Samantha, looking rather bemused.

She poked him playfully in the ribs. "Out with it, La-russo."

"Frankie's on the phone with some boy!"

"It was bound to happen sooner or later," she teased. "She's growing up, Vince."

"Up?" he muttered. "Mostly out, you mean."

"That, too," she said with a chuckle. Frankie possessed the same small stature as her mother. At fifteen, her once-thin frame had filled out rather nicely. Her hair was longer, waving smoothly down to her shoulders, though today she wore it caught back in a banana clip.

Samantha tipped her head toward the kitchen. "You might be interested in knowing her friend's name is Rob. I understand he's on the debate team."

A slow-growing smile edged along Vince's mouth. "The debate team, huh?" He laughed outright. "Well, if he likes to argue, he certainly picked the right girl. They ought to have some pretty stimulating conversations."

Samantha's hand crept into his. "Speaking of conversations, when are we going to tell Frankie about Jane?"

His gaze slid down her body to rest on the slight swell of her tummy. His smile widened. "You mean Joe."

"Jane" or "Joe" was the precious secret they'd shared for the past few weeks. When Samantha found out she was pregnant, they decided to keep it to themselves for just a little longer. Too, they were just a little uncertain how Frankie would react to the news that there would be a baby in the house next spring.

Their worries were for nothing, though, as they discovered when Frankie got off the phone and they broke the news.

Samantha gave her a little hug, trying rather vainly to disguise her anxiety. "You don't mind us having a baby, do you?"

Frankie shook her head. Her gaze bounced between the two adults. "You know what it means, though, don't you?"

Samantha and Vince shook their heads and waited expectantly.

Frankie's lips quirked as she glanced at Samantha. "This time *I* finally get to be a big sister."

Samantha's laugh was shaky with relief.

Frankie started back outside, only to turn around and head right back in. Again she glanced between the two adults. "Will I have to baby-sit?"

Neither Samantha nor Vince was certain what to make of the question. "Well," she paused consideringly. "I suppose we might ask you once in a while."

Frankie's eyes began to gleam. "Would I get paid for it?"

This time it was Vince whose lips quirked. "Yes, Francesca. That's a distinct possibility."

Her eyes lit up like a child's at Christmas. Samantha and Vince convulsed into laughter as soon as she bounced outside again.

It was hours later when his hand slid down to splay possessively over the smooth tautness of her belly. "How's Joe?" he whispered.

Samantha felt a familiar, restless tingle deep inside. Her fingers tangled in the midnight darkness of his hair. She drew his head down so that their lips almost touched, but not quite. "Jane," she emphasized huskily, "is cold. Very, very cold."

His laugh was low and sexy. "We can't have that now, can we?"

His mouth closed over hers, tormenting and arousing. He invited her touch, sweet and eager; she invited his, daringly intimate, always tender and loving. Their joining was a melding of souls, a merging of hearts. Mouths sealed, limbs entwined, they lost themselves in the mindless wonder of loving... and being loved.

And when the fiery explosion was over, he gathered her against his side, sheltering her, protecting her, loving her more with every breath. Raising a hand, she let her fingers drift across the contours of his mouth.

She gave a breathless sigh. "Are you as happy as I am?"

For just a moment, Vince was silent. Looking back on all the empty years of his life, happy was the one thing he'd never dreamed he could ever be.

Now it was the one thing he would *always* be.

He smiled against her fingertips. "I'm happy. Content. Fulfilled. Blessed with everything a man could ever wa—"

"Whoa! I think that answers the question."

"Well," he murmured dryly. "You did ask."

"I did, didn't I?" Heavy-lidded and drowsy, Samantha snuggled closer.

A second later her eyes popped open. Beneath her ear, there was a low rumble of laughter.

She sighed and propped herself up on her elbow. "What now?" she sighed good-naturedly.

"I was thinking about what Frankie said earlier—when she asked if she'd get paid for baby-sitting. What do you think she's got her eye on this time—" He broke off with a groan. "You were right. She probably wants to start saving for a car. Oh, Lord, what next . . . boyfriends . . . cars . . ."

Samantha laughed and snuggled against the hairy roughness of his chest. "Think of it this way. You'll be an old pro at handling all this by the time Jane is Frankie's age."

"Who?" he teased.

"Jane."

"Joe."

A playful punch landed on his chest. "Jane."

Vince relented gracefully. Jane or Joe, it really didn't matter.

The way he saw it, he'd win either way.

S HARLEQUIN SUPERROMANCE®

Books by Sandra James

BSSJ

HARLEQUIN®

Temptation®

Rebels & Rogues

Trey: He lived life on the edge... and wasn't about to be tamed by a beautiful woman.

THE RED-BLOODED YANKEE!
By Ruth Jean Dale
Temptation #413, October

All men are not created equal. Some are rough around the edges. Tough-minded but tenderhearted. Incredibly sexy. The tempting fulfillment of every woman't fantasy.

When it's time to fight for what they believe in, to win that special woman, our Rebels and Rogues are heroes at heart. Twelve Rebels and Rogues, each month in 1992, only from Harlequin Temptation. Don't miss the upcoming books by our fabulous authors such as Janice Kaiser and Kelly Street.

WELCOME TO

The quintessential small town, where everyone
knows everybody else!

Finally, books that capture the pleasure
of tuning in to your favorite TV show!

Join your friends at Tyler in the eighth book, BACHELOR'S PUZZLE by Ginger
Chambers, available in October.

*What do Tyler's librarian and a cosmopolitan architect have in common? What
does the coroner's office have to reveal?*

GREAT READING...GREAT SAVINGS...
AND A FABULOUS FREE GIFT!

Each book set in Tyler is a self-contained love story; together, the twelve novels
stitch the fabric of the community. You can't miss the Tyler books on the shelves
because the covers honor the old American tradition of quilting; each cover
depicts a patch of the large Tyler quilt!

And you can receive a FABULOUS GIFT, ABSOLUTELY FREE, by collecting
proofs-of-purchase found in each Tyler book, *and* use our Tyler coupons to save
on your next TYLER book purchase.
